Dirty Tricks

A novel by

CHAPMAN PINCHER

SIDGWICK & JACKSON

LONDON

First published in Great Britain in 1980
by Sidgwick and Jackson Limited

Copyright © 1980 by Chapman Pincher

ISBN 0 283 98637 9

Printed in Great Britain by
A. Wheaton & Co. Ltd., Exeter
for Sidgwick and Jackson Limited
1 Tavistock Chambers, Bloomsbury Way
London WC1A 2SG

DIRTY TRICKS

Author's Foreword

Though *Dirty Tricks* is a work of fiction it is also a serious account of the operations of Clandestine Intelligence and, in particular, of the 'deception techniques', as the professionals call them, which such work entails. It also offers a close look into the minds of those who devise and perpetrate them.

Counter-Intelligence and especially the deception of hostile Intelligence Services by disinformation – the Intelligence jargon for lies, frame-ups, double-crosses and other 'dirty tricks' – has become of far greater international significance than espionage in its common concept, the surreptitious gleaning of secret information and removal of documents by spies.

It is my view, after many years spent on the fringes of Secret Service and Security work, and occasionally inside it, that none of the incidents presented here, however outrageous they may seem, are beyond the bounds of likelihood, including those 'dirty tricks' which the otherwise friendly British and American Secret Services may play on each other. Indeed, some are based on genuine events which have come to my knowledge through personal friendship with men who have served in the fields I describe.

So, once again, in a work of fiction I have to record my debt to senior officials past and present in the Secret Intelligence Service (MI6), the Security Service (MI5), Defence Intelligence, the Foreign Office, the US Central Intelligence Agency, the Pentagon and to certain members of the KGB.

Except for the historical personages, all the people presented here are entirely the products of my imagination, but I do not believe the peculiarities of their characters to be exaggerated. If the men and women who work in the Clandestine Services seem to be peculiar – as perhaps they have to be to perform their strange and exacting work – let us be thankful, as we continue to sleep reasonably safely in our beds, that such people exist and are prepared to undertake such tasks for small monetary reward and little public recognition.

Of one thing I am certain. As my Secret Service chief, Sir Mark Quinn, argues, the British ought to be the best in the world at the 'dirty tricks' game. 'We have been at it for centuries.'

No doubt I shall be in trouble with some of my friends for some of the 'scenarios' in this novel. I leave it to the readers to make their own decisions concerning the points where fiction may stray into the realm of truth.

CHAPMAN PINCHER

Ewhurst, Surrey
   January 1980

Chapter One

There was a note of finality about the slam of the door as John Falconer, Chief of the Central Intelligence Agency's Clandestine Services, eased his tall, gaunt frame on to the back seat of his Lincoln limousine. That was settled then, he told himself. After hearing the brief of the previous day's meeting of the National Security Council in Washington he had made a firm decision to act.

It would be the most dangerous operation he had ever conceived, loaded with every 'dirty trick' in the book – treachery, assassinations, frame-ups, double-crosses, triple-crosses, plus a few new ones specifically devised and almost all of them rigorously banned after the big CIA clean-up in the 1970s.

Well, someone had to do something and everybody else seemed to be paralyzed.

The level at which he would have to operate was awesome in the extreme, even for him, but it seemed that events had conspired to put a key into his hand. And he was lacking in neither the courage nor the will to use it.

'Straight home,' he said crisply to the driver, who had been locking his briefcase of secret documents in the trunk against the possible danger of a thief-snatch at traffic lights.

Falconer flashed his identity pass at the exit checkpoint of the expansive CIA Headquarters complex at Langley, Virginia, waved his usual friendly farewell to the guard, then settled back for the eight-miles drive to Washington.

What should he call the operation? It didn't much matter because he would be working so independently that nobody else was ever likely to hear it, but it seemed wrong not to have a code-name. 'Operation Swansong'? That would be appropriate on one count. It would be his last effort before taking early retirement. But he would not be the one doing the dying – at least not physically – though he could be obliterated professionally, perhaps even imprisoned for life, if the operation exploded in his face.

How about 'Cliffhanger'? Very appropriate indeed if it went as he expected. It was going to be touch and go until the last moment, with the penalties for failure horrendous, and not just for himself. Yes, he liked 'Cliffhanger'. It reminded him of 'Rockfall', the brilliantly successful operation which had marked him as the future chief of Clandestine Services, the CIA branch, embracing both Espionage and Counter-Intelligence, in which he had spent most of his professional life. 'Rockfall', the assassination of President Gamal Abdel Nasser, an operation so perfectly clandestine that not even the Egyptian dictator's closest colleagues ever suspected that he had died anything but a natural death.

The operation had achieved perfection because only one outsider had been involved in it. How different from the crackpot British scheme to assassinate the charismatic Arab leader at the time of the abortive Suez invasion in 1956! A cache of arms buried in the sand near Cairo! A group of young, blabber-mouth Egyptian officers to do the killing! Secret servicemen from MI6 hovering in the background! What a set-up! With so many in the know it was bound to fail and it did, setting the final seal on the Suez disaster.

Falconer's solution had been so much more elegant with the need-to-know principle so rigidly applied that only the Egyptian, who introduced the poison into the insulin which the severely diabetic Nasser needed daily, was aware of the attempt. Even the poison itself had been superbly sophisticated. Ricin! That incredibly potent extract of castor-oil seed which was not only fatal in minute dosage but left no detectable trace in the body because the tissues destroyed it. A poison so little known then that the forensic experts who carried out post-mortem examinations had never even heard of it. The CIA could have gone on using it for years if those damned, ham-fisted Bulgarians had not blown it by using ricin to kill one of their exiles in London in 1979, and then bungled an attempt on another exile in Paris. Fancy implanting it in pellets fired from a gun camouflaged as an umbrella! Bloody incompetent idiots! It had been bound to go wrong. And to risk exposing such a precious secret like ricin for a target as miniscule as an exile who happened to be broadcasting BBC propaganda which the Bulgarian leaders disliked!

As the fields and buildings sped by Falconer savoured the sophistication of 'Rockfall', and more particularly its splendid results. The need for Nasser's demise had become even more urgent in September 1970 than it had been in November 1956. After yet another of his visits to Moscow, units of the Soviet Air Force had arrived in Egypt not only with more missiles but also with fighters, bombers and reconnaissance planes. Accommodation was being prepared for thousands of ground staff and technicians. In fact, the Russians were setting up what they hoped would be permanent air and naval bases in the heartland of the Middle East, and there was no way that Nasser was ever going to get them out. The entire power structure of the Eastern Mediterranean was changing fast and only the expulsion of the Russians could redress the balance.

The CIA had spotted a successor to Nasser who might eventually be encouraged to do just that – Anwar Sadat. A less forceful politician, devoted to his leader and with no burning ambition to succeed him, Sadat had qualities which could be developed along the right lines given patience and time.

After handing over the tiny ampoule of ricin to the Egyptian 'sympathizer', who was being well paid for his dangerous assignment, Falconer, then a field agent, had been at Cairo Airport making his way back to Washington. It was the afternoon of 28 September, the day Nasser died. He remembered watching the heavily built Egyptian President who had arrived to see off the Sheikh of Kuwait with a smiling embrace after an Arab Summit meeting at the Nile Hilton Hotel. While waving a last farewell Nasser had stumbled, his legs gave way and he was unable to walk to his car, which had to be driven to him. Falconer had seen him helped into the car with such difficulty that he knew his mission had almost certainly been accomplished.

As the Pan-Am plane took off, Nasser was already on his deathbed in the throes of a terminal heart-attack engendered by the effects of the poison on the vagus nerve. By 7 pm he was dead, to the stunned astonishment and dismay of the whole Arab world, but to the delight of the Israelis and to those Americans responsible for defence strategy.

The post-mortem had been a formality because Nasser was known to have a heart condition and a deteriorating disease of the arteries. The perfect target perfectly eliminated! A clean kill with one painless jab of a welcomed needle, administered by someone who had no idea what was in the syringe. A 'termination with extreme prejudice', as the CIA called its assassination projects in those days, executed in such total secrecy that history would never record it. And the CIA assessment of Sadat's character had been just as outstanding as the rest of 'Rockfall'. Not only did he kick the Russians out of Egypt and turn to the West for his support but eventually, after weathering near-defeat in another Arab-Israeli war, visited Jerusalem and made peace with Israel! Nasser could never have brought himself to do any of those things.

Falconer had no residual conscience feelings about political assassination, which he regarded as no more than the necessary removal of a threat to his country's security, or of an obstacle to its progress. In his job he was permanently at war, and to win wars enemies had to be killed. Like pain and rain, any guilt was forgotten within a few hours of freedom from it.

The removal of Nasser had been the highlight of his career to date but that could be totally eclipsed by 'Cliffhanger', which was going to be just as right and just as tight, so far as security was concerned. Better, in fact, because nobody else inside the CIA knew about it. And there would be no outsiders – at least no amateurs. He would have to work with the British Secret Intelligence Service, though only at the highest level with its Director-General, Sir Mark Quinn, in person, and the need-to-know principle would be fully and ruthlessly applied.

Pity about having to involve Quinn, Falconer thought. He was OK, but they had clashed in the past before either of them had held such exalted rank. Like the time when Quinn found out that the CIA and Falconer in particular were doing all they could to help the British Labour Government scrap the TSR2 bomber and other planes, which eventually produced such rich orders for the American aircraft industry. Like a similar disinformation operation, in which he had been involved for the same good American end – spreading totally false rumours about the technical performance of the Anglo-French Concorde airliner.

It had been a straightforward conflict of national interests. Nothing personal. But Quinn hadn't seen it that way. He was a touchy guy, Mark Quinn, and rather unpredictable. You could never be sure how he would react. And his security wasn't all that reliable. Falconer had not forgotten that fiasco of the Enzyme Pill Project or the 'Walking Liquor-still', as the CIA scientists had called it.

Quinn had put up the idea, saying that it had come to him while he was meditating in the bath, which it well might have done, for he was an ingenious guy. The concept was brilliant and, with enough CIA money and effort behind it, it might possibly have been made to work. It involved the development of an enzyme pill which would so alter the human stomach juices for a few hours that sugar, starch or almost any carbohydrate taken in as food would be quickly fermented to produce alcohol. This would be immediately absorbed into the bloodstream, producing all the symptoms of intoxication.

'The stomach is a natural vat with its own built-in heater and stirring mechanism,' Quinn had explained with his usual enthusiasm. 'It is also its own distillation plant because alcohol is almost unique in passing straight through the stomach lining into the blood. So eat apples and you'll intoxicate yourself on cider; bread and potatoes and you'll make your own vodka.'

If the idea worked, anyone taking the pills, secreted in food or believing they were something else, like aspirin, indigestion tablets or vitamins, could be made dead drunk, especially on top of a normal intake of liquor. So the prospects for surreptitious use in espionage or Counter-Intelligence work were promising.

On Falconer's initiative, the CIA had agreed to carry out a feasibility study for which MI6 lacked the resources, and to underwrite most of the costs, though the scientists had greeted the project with scepticism. Then Quinn had fouled it up when he had been questioned by some senior Foreign Office bureaucrat under the new regulations governing MI6's budget. Instead of fobbing him off with some legitimate white lie, he had told the truth, proudly no doubt, believing that at that level his answer would be secure. Instead, the Treasury was alerted and then there was panic. If the secret leaked what was to stop somebody marketing the pills? If that happened, millions who drank alcohol for its effects, rather than for its taste, would switch to booze pills. The Customs and Excise would lose millions. There would be a catastrophic slump in taxes. The entire drinks industry could be ruined. Absenteeism would soar, with thousands stoned out of their minds after lunch, or even after breakfast if they felt like it. And what if the young latched on to it, as they had with LSD?

As soon as Quinn had admitted that the CIA was in partnership with them, the British Foreign Secretary had told his American counterpart and the whole project had been immediately stifled. By the grace of God, nothing had come out about it during the Congressional investigations, but it so easily could have done. No, he wouldn't be taking Quinn far into his confidence, Falconer assured himself.

For another thing, Quinn was even more hamstrung by faint-hearted politicians than he was himself. And had been for years. As witness the occasion in the Fall of 1972 when the revolting Idi Amin had decided to expel 30,000 Asians from Uganda. The CIA had been informed of a secret proposal put forward by MI6 to storm the main Ugandan airfield at Entebbe and fly in sufficient troops to depose Amin and restore reasonable rule. Detailed plans, involving almost a full army division, had been drawn up by the British Defence Ministry, with the approval in principle of Government ministers. An air marshal had been put in charge of the proposed operation. A good guy. What was his name? Cameron! That was it. Neil Cameron, of Scottish origin like himself.

Falconer recalled how the plan had reached a stage at which even a tanker was on its way to the Seychelles in support. And to the CIA's delight it seemed that Britain had got its balls back at last. Then the politicians had taken fright. What about the international repercussions for the infringement of Ugandan sovereignty? What about the Third World? What about the United Nations? The invasion had been summarily abandoned in favour of the cowardly solution of taking the Asians into Britain, with the public never being told of the alternative.

12

That was not the way the Israelis had behaved when the temporary occupation of Entebbe Airport had suddenly been in their interests. They were the boys, Falconer thought. Acting with dash and determination as the British and the Americans used to in the good old days. And what did they get for infringing Ugandan sovereignty? International condemnation? On the contrary. International acclaim!

By contrast, MI6 had even issued an internal memorandum to its headquarters staff assuring them that under no circumstances did the British Secret Service involve itself in violence of any kind. Holy Cow! If I was a British taxpayer I'd want my money back, Falconer thought.

No, he wouldn't be telling Mark Quinn a word more than was absolutely necessary.

As the car entered Connecticut Avenue Falconer looked at his watch. Good! He would have time for a change and a bath before his expected visitor arrived from London. He felt tired and knew that by the end of what – win or lose – was going to be 'Falconer's Last Case' he would probably be exhausted. Yes, it was high time he quit. He was getting too old for Intelligence games. But this one he had to play. There was no escaping it. The lives of millions – literally millions – could depend on it.

By comparison 'Rockfall' had been a parlour game.

Chapter Two

While Falconer soaked luxuriously in his bath, half dozing with a stiff Scotch and soda on the rim, Viktor Kovalsky, his latest KGB defector, who had brought the crucial information which made 'Cliffhanger' possible, was sitting anxiously on a single bed in his room on the fourth floor of a modest hotel in downtown Washington. It was the eighth hotel room he had occupied during the last ten days, not that any of them looked much different with their clinical furniture, plain mirrors, television sets and self-service coffee machines.

It seemed extraordinary to him that, with all its resources, the CIA could not provide a safe house for him. Instead his case officer, no doubt acting on instructions from above, had assured him that since that assassination attempt when a limousine had so obviously tried to run him down the safest thing in a free and open society was to keep moving around.

That experience had been frightening on two counts. The sight of the long-nosed vehicle accelerating towards him and mounting the side-walk, the sudden realization that its speed and direction were deliberate, and the frantic dive to a door which happened to be unlocked were terrifying enough. But that fear soon passed. What remained was the concern about the appalling carelessness of his CIA case officer in allowing him to stand alone in such a vulnerable situation while he made a telephone call.

The CIA knew beyond any doubt who he was. He had used several pseudonyms in the various places where he had worked abroad but Mr Falconer, who had spent much time with him in friendly interrogation, knew that he was truly Viktor Kovalsky, the most senior KGB officer ever to defect to the West, with the rank equivalent to major-general. As evidence of his confidence, Mr Falconer had even shown him the CIA dossier labelled 'Kovalsky' which contained so much personal detail of his prestigious career, including photographs taken surreptitiously.

The case officer had been replaced, presumably as a consequence, but the incident had deprived him of his confidence in the Agency to which he was now pledging his loyalty. He could not think of any of his former KGB colleagues who would have been so careless with such a valuable acquisition. That special item of information, which he had revealed at his first debriefing session three weeks previously, was surely enough in itself to merit the highest VIP treatment. Falconer was pretty poker-faced, but even he had been unable to conceal a look of delighted surprise.

Sitting in his shirt sleeves, the defector drew deeply on a cigarette as he watched the television screen. A diet of Western films and raucous advertisements with their unfamiliar jingles was not to his liking at all. He derived no pleasure

14

from watching Indians die obligingly in the dust in ludicrous circumstances. He had never been able to understand why men who looked after cows should be romantic figures. Surely they must have been dirty and smelly. And at the moment he was rather allergic to guns.

Master of several languages and well-travelled through service in various Soviet embassies as a KGB officer posing as a diplomat, Kovalsky had long regarded himself as something of an intellectual, addicted to classical music, ballet and literature. Trivia and razzmatazz were not to his taste. He was a serious man and, above all, a professional. Hadn't he been in line to become head of the First Chief Directorate, in charge of all foreign operations, until that sudden flight from Helsinki?

He looked at his new American digital wrist-watch. Where the hell was his case officer? He should have called for him more than an hour ago to take him down to lunch. There was no way that he was going to risk going down to the restaurant alone, so he turned down the sound of the television and lay · back on the bed staring at the ceiling.

He would certainly have deserved that promotion with all the fringe benefits it would have brought, he told himself. His record had been one of steady achievement ever since he had so cleverly organized the diversion of a big shipment of Indian-made sub-machine-guns, ostensibly intended for Libya, to the Palestine Liberation Organization in Beirut in 1968.

That first connection with the PLO, which had brought him into personal contact with its leaders, like Habash and Arafat, had led him to make an ingenious suggestion which had been snapped up, not only by the then Chairman of the KGB, but by the Central Committee of the Party. The Committee had been so impressed that it had reversed its policy and authorized the provision of money, weapons, training and planning advice to the PLO terrorists which had enabled them to bring off airliner hi-jacks, kidnaps, assassinations and hostage situations.

The results had been so beneficial to the KGB that the terrorist support was soon extended to the Baader-Meinhoff group in West Germany, the Red Brigade in Italy, the IRA in the United Kingdom and to others under the same secret condition which gave seemingly mindless outrages precise

15

purpose for the Soviet Union. The ingeniously simple arrangement which Kovalsky had initiated was that, whenever possible, the terrorists would give the KGB advance warning of any projected coup. Preparations could then be made for the KGB to use the turmoil and disruption created by the terrorist attack as cover for some operation of its own, while the police and security forces of the country concerned were severely stretched.

In that way the KGB had run caches of arms into West Germany while massive hunts were in progress for the killers of kidnapped public figures; it had infiltrated and withdrawn agents in and out of Greece while attention was concentrated on Athens Airport; it had smuggled explosives into France while all eyes were on terrorists holed up at Orly; and had strengthened its position in Turkey while the Egyptian Embassy there was under a seemingly stupid attack, which the PLO carefully went out of its way to condemn. In Britain the terrorist cover had been used so successfully to introduce arms and subversive agents that, on several occasions, it had concentrated Special Branch and other Security forces on to Heathrow and other airports simply by feeding a false tip into the Home Office or MI5.

The general disorder and debilitation of Western societies by the terrorists had been a bonus for the Soviet Union as a whole, but the big pay-off for the investment had been the extra KGB cover, which could be turned on almost whenever and wherever it was needed.

Such was Kovalsky's reputation as an innovator as well as an operator that his close colleagues must have been staggered by his defection, for he had gone out on the crest of another major KGB triumph – the incredibly successful Soviet propaganda drive against the American manufacture and deployment of neutron bombs.

Contrary to popular belief, the neutron bomb had been under development by the United States since the early 1960s, and from the moment the KGB got a whiff of its potentiality it had become a prime target for elimination by any means that might be engineered. Here was the very weapon the Red Army generals feared most – a small bomb or missile-warhead generating such a flux of lethal atomic particles that it could kill tank crews sheltering behind the thickest armour-plate. The further advantage to a defending army was the minimal damage it would cause to civilian buildings.

The virtual certainty that it would soon be possible to marry this weapon to extremely accurate missiles meant the 50,000 battle tanks, in which the Red Army had invested so much money and so much confidence, could be severely blunted or even neutralized. And it was on them that the Generals depended for maximum shock effect in the event of a war in Europe.

It had been his old friend Sergei Yakovlev, with whom he had first been recruited into the KGB, who, in his sojourn as Chief of the Disinformation Department, responsible for disseminating false reports, had so brilliantly foreseen how to stop the Americans from producing the neutron weapons. What a flier that Sergei had been! What escapades they had enjoyed together! Now, deservedly, he was right at the top, Chief of the entire KGB and a member of the Politburo – a further reason why promotion would surely have come his own way, perhaps eventually to the post he coveted most, one of the six deputy-directorships.

With characteristic insight Yakovlev had seen that the key to killing the neutron bomb lay in West Germany. The weapon was of no value for the defence of the United States, which was never likely to be attacked by tanks. Its sole value lay in preventing or defeating a Soviet strike in Central Europe. It would be pointless for the Americans to make it if the West Germans refused to have it on their soil. So that was the Yakovlev solution, namely a massive propaganda drive centred on West Germany to brand the neutron bomb as a criminal weapon deliberately designed to murder people and save buildings, a capitalist bomb which only a villainous, Imperialist nation could have invented, a bomb that killed slowly by atomic radiation, recalling all the horrors of Hiroshima.

When Yakovlev had sold his propaganda plan to the Soviet leadership he had immediately nominated Kovalsky, his old friend and fellow recruit, to control the operation against West Germany. And he had certainly controlled it with patience and faultless efficiency, the defector told himself as he lit yet another cigarette. Hadn't Yakovlev himself, in front of other superiors, slapped him on the back and talked of 'the Kovalsky touch'?

His first move had been to penetrate the West German leadership, and this he had accomplished through the planting of Guenther Guillaume, a professional Communist spy, into the entourage of the Chancellor, Willi Brandt. Guillaume had operated so superbly that he had become Brandt's closest confidant, and amongst the stream of information he funnelled back to Kovalsky was a continuing assessment that the leading German politicians could be deceived into opposing the neutron weapon which, in truth, could be their best safeguard against Soviet attack.

At the right moment a propaganda campaign against the weapon, which had been carefully planned for many months, was launched by Communist front organizations in Germany, Britain and Washington. After a softening up, which had been greatly assisted by pacifists, nuclear disarmers and others, the Kremlin leadership itself joined in the struggle. In the result, Jimmy Carter, the US President of the day, publicly agreed to delay production of neutron weapons and never to deploy them in Europe without the agreement of the countries concerned. And, as Yakovlev had cleverly foreseen, none of those countries would want to be the first to acquiesce.

In Moscow the campaign had been hailed as one of the most significant propaganda victories of all time. It had marked out Yakovlev as the next Chief of the KGB, the appointment being sure of the backing of the Red Army generals who, for the foreseeable future, could continue to put their faith in massed tank attack.

Ah, Kovalsky thought, that had been a triumph indeed! And he had played a pivotal role in it. Now, instead of reaping his rewards, he was lying bored stiff in a lonely hotel bedroom in the capital of Russia's most powerful enemy.

He had arrived on an American cargo ship from Helsinki where he had been visiting the Soviet Embassy for routine discussions with the KGB Resident there. The Resident was such an old friend that he could only have believed he had been kidnapped. Yet here he was, haggard, hard-up and looking older than his fifty-two years with his balding hair and rimless glasses, a full-blown defector apparently being hunted down by his former colleagues.

Kovalsky had often wondered about the defector's way of life: what it must be like to be suddenly and permanently cut off from one's roots. Now he knew and it did not suit him. Gone were the dignity and the security of belonging to an élite corps. Gone was the sense of belonging to anything; of any continuing purpose. Instead of a desk diary filled for weeks ahead with appointments and assignments, he faced a desert of empty days. Even the countryside, which he had admired during a brief professional visit to Washington some years previously, seemed alien and unfriendly, even though in late May it was lush and green, the woods being particularly splendid. The Russia with which he was familiar was mostly flat and featureless but, like the North African desert, which he knew from his service in Tripoli, it engendered a deep-seated longing. Who was that British poet who had written:

> Breathe's there the man, with soul so dead,
> Who never to himself hath said,
> This is my own, my native land!

It would be no good asking his case officer for the name – if ever he arrived. His mental processes seemed to be limited to one purpose: that of extracting every possible item of information from his charge's memory store. They had gone over the same ground so many times, not only in formal interrogation sessions, but while they were taking exercise or dashing from one address to another in fast cars.

Kovalsky had interrogated enough people himself in his time to be familiar with the routine, and he admired the case officer's skill and persistence in posing the sudden question which seemed innocuous but was ingeniously loaded. Still it was unbelievably tedious when one was on the receiving end.

The case officer's excuse was that the questions might stimulate the memory to release some half-forgotten fact or incident which might be of significance. But Kovalsky understood their prime purpose well enough. There was still suspicion that he was not genuine, but what the CIA called a 'mole', a double agent still loyal to the KGB sent to ingratiate himself with secret documents and information and then to mislead and disrupt. Well, he could cope with such doubts, however long they lasted; however searching the inquiries.

What could possibly have happened to the case officer? He had never been late before. A car breakdown perhaps? But he should have telephoned.

He stubbed out his cigarette, stood up, stretched and bent down to look at the snapshot of his wife and daughter which he had propped against the hairbrush on his dressing-table. He had taken it on that wonderful holiday at Sochi on the Black Sea where he and his family had been sent by a grateful Government for a mission well achieved. Tamara, his wife, a dumpy woman with blonde hair in plaits wound above her head, posed no great loss to him. They had married too early – 'when he was a corporal', as that scoundrel Napoleon would have put it – and he had been out of love with her, and certainly out of lust, for years. But his fourteen-year-old daughter, who had arrived late in a marriage he had written off as childless, was a different matter. Leaving her had been a major sacrifice for him and a cruel blow to her. He could only hope that it would be worth it.

He glanced again at the watch which, together with his American clothes and his latest American name, had been given to him by his new masters. He put on his jacket for something to do and put the snapshot in his inside pocket. The case officer had told him to carry nothing that could identify him, but he needed a physical link with the person whom he still regarded as his real self.

As he moved to turn up the television again there was a knock on the door – five knocks in fact. It was the pre-arranged signal, two knocks, pause, one knock, pause, two knocks. At least he would have some company even if it meant coping with the fractured Russian, which the case officer was cramming, obviously for some coming assignment in Moscow.

Kovalsky opened the door with a broad smile, but did not see the case officer. A stranger stood there. A weasel-faced man with a rather large-brimmed trilby hat. He was pointing a Luger Parabellum pistol ominously fitted with a fat silencer.

Concentrating his gaze on the pistol, Kovalsky was

momentarily too terrified to speak as he recognized it as the weapon favoured by Executive Action hit-men of the KGB when they wanted to leave evidence that an execution had been their work.

The stranger motioned him inside with threatening stabs of his gun and shut the door behind him. Then, keeping Kovalsky covered, he turned up the television set as loud as it would go. He made no reply to Kovalsky's Russian protestations as he pumped two bullets into his captive's chest and then shot him in the head for good measure.

If anyone was passing in the corridor at that moment the muffled shots raised no interest. They were a standard component of the television violence which was the normal environment for a modern hotel bedroom.

The assassin searched his victim's clothing but found nothing except the snapshot, a wad of dollars and some small change. He took the snapshot and slipped it into the briefcase which already concealed his pistol, but left the money. He checked there were no identification marks on the clothing. Then he opened the door gently, saw that the corridor was clear, hung the 'Do Not Disturb' sign on the knob outside and walked slowly out of the hotel, avoiding the lifts.

Chapter Three

As Ed Taylor, chief of the Central Intelligence Agency's mission in London, stepped down from Concorde at Dulles Airport on that warm afternoon, the extreme humidity proclaimed that Washington had been built on a swamp. Carrying the raincoat he had needed in London and swinging a pigskin hold-all, he walked briskly to the cab-rank, a sturdy, somewhat overweight, soberly dressed figure with a pleasant face which smiled easily. As he directed the driver of the Yellow Cab to an address off Connecticut Avenue, he was still wondering not so much why he had been recalled so hurriedly for a meeting with John Falconer, but why it was to be held at Falconer's private house instead of at the Langley Headquarters.

Like all the officers of the Clandestine Services, where the very nature of the work bred exaggerated caution and suspicion, Falconer was intensely secretive at any time, so much so that some regarded him as near-paranoid. However, Taylor was puzzled by his insistence that nobody at Langley or even in London should know of this sudden recall. It had to be something of exceptional sensitivity and urgency. After turning over every likely possibility during the flight he felt sure that it could only be about the international situation, which seemed to be sliding towards disaster hourly. But there was little about it that was not common knowledge and the main subject of current newspaper comment.

He opened the *Washington Post* he had bought at the airport. Though Iron Curtain censorship had never been more rigorous, the evidence of serious unrest in the Warsaw Pact countries was undeniable. There were strikes in Poland, Hungary and Czechoslovakia, and dissidence bordering on riots in the Soviet Union itself – in Georgia, Armenia and the Ukraine. There was even evidence of disaffection in the Red Army, with growing resentfulness against the three years of compulsory service under conditions which the young soldiers knew to be extremely harsh compared with any Western force.

The signs all pointed to the probability that the Soviet empire was beginning to crack under the strain of internal pressures. And that was bad. Any destabilization of the relationship between East and West was dangerous to peace. It would suit the West, as well as Russia, for the dissidents to be suppressed, however brutally, though Western politicians would have to continue to make noises about it.

As Taylor adjusted the tie he had loosened in the cab and rang the bell at Falconer's residence, Dan, the negro butler, was casting a final eye over the living-room, a room which clearly reflected the excellent taste of a wealthy man. He lifted the soda siphon to ensure that it was full, peeked into the ice-bowl, checked the bottles on the large drinks tray and repositioned the ashtrays before opening the door to admit the visitor, whom he had not met before. Falconer, a

22

bachelor, was something of a recluse and only a few select friends were ever invited to his home.

'Mr Falconer's apologies, Sir, but he's been out at Langley and got back later than he expected.'

'But he is back?' Taylor asked, gratefully appreciating the air-conditioned atmosphere.

'Oh, yes Sir, but he always insists on bathing and changing all his clothes after he's been out at Langley.'

Taylor smiled. 'Maybe it's a symbol. Maybe he finds the work dirty. You are not on the CIA payroll yourself?'

'No way, Mr Taylor!' the dignified, grey-haired negro replied almost with indignation. 'I've worked for the Falconer family in Virginia all my life until now. Or what I should say is that I have worked *with* the Falconer family. I was born in it.'

Taylor inclined his head towards an oil-painting of a man with Falconer's hawk-like features which, it was commonly said in Intelligence circles, matched not only his name but his nature. 'Is that Mr Falconer's father?' he inquired.

'No Sir. His grandfather. His father was killed in a riding accident when he was quite young and Mr Falconer was brought up by his grandfather. The old man was very strict, very strict indeed, but he was a good master. You could say that Mr Falconer and me were raised together. We certainly played together as kids. That was natural then, but the world's so crazy now that other coloured folk don't like it if you mention those good times. Would you like a drink, Sir?'

'No, thanks. I'll wait until Mr Falconer shows. What happened to your predecessor? He was employed by the CIA.'

'It's not for me to say, Sir, but he put his loyalty to the CIA before his loyalty to Mr Falconer. After all those terrible investigations into CIA executives Mr Falconer decided that he didn't want another Agency man living in his house.'

Taylor, a career CIA officer from a family of career diplomats, nodded sympathetically. 'Yes, it's been a very sad business for us all and, not least, for the Agency itself.'

'Mr Falconer was so angry that I thought he might quit, especially when that Congresswoman, that Mrs Jansen, started hounding him on Capitol Hill,' Dan said. 'He used to come down to Virginia at the weekend and walk round the estate without saying a word to anybody. And him always so kindly. I never understood why he went into the spy game in the first place. He's such a gentle man and he didn't need the money.'

Taylor smiled inwardly knowing the devious and ruthless nature which that aura of gentleness concealed, though more by hearsay than by personal contact. He had met Falconer only once since he had taken over as Chief of Clandestine Services, some three years previously, and only a few times during his own brief service in Counter-Intelligence.

'Oh there's no money in the "spy game",' he said. 'But if there's any excitement I suppose it's in the area Mr Falconer controls.'

He was admiring the red and white Chinese ivory chess set deployed on the mother-of-pearl chess-table and wondering who was Falconer's opponent, since the pieces were halfway through a game, when his host entered the room.

'Hi, John,' Taylor cried, seizing the hand thrust out by the rangy Virginian who always had an air of world-weariness about him. Observant by nature and by training in his field-agent days, Taylor noted that Falconer was wearing a dark-grey lounge suit and black Oxford brogues, hardly the clothing for Washington in such weather in spite of the coolness of the room. He also saw that he was carrying a slim red folder which he placed on his knees after tugging up his sharply creased trousers.

After the servant had left the room, closing the door behind him, Falconer offered Taylor a cigarette, which was refused in preference for a well-loved pipe. Then he spoke. 'Sorry to drag you over here at such short notice, Ed, and apologies for the cloak-and-dagger stuff, but I have some very hot information for you. I think you should have a drink before you hear it. You may need it. Scotch or Bourbon?'

'Scotch. No ice.'

Falconer poured two Scotches and handed one to Taylor.

'You're not going to believe this, Ed,' he said, sitting forwards in his black leather armchair and staring fixedly through thick-lensed, thick-rimmed spectacles. 'We have positive proof that Albert Henderson, the British Prime Minister, is an agent of the Soviet Union!'

Taylor, who had a habit of smoothing his crinkly red hair

24

when lost for words – as a boy he had inevitably been nicknamed 'Red', which he dropped on becoming an anti-Communist agent – stared back disbelievingly, then murmured, 'My God, John! At a time like this!'

'Right! At a time like this!' Falconer echoed. 'If there was ever a moment in history when the Soviets would like to know our intentions this is it. And who better to provide them than the British Prime Minister? He's forever on the hot line to the President.'

'But John, when you say he's an agent, do you mean an agent of sympathy because that wouldn't surprise me about several members of the British Left?'

Clasping his long, slim fingers and looking Taylor in the eye, Falconer said very deliberately, 'I mean he is a full-blown agent who passes the most secret information to the KGB for use by the KGB whenever he gets the chance. As you know, we've had our suspicions for years – ever since he was a junior minister. And before then, when he was forever marching with those nuclear disarmers. But now we have the full low-down on Henderson from a defector. It's all in here. He's given us a mass of evidence against him.'

He passed the red folder to Taylor who skimmed through it murmuring, 'Jesus Christ! Jesus Christ!'

'There's no doubt that the defector is genuine?' he asked.

'None whatever,' Falconer said emphatically. 'He's spilled some stuff we know to be accurate from other sources, and provided a mass of authentic documents including information about laser-beam weapons. The Soviets would never have sacrificed information as sensitive as that to establish the credibility of a phoney defector. And there's another reason why we're sure he's genuine.'

'What's that?'

'There's been an attempt to assassinate him.'

Taylor puffed at his pipe without commenting. He knew that when a defector was truly dangerous it was standard practice for the KGB to kill him if they could, and in such a public way that other would-be defectors were left in no doubt that they would be hunted to destruction. He tapped the open file on his knee and said, 'I see that Henderson was recruited way back when he was an undergraduate at Cambridge.'

'Yeah. And they've jollied him along ever since, waiting for the day when he might make the top and now he has in a big way. What a catch! He's still in his fifties.'

'What's his objective, John? To put Britain under Soviet rule?'

'No. It never is, is it? He genuinely believes that some link-up, some pact with the Soviet Bloc, which he would like for trade purposes in any case, is the only way of preventing a nuclear war. He's pathological about nuclear weapons. He was a member of that nuclear disarmament lot in Britain.'

'So he's spying for purely political motives. There's no blackmail or anything like that?'

'Correct, as far as we know. He's been conned into believing that if the Russians do attack in Europe it will be a swift prophylactic strike to prevent a nuclear war, which could become global. As a former professional historian he's convinced that the reunification of East and West Germany is inevitable.'

'Under Communism?' Taylor interrupted.

'Of course. Reunification the other way is just not on.'

'And I sure hope that nobody tries it,' Taylor said emphatically. 'Moscow would never allow East Germany to reunite with the West. A Fourth Reich would be far too strong for the Russians' peace of mind.'

'That's why Henderson sees armed conflict in Europe as inevitable one day. He's been sold on the idea that the Russians could occupy so much of West Germany in two or three days that we and the rest of NATO could recover it only by going nuclear. He believes – with some justification, I think – that the West Germans would then surrender rather than have their country devastated by the nuclear weapons we would have to use to recover it.'

'Better Red than dead, John?'

'And better Red than roasted! In any case, Henderson believes the President of the United States would not permit battlefield nukes to be used, for fear of strategic long-range missile retaliation on American cities.'

'Is that the way you think he would react?' Taylor asked.

Falconer was silent for a moment, then commented, 'The most I will say on that score is that famous men do not obey the laws of optics. The nearer you get to them the *smaller* they become.'

Taylor smiled in agreement, thinking that as far as his new Ambassador in London, Her Excellency Mrs Jane Jansen, was concerned, the aphorism also applied to women. He knew what Falconer and most of the Agency chiefs thought of the President. He meant well but in his bid for re-election was over-concentrating on domestic affairs, leaving foreign policy decisions in the hands of a Secretary of State who seemed satisfied with an outward show of good East-West relations. The Intelligence men were convinced that, in consequence, the administration was being taken for a ride by the Kremlin, but their evidence was dismissed as alarmist.

'How crazy can Henderson be to buy the idea that the Soviets would be content with Germany and wouldn't take the UK?' Taylor asked.

'He's even been assured that, if a lightning strike against Germany went according to plan, they would refrain from attacking the UK or France or Norway in return for a quick settlement accepting that West and East Germany should be demilitarized and reunited.'

'Good grief, John! That would be the end of NATO and the end of the United States in Europe. France wouldn't have us. I've never agreed with much that Henderson has said but I've always thought he was intelligent.'

'Oh, Communism's like religion, Ed. It cuts right across intellect. You have to believe what you are told. From above,' he added, pointing skywards.

'What does the President think about his good friend Henderson now?'

'He hasn't been told,' Falconer answered.

'Hasn't been told!'

'Well Ed, what could the President do if we told him? Ring up Downing Street on the hot-line and say, "Hi! Prime Minister. We've found out you're a spy." Telling him would put him in an impossible position.'

'But surely he'll have to be told eventually?'

'Correct. But not by us. There's only one way to handle this, Ed. We've got to tell British Intelligence so that they can sort it out for themselves.'

'You mean tell Mark Quinn?' Taylor said, referring to the

Director-General of the Secret Intelligence Service, with whom he was in regular touch while based in London.

'Yes. Then the news can come from him to the President by whatever channel he cares to choose. The whole thing's going to be hushed up anyway. You can imagine what it would do to Anglo-American relations, and to NATO morale, if it became public.'

'It would be the end as far as Congress is concerned,' Taylor, a confirmed Anglophile, said sadly. 'The Philby affair was bad enough, but the Prime Minister ... '

'You couldn't be more right, Ed. However, if we play this properly the public need never get a whiff of it on either side of the Atlantic. Why the hell should they have the pants scared off them for no good purpose? Can anyone doubt that we were right to keep the truth from the public when we nearly went to nuclear war with Russia over Berlin in 1948, and on several dicey occasions since?'

Taylor knocked out his pipe gently into an onyx ashtray surmounted by a silver model of one of the racehorses bred by Falconer on his Virginia estate, and then said, 'I sense that you don't want *me* to tell Quinn about Henderson.'

'No, Ed, and I'll tell you why. There's going to be no credit in this for anybody. Bearers of bad news are never welcome, and if it all goes sour the President will want somebody's head for not telling him right away. I'm fifty-eight, battle-weary and quitting soon. You have plenty of career time in front of you, and you are someone the Agency can't afford to lose.'

Taylor smiled his appreciation. Falconer was not noted for handing out compliments.

'So there are two ways you can play it, Ed,' Falconer continued. 'You can stay here for a few days on some trumped-up vacation while I fly to see Quinn. Or you can come with me. But I do all the talking and take all the responsibility.'

As a mission chief who was usually desk-bound, Taylor was not going to miss any action, particularly on his own territory, even if limited to being a spectator.

'I'll come with you,' he said without hesitation.

'I knew you'd say that, Ed. That's why I've booked two seats on the Concorde return flight to London today. But we'll be travelling separately, and I'll be listed as John Middleton. The airlines almost require a phoney name these days for anyone who's likely to be on a terrorist death-list. Officially I'm taking a week's vacation. If anybody finds out I'm in London, I'm there on a private visit.'

As Taylor handed back the Henderson dossier, Falconer treated him to one of his rare broad smiles, the twinkle in his eyes magnified by his pebble lenses. 'Ed, the time has come for a little private enterprise,' he said almost with boyish glee.

Of all the CIA branches, Falconer's Counter-Intelligence section had suffered most from the crippling restrictions imposed on the Agency following the inquisitions and resignations of the 1970s, including that of James Angleton, one of his most distinguished predecessors, and he deeply resented the limitations which, in his opinion, helped nobody but the KGB. So any opportunity for executive action had to be welcome to such a determined operator.

'I take it you won't be showing at the Embassy?' Taylor asked. 'You won't be wanting the Ambassador to know you are in London?'

'That interfering bitch!' Falconer exclaimed, with the arrogant look of a bird of prey. 'You are dead right. We don't want her poking her nose into this stinking midden.'

Falconer had compelling reason for disliking Jane Jansen, the recently appointed United States Ambassador to the Court of St James. As a Democratic Party Congresswoman, married to a campaigning and ambitious Democratic Senator, she had chaired the Congressional Committee which had made the check inquiry into the activities of the CIA, ostensibly to see whether the restrictions placed upon it some years previously were being observed. In Falconer's view Mrs Jansen's questions, which concentrated on anything she could label 'dirty tricks', amounted to a witch-hunt motivated not only by exaggerated antipathy to secrecy but by the political opportunity to make a name for herself.

For her part, Mrs Jansen had fair reason to detest Falconer. He had been the only witness to score off her repeatedly during the televized hearings on Capitol Hill, and she had failed to secure his dismissal, though she had pulled every possible string in public and private.

The main thrust of her allegations was that the CIA was

29

'still spying on our friends and allies', and that Falconer was the man mainly responsible for those reprehensible and dangerous activities. Falconer, who was vulnerable on that issue, had kept his cool and parried all the charges with replies so adroit and often so astringently witty that they won grudging praise even in the *Washington Post*.

'If she does find out I am in London and questions you, just say I'm there privately to watch the Derby and maybe buy a horse or two for my stud. Better still,' Falconer told Taylor, 'let her know I'm quitting the Agency and I'm there to say my farewells. That should please her. God in Heaven what a crazy appointment to put her in charge in London – or anywhere else! She's the most undiplomatic person I know. She ought to write a book called "How to Lose Friends and Alienate People". How are you getting on with her?'

'She just ignores me and the rest of the mission. She hates having the CIA under her roof, but there's nothing she can do about it so she pretends we are not there. It suits me. I hate having to work with a woman. A man is so much easier in our game.'

'I agree with you,' Falconer said emphatically. 'Women are far too nosey.'

The less any ambassador knew about the day-to-day operations of the CIA the better Falconer was pleased. And that was particularly true in Mrs Jansen's case. He was by no means sure of Taylor, not in the sense that he was insecure but that he might be averse to involvement in some of the more reprehensible deception techniques. There were far too many of that ilk in the CIA these days for his taste – younger men burning to re-brighten the organization's tarnished image. Taylor could be one of them.

Taylor had a reputation in the Agency of being 'popular' and a 'nice guy'. Neither tag was a recommendation to Falconer. In his dictionary of experience being 'popular' meant 'being easily understood by other people'. The implication was that other people could make some assessment of what was going on in a 'nice guy's' mind and how he would probably react in given situations. For security's sake, Falconer liked his subordinates – and his bosses – to be ice-cold, inscrutable loners. The Agency was no place for gregarious 'nice guys' whose judgement and determination might be warped by pity, sympathy, generosity or some other extraneous sentiment. It was about the realities of politics, not the equities. Do-gooders could foul up an operation and endanger their colleagues.

No, he wouldn't be telling Taylor too much either.

'I understand that Jane Jansen was the President's choice,' Falconer continued. 'He knew she was friendly with Henderson. They met at a White House party when Henderson came over to see the President after he became Prime Minister.'

'The buzz in the Embassy is that they knew each other before that. She's already been to dinner twice at Number Ten. I've developed a good source there – one of the servants.'

Falconer's face registered appreciation of his colleague's initiative. 'They should get on. They have a lot in common. They are both "liberals", whatever that may mean. "Socialists" they call them in Britain. Both are allergic to nuclear weapons and they are both sold on the belief in peaceful co-existence with the Soviet Union.'

'I wonder if they have anything else in common,' Taylor ventured. 'KGB-wise, I mean.'

'Huh,' Falconer grunted. 'Nothing would surprise me about that bitch after her crash programme to ruin the CIA. And the same goes for that Bible-punching husband of hers. Sanctimonious bastard!'

He might have allowed himself the luxury of savouring his hatred for a while longer had not the telephone started to ring. After Dan had answered it, a light flashed by the instrument in the living-room and Falconer picked up the receiver. The conversation could hardly have been more monosyllabic. 'Yes ... Good ... Understood.'

He put the receiver back without explanation, but Taylor could see that while very serious he seemed relieved. 'Now, Ed, we're going to have to work to very tight deadlines,' he said. 'Everything could blow up in our faces within the next few days. What's the latest Intelligence at your end?'

'Same as yours, I imagine. I've brought copies of the latest MI6 reports. I picked them up from Mark Quinn this morning.'

As he reached to open his holdall Falconer waved a well-manicured hand saying, 'Later, Ed. Just tell me about them now.'

'Their Foreign Office stuff confirms ours. Big trouble in the satellite countries and in the Soviet Union itself. The Politburo's deeply worried and there's a big split between the old leaders and the young thrusters.'

'That's hardly surprising. Most of those old hacks should have been pensioned off, or sent to the knacker's yard years ago. What's their average age, seventy?'

'Something like that. Quinn's really boned-up about the split, which he sees as a clash between the remaining protégés of Stalin and those who want a new approach to Communism. As you know, he's developed a source with excellent access right inside the Kremlin.'

Falconer nodded. 'Yes, "Uncle Vanya". The best source he's ever had and, thanks to him, the best Soviet source we've had for a long time. It was because of his success in recruiting "Uncle Vanya" and running him so well that Quinn got the top job.'

'Any idea who "Uncle Vanya" is?' Taylor asked.

'Not a clue. We've tried to find out, but our friend Mark O'Toole plays the "Uncle Vanya" operation very close to his chest,' Falconer replied, using the middle name which Quinn tried to conceal because it advertised his Irish origin. 'What's "Uncle Vanya's" latest, Ed?'

'The senile leadership – what Quinn calls the "gerontocracy", particularly Borisenko and Volkhov – are blaming the KGB for failing to stop the unrest, but they won't allow troops to be used for fear of triggering off a full-scale revolt.'

'So Yakovlev's getting the stick,' Falconer commented, naming the recently appointed chief of the KGB. 'Anything that takes his concentration away from us is good news.'

Taylor was aware of the admiration-hate relationship between Falconer and Sergei Yakovlev. They had first met when both were serving in cover-jobs in their respective embassies in Ankara. Each had known exactly what the other was doing to undermine his opposing country. And each enjoyed the bantering encounters on the cocktail circuit – Yakovlev had a lively sense of humour – a situation which had continued when Yakovlev had been posted to the Soviet Embassy in Washington.

Some dialogue with the KGB was encouraged at middle level by the then Director of the CIA, and Falconer had always believed that to know the enemy one needed to be as near him as possible. That was how Ambassadors behaved and even at that exalted level many of the Soviet envoys were KGB. So, years previously, Falconer and Yakovlev had even been seen together at race meetings and, on the Russian's surprise promotion to head the KGB, which had made him CIA Enemy Number One, Falconer had been moved to remark that at least there would be a civilized man in charge instead of the usual Party thug.

'Quinn says that the Kremlin leadership has intensified its hate against the United States and Britain for arming China,' Taylor recounted. 'They want to secure their front in Europe before their war with China, which they regard as inevitable.'

'That's our information too, Ed,' Falconer said. 'The old boys see a quick non-nuclear attack to occupy West Germany and push us out of Europe as the only means of resolving both their domestic and military problems. By claiming that it's Russia which is being attacked and is defending itself against the German aggressor again, they could unite the country under the guise of another "Great Patriotic War".'

Falconer rose to refill their glasses. 'It's the "worst case scenario" we've always feared, Ed – a war by political miscalculation at a time when our combat-readiness is at rock-bottom after a decade of neglect.'

'Yes, there's been too much butter and not enough guns.'

'Right!' Falconer agreed. 'All the miscalculation's been on our side. The Agency and the Pentagon have been pointing to the writing on the wall for years, but the politicians never see it until they have their backs to it.'

'And even then they ignore it,' Taylor said, scathingly.

'Right again! The NATO Supreme Commander is crying out for reinforcements, but the National Security Council is adamant. They reaffirmed their position yesterday. The Secretary of State argues that if we start to fly troops and arms to West Germany, or even just to Britain, it will give the Kremlin just the excuse it's looking for to "prove" we are preparing to attack.'

'They'd rather go on dishing out the crap about détente?'

'Sure, yet it's as clear as a glass of vodka that the central core of détente is appeasement. It's like Munich on a long continuing scale. While we sign scraps of paper the Russians churn out tanks, planes and warships by the thousand.'

'And KGB agents,' Taylor added.

'How right you are. Yakovlev's never had it so good.'

'Yet "Uncle Vanya's" information is that Yakovlev is strongly opposed to a Soviet adventure in Europe,' Taylor pointed out. 'He thinks Germany will fall to Communism through subversion alone.'

'Well subversion's his game, isn't it?'

'Sure, but it also seems to be the view of most of the young members of the Politburo. They believe that the only sensible answer to the dissidents is not a war but a relaxation of the régime, which is inevitable anyway.'

'All very encouraging,' Falconer said with a note of sarcasm, 'but it's the old men who are in command and they are too fossilized mentally to cope with internal changes. The only solution they can think of is trying to unite the people by whipping up a phoney fear that they are about to be attacked by the wicked capitalist West.'

'And the Red Army will do what they say,' Taylor commented.

'Yeah, all the cards are now in the Kremlin's hands – including the Joker I've just told you about.'

'The British Prime Minister?'

'Yes, Ed. The British Prime Minister! Our country has never been in such a dangerous position. You know I think you should get your wife and kids out of Britain. If the Russians do attack they'll strike at the UK simultaneously because it's our main reinforcement base. Your mother still lives in Idaho doesn't she?'

'Yes, at Boise.'

'Then I suggest you think about concocting a telegram from her with some family excuse for your wife and kids to visit her. You can send it from the airport. Then fix it with her for them to stay until we see how things pan out.'

'That's a good idea, John,' Taylor said gratefully.

He was deeply devoted to his wife, who was English, and from what Falconer had told him there was to be no general recall of the Embassy staff, at least not until it might be too late.

Falconer rose from his armchair and looked at his watch,

while Taylor noted that he was more stooped than when he had last seen him, the usual ageing penalty for great height.

'We haven't a lot of time to get to Dulles Airport,' he said.

'But I'm all packed and there's a car waiting.'

He took the red folder and placed it in his briefcase, which he locked.

'I reckon Mark Quinn is in for the biggest shock of his life, and he's had a few,' Taylor commented as he bestirred himself. 'What do you reckon he'll say?'

'He won't say much, although he'll be delighted. He hates Henderson. They've got a thing about each other. How is the great Sir Mark?'

'Same as ever. Full of quiet confidence and British calm. And more loaded with charm than ever.'

'Yes, and you watch that charm, Ed,' Falconer said, wagging his finger. 'He's as ruthless as they come. I always think he would have made a good gauleiter with those sharp, Nordic features. Have you ever heard the story about the ambassador's report on him when he was serving in Rome? It simply said, "I wouldn't breed from this officer." '

Taylor's freckled features creased into a laugh. 'Well, it didn't do him much harm.'

'No. Neither have his sexual proclivities. Does he still have a girl-friend in the office?'

The remark harked back to what Falconer had called 'an international incident' when Taylor's predecessor had taken away Quinn's mistress, who was also his personal assistant in MI6, and married her. Quinn had been more astonished than angry because he had always been the one to break off his romantic attachments. In any event the lady's place had been smartly filled by his next personal assistant, who had already been established as a secretary in MI6 and had previously caught the master's eye.

'He sure does have a girl-friend in the office,' Taylor replied. 'Angela, she is called, Angela Strickland, and apart from being a blonde she's something of a Chinese copy of her predecessor. Tall, long legs, and looks like she might be exciting in bed.'

'Does he confide in her to the extent that he did in his previous lady friend? She's proved very useful to us.'

'Yeah. He's quite open about it. "Who better to confide

in," he says, "than your mistress, when she also happens to be your personal assistant, cleared for Top Secret and daughter of a famous diplomat into the bargain?" '

'Then you should work on her, Ed. He must put a lot of secret eggs into that basket and there must be a few you could suck.'

Taylor grinned and shook his head. 'My wife wouldn't like it. Anyway, I reckon Angela might be more impressed by you. She obviously goes for older men.'

'No. I spend too much money on slow horses to be able to afford fast women.' He waited for the laugh then added, reflectively, 'I have no regrets, though I suppose I have missed out by having nobody to confide in, especially during a critical situation like this one. It has helped me to be able to confide in you.'

Momentarily Taylor felt a pang of sorrow for Falconer's legendary loneliness, but he felt the compliment was without much foundation. Falconer was so obsessed with the principle that only those who needed to know should be told anything that he would be incapable of taking anyone into his confidence purely to relieve himself of some of the burden of his frightening knowledge. No truly intimate relationship with a woman or a man was possible without trust, and Falconer trusted nobody. By nature, by training, probably by both, he seemed immune to the normal human need to share his secret life. If a rudiment or a vestige of that need was there it was more than recompensed by the exquisite gratification of wielding power in total secrecy.

No, Taylor thought, there was no purpose in feeling sorry for him. His loneliness was self-inflicted and almost certainly enjoyed. Why he even appeared to play chess with himself!

'Who's your opponent?' Taylor asked, nodding towards the chess table. 'You seem to be headed for a draw.'

'With that guy one always is,' Falconer said without answering the question. 'The only way I could win would be if he could win, too. And that's not possible at chess.'

There was a knock on the door and Dan appeared to announce, 'Time wheels were turning, Sir.'

'Thanks, Dan,' Falconer said, picking up his briefcase. 'Come on, Ed, let's go.'

Chapter Four

As the Concorde bearing Falconer and Taylor was touching down at London Airport, a military version of the supersonic Tupolev 144, known in the West as the 'Konkordski' because it owed so much to early information about the Anglo-French plane secured by agents of the KGB, was awaited at a military airfield near Strausberg-Eggersdorf in East Germany.

The airfield was the headquarters of the East German Air Force, the Luftstreitkräfte, but the most important person waiting there was a Russian, Marshal of the Soviet Union Andrei Andreievitch Dominowski, Chief of the United Armed Forces of the Warsaw Pact, First Deputy Minister of Defence, and a Member of the Central Committee of the Communist Party.

He waited with some impatience, a squat, clean-shaven Ukrainian with near-shaven hair and not much neck, except at the back where his nape was double. Standing with his jackbooted legs apart, the broad shoulders in his high-buttoned khaki jacket braced back, he shared his gaze between the clock on the wall of the Operations Room and the maps spread on the trestle-tables in front of him.

The person he awaited, and who was already several minutes late, was of even higher rank – Marshal of the Soviet Union Vladimir Davorin, Minister of Defence and Member of the Politburo, the main policy-making body in Moscow.

Dominowski, a soldier's soldier of modest origin involved for many years in building up the Red Army's mighty tank forces, had served in East Germany fairly recently as Commander-in-Chief Soviet Forces there before his promotion to be the youngest Chief of the entire Warsaw Pact Forces at fifty-one. Davorin, too, had served in East Germany, but only in the thrust against the retreating Nazi Forces in 1945 and during the ensuing occupation. Now aged seventy-two, he had served with the great Marshal Zhukov, whose tank tactics Dominowski had done so much to develop and modernize.

Dominowski did not approve of Davorin. He had been a great soldier – in his day – but that day was long past. With his heavy, drooping, grey moustache and roisterous, back-slapping manner, he looked like something out of *War and Peace*. And his ideas were as dated. New weapons with old men controlling them made no sense. And Davorin did control them. For the First Secretary of the Communist Party and Chairman of the Praesidium of the Supreme Soviet, Anatoli Borisenko, was a contemporary and old comrade of Davorin's and, as far as Dominowski was concerned, both were living in the past and living there dangerously for their country.

Dominowski looked again at the maps of 'Exercise Sword-thrust', the biggest peacetime manouevres ever attempted by the combined Warsaw Pact Forces, which Davorin was coming from Moscow to inspect. To the right of those unfolded on the table was a pile of maps which the German Chief of the Luftstreitkräfte, who was waiting with him, would not be allowed to see, certainly not on that day or on any other if Dominowski had his way.

There would be no difficulty there. The German knew his place. With the East German Forces there was not even a pretence that they were under national command. They were under total control of the Group of Soviet Forces in Germany, an enormous machine with tremendous potential fire-power. In the event of war, the East German Air Force would become part of the 16th Soviet Air Army, which alone fielded 1200 planes in the Democratic Republic.

'The Marshal's aircraft is in sight,' the control tower announced over the public-address system. Dominowski picked up his gloves and led out the dozen or so officers detailed to receive Davorin on the airfield. He hated being accompanied by a 'long tail', particularly when it included, as it always did on such occasions, a commissar from Glavpur, the political indoctrination outfit, and a senior officer of the military branch of the KGB, responsible for the 'reliability' even of the top commanders, but he knew that Davorin loved bullshit. No doubt the old boy would arrive decked out in all his medals!

38

He did. His chest was a mass of shining metal surmounted by his three Gold Stars, of which Dominowski could boast only one, awarded by the Central Committee for his work on the tank forces.

As the short, but still robust, figure of the Defence Minister appeared at the top of the airplane steps there was a cheer from the guard of honour and assembled troops, which he acknowledged with a smart salute and a wave. He had always been popular with troops, who called him a 'polkovodets' – a 'real commander'. His fine reputation as a fighting general in the 'Great Patriotic War' of the early 1940s had been well deserved. He had worked on the principle that he didn't mind how his troops pillaged or raped so long as they were smart and ready to fight next day. Dominowski took the view that modern weapons were so sophisticated and demanded such expertise to operate them that drunkenness and licence were completely out. Being untried in high battle command, he was jealous of Davorin, who was continuing to walk the high wire between political popularity and professional disgrace with remarkable agility.

After inspecting the mixed Soviet and East German Guard of Honour, Davorin gave the troops and airmen a brief pep-talk larded with suitably coarse Russian proverbs, and stressed the utmost importance of treating 'Exercise Swordthrust' as though it were a full-blooded thrust into Western Europe in defence of the Soviet Homeland and the Warsaw Pact countries. He ended on the note that, 'One day – it could be any day – you may be called on to risk your lives in the defence of your Motherland and your Party. So it is in your interests to learn as much from this Exercise as you can about the terrain, your weapons, your officers and about the enemy. Treat "Exercise Swordthrust" as though it were the real thing.'

Davorin seemed so intense that many listening to him, particularly those who had been involved in the invasion of Czechoslovakia, suspected that he was giving them a broad hint and they did not relish the prospect. Taking over Czechoslovakia had been an exciting and rapidly successful adventure but, apart from a few stones thrown by angry people, there had been no resistance. Indeed, they had been assured by their Glavpur officers, as they moved into Czechoslovakia, that there would be no effective resistance because the Americans would not intervene. Whether it was true or not, they had been told that Washington had consented to the occupation to preserve the stability of the East–West Iron Curtain line. But West Germany was a very different matter. Whatever they might be told by their political indoctrinators, if the Exercise was suddenly switched to an attack, they could not be sure that fear of reprisals would stop the Americans using their nuclear weapons.

As Davorin marched away to the Operations Room, some men who hailed from distant cities were wondering whether they would see them again or return to blackened ruins.

'Let's look at your plan, Andrei Andreievitch,' Davorin said, after being introduced almost cursorily to the East German Commander. For more than twenty minutes they pored over the maps, with black arrows showing projected pincer movements, concentrated thrusts, river crossings, tank-assembly areas and air drops of Soviet troops – all pointing towards the West German border.

'Where are your designated areas for "prisoners of war"?' Davorin asked.

Dominowski took one of the maps from the pile, opened it and pointed out the areas.

The East German Commander and his contingent were then dismissed on the pretext that purely Soviet matters were about to be discussed.

'What is your estimated rate of advance?' Davorin asked.

'Twenty to forty kilometres a day in the break-through phase,' Dominowski answered briskly. 'Fifty kilometres if we use nuclear weapons.'

'And in the exploitation phase?'

'Fifty to eighty kilometres a day.'

'Good,' Davorin commented, tugging at his moustache. 'You should be able to do that all right with the tanks, artillery and rocket fire at your disposal. What we must have is a war – I mean an exercise – of fast-moving advance. There is one other question. What are your plans for dealing with the refugee problem? Refugees streaming along the roads can't be allowed to stand in the way of your advance.'

'They won't,' Dominowski assured him grimly. 'My tanks

40

are all designed to operate fast off the roads. But if they can only operate on the roads they'll operate – whatever is in the way.'

He unfolded another and larger map and laid it down for Davorin's inspection. It showed thrust lines taking in Hamburg, Kiel, Hanover, Frankfurt, Nuremburg, Regensberg in West Germany and Linz in Austria, with projected areas where enemy troops were to be encircled.

'Excellent. Don't forget that any people in the way will all be Neo-Nazis. Your troops should be told that – and reminded how the Nazis behaved in the last war.'

'They will.'

'Good. So let us start the tour. We have to be back in Moscow tonight. The meeting of the Main Military Council is fixed for tomorrow morning.'

Dominowski led the way to the Mi 24 battlefield helicopter which had arrived outside the Operations Room. A gun-ship, it had room for the two Marshals and their adjutants. With a noisy swish of its five rotor-blades it took off for the nearest tank-assembly area, a few minutes flying time to the north.

The perimeter of the airfield they had left was packed with Soviet Mig and Sukhoi combat aircraft, including many of the latest marks recently flown in from Russia, together with Swidnik helicopters armed with anti-tank missiles.

As they approached the assembly area the two Marshals looked down on paraded ranks of T 72, T 62 and T 55 tanks, with their supporting BMP infantry combat vehicles designed to accompany the tanks all the way to their objectives. Davorin seemed most impressed.

'They'll be dispersing tomorrow for the local assembly points,' Dominowski shouted above the roar of the machine.

They landed briefly for a close-up inspection of one of the heavy tank battalions with a unit of battlefield SAM 4 anti-aircraft rockets alongside. The paint of the vehicles had been touched up and the crews were spotlessly smart and seemingly at peak morale.

'I see you believe in keeping your men well occupied when there's no fighting to be done, Andrei Andreievitch,' Davorin said. 'But that problem may soon be resolved, eh,' he whispered with a nudge.

Dominowski nodded, rather unenthusiastically to Davorin's mind. 'Right Marshal,' he said looking at his watch. 'It's time we returned for the trip to Milovice.'

A similar reception awaited them when they landed at the headquarters airfield of the Soviet Air Army based in Czechoslovakia, north-east of Prague. Davorin was first out of the Tu 144, anxious to see as much as possible of the preparations for 'Swordthrust' on which he was to report in person to First Secretary Borisenko. They watched aircraft operations, including landings on hard roads pressed into service, they inspected units of a Soviet Motorized Rifle Division and concentrations of multiple rocket launchers and 130 millimetre artillery.

There was also a special inspection of a chemical munitions unit, of which many were to be involved in 'Swordthrust', as they had been in the previous exercises leading up to it.

'Chemical weapons could be very important, Comrade, particularly against enemy air bases and storage areas,' Davorin counselled. 'We didn't have to use them in the last war, but with the nuclear threat speed is of the essence this time. The more of capitalist Germany we can occupy in forty-eight hours the less likely the enemy is to attack us there with nuclear weapons and it'll take them that long, at least, to carry out their crazy consultations.'

After one hour on the ground they were away to Legnica, the Polish headquarters of the 37th Air Army of Soviet Frontal Aviation, battlefield planes on which so much would depend as they bombed in advance of the tanks.

'How do you feel about the reliability of the Czechoslovak and Polish Forces, Andrei Andreievitch,' Davorin asked as they examined still more maps during the journey. 'After all these riots and strikes, I mean.'

'So, so,' Dominowski replied, making a see-saw motion with his hand. 'But they'll be firmly under control once the Exercise starts. KGB troops will be with them in some force.'

Davorin hoped that would be so. Poland had the largest Warsaw Pact air force outside the Soviet Union, and it was essential that it should pull its weight.

They made one quick stop at an air base well inside the Soviet Union to inspect a unit of SS 20 mobile ballistic nuclear missiles and briefly to watch tanks, waterproofed within thirty minutes, crossing deep rivers.

'You must be very proud of your tank crews,' Davorin said as they mounted the steps of the Tu 144 again for the final flight to Moscow.

'I am indeed, Marshal,' Dominowski replied. 'I would be sorry to lose any one of them.' He almost added, 'At least in an unnecessary cause', but deemed it dangerously impolitic to do so.

They left for Moscow with Davorin seemingly as fresh as when he had started. He appeared to be made of old leather. At that rate Dominowski could see no reason why he should ever retire.

'Do you think we'll reach a firm decision tomorrow?' he asked, when they were seated, referring to the special session of the Main Military Council, which was to be chaired by Davorin and would report directly to the Council of Defence chaired by Borisenko.

It was clear that Davorin was not prepared to give a view. 'We'll have to wait to see what the meeting says, Comrade. It will be a good democratic decision.'

At that moment it seemed that 'Swordthrust' might after all be no more than a genuine exercise, with naval units far out at sea also in position to stage the pretence of all-out war. However, as Dominowski knew, thousands more battle tanks and self-propelled guns and missiles than could possibly be needed for manoeuvres were clanking their way across great stretches of the Soviet Union, and the clear sky was loud with thousands of jet aircraft – all progressing purposefully in a Westerly direction.

Chapter Five

In the basement cinema of Century House, the twenty-storey monolith which served as the London Headquarters of the Secret Intelligence Service, Sir Mark Quinn, the Director-General, was sitting with his personal assistant, Angela Strickland, for the screening of two films which could only be described as 'blue'.

The first, which had been shot surreptitiously by MI5, the sister Counter-Intelligence organization, showed the ambassador from a rather hostile Middle East country taking enthusiastic part in a succession of deviant sexual activities, involving attractive young prostitutes in a large London flat. There was much alcoholic liquor about the place, from which His Excellency was seen to imbibe, and one of the girls looked very Jewish. In his public life the ambassador, who was married, made a show of condemning alcohol, declining to serve it to his Western guests at his embassy, and his country's leader, who leaned heavily on the Koran, was so antipathetic to adultery that his guilty citizens could face death by a thousand lashes.

Quinn had enjoyed the twenty minutes of action-packed voyeurism, which contained shots commanding his technical admiration. He would also have admitted to himself that the presence of Angela enhanced the pleasure. For her part she treated the experience, which was by no means new to her, as a routine part of her job. Her master wanted a woman's view of the likely reaction to such films, should they be 'made available' to parties who might be unusually interested, such as the ambassador himself, in this case, or his leader.

'That's certainly one to keep at the ready,' Quinn remarked, as the film ended in a riot of writhing bodies with the ambassador totally deflated. 'The villainous way he and his wretched country are behaving towards us these days, we

44

could need it any time. A good effort by MI5, though it irks me to have to say so. Damned clever the way they insinuated that Jewish tart into the set-up. She seemed to set him alight more than the others. Perhaps he fantasied that he was taking it out on the Israelis.'

'In that case, I reckon the Israelis won again,' Angela said, slyly.

The second film had been specially contrived with hired actors by Quinn's own film unit for showing to recruits to the Service, and as a refresher for established personnel, anyone of whom could be posted abroad. It featured a young British Intelligence officer, posted to Warsaw, meeting a pretty Polish girl said to belong to the underground movement there. She had much to say, in fair English, about the hated Russians and their army of occupation.

Lonely in a sad city, the Briton was shown, rather explicitly, falling prey to the girl's charms, a scene which excited Quinn even more than the ambassador's antics, for in recollection he could identify himself with the young officer. By repeatedly assuring the MI6 man of her pro-Western sympathies, as well as her affection, the girl induced him to part with information which in his judgement was not very important yet it could be used against the Polish section of the KGB. Sadly, it transpired that the sexy and obliging girl was a KGB officer herself, and the young man was quickly faced with giving further and more concrete assistance, or with denunciation.

'Not very original,' Quinn commented while Angela noted his remarks in her shorthand book. 'And not very sophisticated. Still it's the eternal bait that goes on trapping them.'

'Do you want it sent over to the High Street?' Angela asked, referring to the separate building used for training, so that any rejected recruits would not have been exposed to the secrets of Century House.

'Yes. They can show it in the next security pep-talk,' he replied, as he made briskly for the stairs.

Quinn was rather proud of the desk he had designed for his spacious private office on the fifth floor, a room with a panoramic outlook over the Thames taking in Whitehall and

Parliament just across Westminster Bridge. The desk was a ten-foot circle of mahogany with a four-foot diameter hole in the middle housing a comfortable swivel chair. Access to the centre was through a lift-up section and, once inside, Quinn could swing himself round to any other section of the desk. This was a great convenience for the top was usually laden with files, in-and-out trays, piles of diplomatic telegrams, reports from agents abroad and intercepts of foreign radio communications, provided round the clock by GCHQ – Government Communications Headquarters. GCHQ was the all-important network of electronic eavesdropping and decoding stations working in close co-operation with the American National Security Agency, which operated several American-built intercept stations in Britain. It had once belonged to MI6 but had been filched – as Quinn put it – by the Foreign Office.

For making his routine reports to the Foreign Office, controlling some espionage operation abroad or assessing the flow of Intelligence reaching Century House, Quinn liked to have every scrap of relevant information within arm's length and he liked it 'raw', not processed by passage through some underling's mind.

'Information is what we are about,' was his continual guidance to his staff, both in the field and at headquarters. 'We have no executive powers. We are a dredging outfit and we must dredge deep and wide. Information, information and yet more information!'

There was plenty of room on the desk for the four differently coloured telephones, and the office inter-communication box. Beneath it were the switches operating the well-hidden microphones connected with a concealed tape-recording machine in the ante-room, so that any visitor's conversation could be kept on record for analysis later.

By swinging his chair through 180 degrees he could face the large world map showing the position of his officers and agents abroad, a reference aid which was covered by a security curtain when not in use. To his right, outside the desk, was the television console which, at the touch of his remote-control hand-set, provided military information or the latest picture of Soviet Intelligence-gathering operations by ships and aircraft.

46

In front of him, at a distance which would look respectful to visitors, was the desk occupied by Angela. She had a private office in the ante-room, but Quinn preferred her to be close by because he used her as a sounding-board for his ideas and assessments, and valued her views as he was 'thinking things through'. Quite simply, he just did not like being alone.

'You look like a spider in the middle of a web,' Angela had remarked when the desk had first been installed and her master sat, rather proudly, inside it. The comparison was apt, though for a spider which pulled strings rather than one that pounced and killed.

Anyone entering the room was treated to the pleasurable smell of coffee, which Angela brewed in an electric apparatus providing a constant supply. Angela was tall, naturally blonde and slim, with the good legs to which Quinn responded so much more positively than to any other feminine attribute. In fact, he emphatically forbade her to wear slacks. With the self-assurance of a much-travelled background, through her father's foreign service, and fluent in several languages, she was no less astute than her predecessor had been, and what Quinn called her 'feminine intuition' was, as often as not, native intelligence. Indeed, she was capable of putting forward her sometimes ingenious suggestions in such a way that her master was able to believe they were his own.

It was no secret to the Century House staff that Angela was Quinn's mistress, though they took care to have separate establishments 'to preserve appearances', his flat being in Cadogan Gardens, hers in Clarges Street, off Piccadilly. The requirement of the night-duty officer at Century House to know the whereabouts of the Director-General in case of emergency put the situation into the realms of farce, but illusive appearances played many roles in the Intelligence game.

Well-meaning friends, including senior colleagues, who heard the illicit relationship being discussed by junior staff in the Century House Social and Welfare Club, had frequently pointed out its danger with the ever-present threat of KGB blackmail, but Quinn simply argued that as so many in Whitehall also knew of it there could be no risk. He kept stubbornly to this opinion, even while being party to the use of evidence of embarrassing sexual relations, or even its fabrication, to apply pressure on some foreign diplomat or other who might be causing trouble. If severely pressed, he could always cite a previous example of a Director-General of MI5 who had enjoyed a precisely comparable situation, making no effort to regularize it until his retirement, when he had divorced his wife and married his former personal assistant.

Angela had little hope that this would happen in her case. She was never likely to be Lady Quinn, even if she stayed the course. She knew that one day when it suited him her lover would ditch her, but she put up with the bleak prospect and much more besides, for the big lesson she had learned from her upbringing in a diplomatic environment was that life was all about making concessions. There was no way every desirability could be satisfied. Internationally, nationally and in domestic life one had to settle for a fair compromise, and she felt she had found hers.

She had been quickly captivated by the piquant satisfaction of being so exclusively in the know about the most secret matters of State, through the documents which had to pass through her hands, and from what Quinn told her. Undercover operations fascinated her. She could think of no job which could possibly supply such a constant stream of intriguing circumstances, and she knew that if she lost it she would miss it terribly. She would also miss Quinn for, like many attractive women of spirit, she happened to like bastards. Her father, whose diplomatic activities had occasionally intruded into the demi-monde of MI6, had also qualified for the epithet and she had admired him enormously.

Quinn had also been warned many times of the risk that some journalist might hear of the relationship and write about it, stressing the security danger, which could lead to embarrassing questions in Parliament. His reaction was even more robust. The journalist would be damned sorry, whoever he was!

He had a vengeful habit of fixing journalists who crossed him. There had been one occasion recently where a national newspaper had printed a true report about a minor MI6 disaster and, through a distinguished intermediary, Quinn had warned the Fleet Street proprietor concerned that his reporter was not only ill-informed but was suspected of working for the KGB. Under the circumstances, it was pointed out with consummate tact, any further problems of a similar nature might force the security authorities into ensuring that neither the proprietor nor the editor would ever appear in an Honours List.

The name of that journalist, famous as it was, rarely appeared in the newspaper again.

Whatever arguments might have been arrayed against his sexual habits, Quinn was not going to be deprived of a private life simply because he chose to remain unmarried, if only for a peculiar reason which he kept secret from everybody and especially from Angela. He needed close feminine companionship because, as his intimate friends soon discovered, behind the aura of supreme confidence and the resolute set to his features there lurked much doubt. By nature he hated being in a state of doubt, yet he had chosen a profession so beset with it that the best he could usually hope for was a correct assessment of a balance of probabilities. He therefore needed a confidante not only to assist with his professional problems, which were always complex, usually urgent and often daunting in the extreme, but to minister to his psychological need to discuss his secret life with somebody and to support him emotionally, though he would never have admitted that, even to himself. His explanation for confiding in a woman was that the feminine mind worked differently:

'My job may seem to be about events but it's really about people. I need to know as much as possible about their characters and how they are likely to react. The feminine mind, which is differently constructed from a man's, sees things I may miss.'

His relationship with Angela also meant that he received much of her guidance in private and so could avoid giving the impression to his colleagues of being swayed by her, though few of them were fooled.

At fifty-five, Quinn still had an air of youthfulness with his blue eyes, fair, fresh complexion, firm jaw and ready smile, the silvering of his blonde hair being the most observable clue to his age as he sat in the centre of his 'web'. He had been 'thinking through' a projected Intelligence operation in Kenya and was burning his notes in a large glass ashtray, selected for its transparency so that no KGB 'bug' could be concealed in it, when Angela entered the room bearing an oblong, yellow dispatch-box. He unlocked it with a key attached to a long gold chain secured to his belt. An Italian belt suited his 'with it' appearance for which he took such care that he had his jacket made by one tailor and his trousers by another.

The box was so full that the papers welled out of it as Quinn released the pressure of the lid.

'You know what the coroner's verdict on my inquest will be?' he asked rhetorically, in a voice which still retained a trace of Irish brogue in spite of his efforts to eliminate it. 'Found dead – under a pile of paper!'

He picked out the top document, originating from the Cabinet Secretary, read it and announced, 'The President's been on the hot-line to Downing Street again. The National Security Council met in Washington yesterday. They decided to continue playing the international situation cool. No military alerts. No reinforcement in Europe. Nothing that could be misinterpreted as mobilization. No political speeches drawing attention to the danger. Nothing that might provoke the Kremlin. The PM's in full agreement. He would be, wouldn't he? Meanwhile things go from bad to worse – and fast.'

'What else could you expect from "The Prince of Peace"?' Angela asked, using Quinn's cynical description of the Prime Minister. 'He's so starry-eyed about Anglo-Soviet trade and cultural relations that he would never do anything to offend the Kremlin.'

Quinn grunted his agreement as he initialled the document with the green ink which he alone in the department was allowed to use. 'Happily there are some who are more realistic,' he said. 'The Home Secretary is making preparations to evacuate the Government, if needs be, to the underground regional seats, and that cavernous shelter near Bath is being warmed up to receive the Royal Family. Meanwhile, we have all the evidence here of what's happening behind the Iron Curtain.'

He swivelled his desk slightly and picked up a sheaf of papers. 'These are further reports of insurrections. There's every sign that the Politburo will try to resolve its problems by fabricating an excuse for a military adventure against NATO. And what are the gutless politicians doing? Sweet fuck all!'

Angela, who had come to terms with Quinn's use of coarse language, though such obscenities still jarred, remained silent as he slammed the papers back on the desk.

'Most of that bumf originated from across the bridge,' Quinn continued angrily, referring to the Foreign and Commonwealth Office in particular. 'So they know the form. Yet one can never make them understand that the only thing the Russians respect in a potential enemy is resolution. Toughness! They'll still go on trying to appease the Kremlin when we get proof positive that the Red Army's on the march. That silly sod Henderson is prepared to see Britain decline to a tiny dot on the map so long as he can go on avoiding war. Politicians! I wouldn't employ one of them to sweep up!'

One of Angela's less pleasant functions was to serve as target for Quinn's tirades against the Labour Government which had pushed Margaret Thatcher from office after two Parliaments. Her hawkish stand against the Russians and their sycophants had been rapidly replaced by a Labour administration fawning on them to 'make amends', the Foreign Secretary being second only to the Prime Minister in his longish list of ministerial aversions.

Hoping to calm Quinn down, for she was convinced that such outbursts must be bad for his blood pressure, Angela moved to his desk to replenish his coffee mug. But he was not to be assuaged so easily.

'What in God's name is the use of spending millions and inducing people to risk their lives to produce prime-grade Intelligence when it is promptly ignored? All I get back from Whitehall for all our efforts are anodyne decisions with which I am required to agree, the essence of genius in that cloud cuckoo-land being the ability to align oneself with the inevitable. All I shall be able to say when I retire is, "I came, I saw, I concurred!" '

'You need a haircut,' Angela remarked as she returned to her desk. 'I'll make you an appointment.'

A flicker of a smile crossed Quinn's face at this deft deflation.

51

As he returned to his documents, Angela's telephone rang to announce the arrival of two expected guests, who had telephoned previously.

'John Falconer and Ed Taylor are here,' she announced.

'Ah, I wonder what they are after,' Quinn said, as he pressed a switch under his desk. 'Falconer never moves from the centre of *his* web without damned good reason.'

'We meet in troubled times, John,' Quinn remarked after extricating himself to welcome his visitors.

'Can you remember when they weren't troubled, Mark?' Falconer asked.

'No, but this is looking like a real flash-point situation – maybe a nuclear flash – and I can't get my political masters to face it.'

'It's the same story in Washington, Mark,' Falconer said, seating himself after the handshakes. 'It's words they are interested in, not facts. The trouble with politicians everywhere is that they confuse the two. When they've said something they believe they've done something.'

'Would you like some coffee, gentlemen?' Angela asked.

'Sure would,' Taylor replied. 'You'll be glad to know, John, that tea isn't the regular brew in these parts.'

'No. Whitehall's the tea centre – down the road,' Quinn said. 'Nothing to do with this firm. Well, John, how long do you reckon we've got before the Russians claim they're being attacked by West Germany and invade Europe?'

'Could be a week. Not much longer. They can't hold things together for many more days without generating another "Great Patriotic War".'

'That's our assessment,' Quinn said. 'We had a meeting of the Joint Intelligence Committee this morning and came to just that opinion. But the Prime Minister rejects it. He can't bring himself to believe that the Russians will attack anybody. "They defend themselves but they don't initiate attacks," he insists. Of course, Hungary and Czechoslovakia are conveniently forgotten. He's just besotted with holy hope!'

Falconer saw his chance. 'There could be another explanation, Mark. The details are in here.'

He took the red folder from his briefcase and made a flick of his eyes towards Angela, suggesting that, for secrecy's sake, she should leave the room.

'No, that's all right,' Quinn assured him. 'I have no secrets from my personal assistant. Whatever it is she would have to know anyway.'

Falconer gave a slight but discernible shrug of disapproval and passed the folder to Quinn. 'The blunt truth is that you have a KGB agent inside your Cabinet – in the shape of the Prime Minister himself.'

Angela was obviously startled by the assertion, but Quinn remained impassive as he thumbed through the summary and the supporting documents.

'You don't seem to be surprised, Mark,' Taylor could not resist commenting.

'In this game nothing surprises me any more! Not after Philby,' Quinn responded quietly, referring to the so very British senior Intelligence officer who had shattered MI6's belief in itself when he had turned out to be a KGB spy.

While Quinn turned the pages at his usual rapid rate, Falconer gave Angela a closer inspection, noting that she had a good head, bold eyes and fine legs which, in his experience of both horses and people, were signs of good breeding.

Quinn made a mental note that some of the defector's statements could account for unexplained leaks which had worried him in the recent past. Then he said, 'You know, John, since I took this job on I've frequently thought that if Kim Philby could have become Director-General of the Secret Intelligence Service – and there's no doubt that he could – then the KGB can get an agent into any political position. Indeed, it should be much easier. Given a dedicated man with unlimited patience and nerve, the door to Number Ten Downing Street is wide open. That MI5 bastard, Anthony Blunt, even got into the Palace!'

Falconer nodded. 'Well you know, Mark, we've often taken issue with the superficial way you check out politicians with access to secrets.'

'And quite rightly,' Quinn responded, keeping his eyes on the documents. 'But we are not permitted to do anything about them. And it's not just politicians either. Remember the British ambassador we had to pull out of Moscow because he fell for the crudest KGB trick in the book – the all-too-willing chambermaid. And all those heart-searchings about a certain head of MI5, though nothing would surprise me about that outfit ... '

Falconer and Taylor exchanged glances. They could appreciate the rivalry between MI6, responsible for Intelligence operations abroad and MI5, responsible for security in Britain, for they had similar problems back home with the FBI.

'You are completely satisfied with your defector's information?' Quinn asked.

'Absolutely. He was a high-level KGB officer. He's been feeding us with prime source information for months. You've already had most of it. Now he's come over.'

'As you've got him, I assume you can now give him a name.'

'Fair exchange for "Uncle Vanya's"?' Falconer asked without much hope.

'No way! *He* hasn't come over yet and I hope he never has to.'

'OK. It's Victor Kovalsky.'

'Kovalsky! I thought he was being groomed for stardom by our dearly beloved Comrade Sergei Yakovlev, God rot his soul. What made him defect?'

'He claims that he was for the high jump. Once Yakovlev reached the top he got scared that Kovalsky might oust him. Apparently our defector has an admirer in the Soviet Premier, Volkov.'

'So Yakovlev was going to purge him! Sounds in character. When am I going to get a sight of him?'

'We'll turn him over to you as soon as we've finished debriefing him. That is if he stays alive.'

'Why? Is he ill?'

'Not yet. But the KGB has already made one attempt to kill him.'

Quinn looked suitably impressed. 'The KGB gets all the executive action and we get none. I used to envy you your freedom in that respect. It can solve so many problems. But now you are as ham-strung as we are.'

'Yeah, but it's no good longing for the good old days,' Falconer sighed. 'They'll never return. But what do you propose to do about Henderson? I felt he was your pigeon.'

'He certainly is,' Quinn agreed. 'And we will move smartly.

But you do realize, don't you, that whatever we discover will have to be hushed up? We did an in-depth study some time ago as to what would happen if we found out that *any* senior minister was a KGB agent. The view here was unanimous – "Operation Cover-Up".'

'Yes, I do realize that the public won't be told anything, but Henderson will have to be removed,' Falconer asserted.

'It won't be that easy,' Quinn replied. 'If I telephoned the Leader of the Opposition now and told him that Henderson, whom he detests, is a spy, he'd insist on secrecy. Parliament's a club you know, and a scandal of this magnitude would be regarded as devastating for the whole membership. So you can imagine what members of the Government would do to convince themselves that your claim is false. The civil servants would take the same line. I promise you, John, that the noise of various ranks closing would be deafening.'

'It would be just the same in the States,' Falconer said quietly. 'But surely we are not going that public. We don't want to repeat the political mess the West Germans made when they insisted on prosecuting that guy Guillaume. That should have been handled under the counter. The public trial put Guillaume in jail, but it ruined Chancellor Brandt and sent the KGB's stock soaring.'

'That's the last thing I intend to do,' Quinn said firmly. 'That bastard Yakovlev's doing too well as it is. No, if there is going to be any swift executive action on this at all we shall have to take it ourselves. In the old days we might have arranged for Henderson's accidental demise. He might have "caught measles", as I believe you used to put it. So would Yakovlev, if I'd had my way.'

'I'm not sure that it would have been wise to liquidate Yakovlev, Mark,' Falconer demurred. 'At least he's civilized, and a dog you know is always better than a dog you don't know.'

Wondering whether Falconer's use of the word 'dog' in connection with Yakovlev might be deliberate in view of a lacerating memory it held for him, Quinn replied tersely, 'Our criteria of civilized behaviour must be different, John. I only hope that one day the Good Lord will deliver him into my hands. But as regards Henderson I must first go through the motions of getting confirmation of your allegations.'

'But won't that mean surveillance?' Falconer asked anxiously. 'And won't that take more time than we've got?'

'It *will* mean surveillance,' Quinn replied quietly. 'But with the Prime Minister that's no problem.'

'How come?' Falconer inquired.

'Oh, it's never been all that difficult in Downing Street, though it varies with circumstances, as it must with you in the White House. One of the best runs we ever had was in Harold Wilson's day. MI5 had a steady informer on the Downing Street staff and they used to send us copies of all his reports – details of where the Prime Minister went, who he saw ... Marvellous stuff.'

'Is that informer still active?' Falconer asked hopefully.

'Sadly not. There was a bad leak in this building, I'm sorry to say. Somebody gave a journalist details of one of the reports MI5 had sent us and he published them along with a claim that Wilson had been bugged. There was quite a nasty inquiry by Callaghan when he succeeded Wilson as PM.'

'I recollect it,' Falconer said. 'There was some suggestion that we were involved. Didn't Callaghan categorically deny that Wilson had been bugged by anybody?'

'After a lot of consultation he issued a statement denying that Downing Street had been bugged *electronically*. Nothing was said about the "human bug".'

'You don't still have him, do you, Mark?'

'No, and I don't suppose, after that row, that MI5 had the nerve to replace him. In any case, our relations with MI5 have never been quite the same since. They are still sore at the way the leak here fouled up their operation.'

'So how will you cope with the Prime Minister now?' Falconer asked.

'We have our own informer – the PM's private detective. He belongs to Special Branch but we offered him some fringe benefits to keep us in the picture. He goes everywhere with the PM, knows how he spends every minute, who he meets and where.'

'He defected to you,' Taylor could not resist exclaiming in admiration.

'You could say that. Regrettably, it doesn't happen often. But it's damn useful when it does. You must have similar situations with the FBI, John?'

Falconer raised his hands in mock solemnity. 'I wouldn't know anything about that. Has your detective come up with any lead?'

'No. The PM doesn't seem to be seeing anyone he shouldn't. But our friend will now be taking a closer look.'

'But will that be enough?' Falconer persisted. 'It might be days before the PM has reason to make contact with his KGB connection.'

'No, John. It will not be enough,' Quinn replied.

'Then what else do you propose? A disinformation gambit?'

'Of course. What else? I'll feed the PM some false Intelligence that sounds really hot. If he is as active as you say he'll be driven to pass it straight to his contact, and it should be in the Kremlin in hours. Our contact will then inform me.'

' "Uncle Vanya"?' Taylor asked, receiving a slight frown from Falconer for interrupting.

'Yes, "Uncle Vanya". He is superb. He makes Kim Philby look like a village sneak. He's also got a sense of humour, which is rare enough for a Russian. As evidence of the authenticity of his messages he always adds the latest anti-Kremlin joke.'

Quinn took a piece of paper from a small strong-box, which was usually locked in the office safe, and read: 'Question. What is fifty metres long and eats cabbage? Answer. A queue outside a Russian butcher's shop. If dear old "Uncle Vanya" plays back the false information to me we need no further proof.'

Falconer seemed encouraged. 'Any idea what you will use – as disinformation, I mean?'

'None whatever at the moment, but ideas grow out of facts and you've given me a most interesting fact. I shall have to make use of the think-tank,' Quinn added, rather mysteriously.

'The think-tank!' Falconer said with some alarm. 'Surely you're not going to bring anybody else into this?'

'Of course not. And nothing whatever is going down on any report. Nothing that anybody can ever demand to see under this blasted Freedom of Information Act, or that some Prime Minister might find it expedient to blow, as Mrs Thatcher did with the Blunt case.'

Falconer was relieved to hear it. Under the American Freedom of Information Act, members of the public, which usually meant prying journalists and politicians, could demand to see departmental documents. This meant that informants and spies could never be certain, as they had been in the past, that their identities would remain secret. So many who could have volunteered help or been recruited for money had shied away, leaving the CIA officers themselves, including Falconer, to perform such clandestine tasks as they could.

'But what about this think-tank?' he asked with continuing concern.

'That couldn't be more secure or more private,' Quinn replied. 'Almost as private as the grave! My think-tank, John, is my bath. I get my best ideas, especially for disinformation exercises, lying quietly in a hot bath. I never take a bath without having my portable tape-recorder handy. I would no more move without it than without a toothbrush. So, with any luck, I'll have something in the pipeline before the evening's out. And if I know "Uncle Vanya", we'll have a feedback by tomorrow. That is if the PM's guilty.'

'He's guilty, all right,' Falconer insisted, standing up to depart. 'Right, Mark. The ball's with you. Let us know soonest when you get a result. I daren't hold our information back from the President much longer. You can get me through Ed, or ring me direct at the Grosvenor House Hotel. I'm booked in there under the name John Middleton.'

They said their farewells to Angela and left the office while Quinn returned to his 'web'.

'That's all we needed, Angela,' he said wearily. 'As though I haven't got enough on my plate. And to be told about the Prime Minister by the CIA, though we've had our suspicions as you know.'

'What will you do if they prove to be true?'

Quinn stroked his chin. 'I may have to confront him. I have a constitutional right to see him privately. But I don't relish the prospect. If he's as close to the KGB as Falconer says they will have gone into this contingency with him – what he should do if he's caught. They must know that we can't arrest him, that there couldn't be a public trial. By comparison, Watergate would look like the triviality I always thought it was.'

To Angela the idea that any traitor should be pardoned and escape public censure because of his position in society seemed preposterous, and she said so.

'Look Angela,' Quinn said patiently, avoiding any endearments as was their mutual custom in the office, 'when you've been in the Intelligence game as long as I have you'll realize that it's not about catching spies but preventing the other side from doing you damage. Which would cause more damage – letting Henderson go or taking all the backwash of an international scandal?'

'But what about justice?'

'To hell with justice!' Quinn barked. 'The trouble with justice in this country is that it has to be seen to be done and that demonstration could do so much harm. That's why my predecessors never wanted Philby in the dock. There's no point in making the whole country suffer just to send one man to prison.'

Quinn regarded his power to ignore laws, or at least bend them, as his last remaining privilege.

Reluctantly Angela accepted his argument. 'What about informing the Queen and ... '

'No. No. One can't bring the Monarchy into a filthy mess like this. Not after the Blunt disaster. The Queen didn't mind being used but Parliament was furious. The way I see it at the moment, the best we can hope for is to neutralize the bastard and leave it at that. Of course, we are assuming that Falconer is right.'

'He seemed totally convinced.'

'A little too convinced for my liking,' Quinn said rather sourly. 'He could be plain wrong. The CIA has a record of tripping over its cloak and falling on its dagger. As we all have,' he added grudgingly, remembering how his own career could so easily have been curtailed if Ian Smith, then Prime Minister of Rhodesia, had insisted on 'going public' when he discovered, through an appalling gaffe, that a British Government official in Salisbury was really a full-blown MI6 spy, instead of reluctantly agreeing to the man's removal on the fictitious grounds that his father was dangerously ill back in Britain.

'There may be a lot more to it than we know, Angela. I haven't really fathomed why Falconer came all this way to tell me about Henderson when Ed Taylor could have done it.'

'Protocol, surely,' said Angela, being knowledgeable in that field through her experience as an ambassador's daughter. 'The information was too important to be handled except by a senior man.'

Quinn grunted his doubt. 'John Falconer cares as much about protocol as I do. No, there's more to it. I'm not entirely convinced about the bona fides of that defector, Kovalsky. He's a high-level chap and he'd be expended only for a really big cause, though you never know with the KGB. Did I ever tell you how the KGB once connived at the sinking of a boat in the Black Sea, drowning 1500 Russian soldiers, just to establish the credibility of one agent they wanted to plant as a double?'

'Good God! Do they really go that far?'

'They do. And with that sort of licence you can go places. With our politicians you don't begin. When you think of the way they threw out my machine-gun idea!'

Quinn was referring to a project he had put forward for dealing with caches of IRA machine-guns found from time to time in Northern Ireland. The Army simply removed them which to Quinn was a crazy waste of opportunity. He wanted to replace the ammunition with specially faked rounds which would blow the guns up in the faces of the IRA men as they fired them. The politicians, though, wouldn't countenance it. What if some innocent person happened to find one of the doctored guns and fired it? Quinn had been unable to repress his contempt for such a flabby response. 'Dear God! What game are we supposed to be playing with these murderous little bastards? Pat ball?'

Being so keen to hide his Irish origin – Angela could guarantee to annoy him by referring to him as 'himself' – he was more English than the English in detesting the IRA. But the only 'dirty tricks' he could begin to consider in any part of the world were those he could conduct himself without political backing. And that, sadly, was also Falconer's position.

'He's a devious sod, John Falconer,' Quinn remarked, rubbing his chin. 'Machiavelli with a touch of Torquemada. Do you know why?'

'Tell me.'

'It's a sad story, really. He was an only child and he lost

both his parents when he was a boy. His father was killed in an accident and his mother was so devastated that she committed suicide. So, after being spoiled rotten, poor little John was suddenly left in the care of his grandfather who was an eccentric who only cared about horses. This meant that John grew up on his own, apart from an odd negro pal on his grandfather's estate, and he seems to have spent the rest of his life alone conspiring with himself.'

'It is a sad story, but all the more reason why I wouldn't trust him an inch. He's a weirdy,' Angela said with a disapproving twitch of her straight little nose.

'What about Ed Taylor?' Quinn asked mischievously, ever mindful that it was Taylor's predecessor who had enticed away his former assistant.

Angela knew how to deal with that bait, which had been dangled at her so often before. 'He's much more trustworthy, I'd say. But then he has the advantage of being happily married, with the gentling influence of a good woman.'

Quinn did not reply, although the narrowing of his rather penetrating, sky-blue eyes and the set of his mouth suggested that in his view few people, if any, were entirely to be trusted.

'Angela, I'd like you to transcribe the tape-recording of the conversation with Falconer. One top copy only for me. Nothing for any files.'

Quinn was punctilious about studying the written record of a conversation as well as listening to the play-back. Sometimes a phrase or even just an exclamation suddenly assumed special significance, and he particularly wished to check the intonation of Falconer's insistence on immediate action over Henderson.

As Angela went to her ante-room, where she did her typing, her telephone rang and she returned to report, 'Your Washington Special Intelligence, which came in with the last Concorde flight, has now been processed. Do you want it right away?'

'Yes indeed. There might be something from "D.J." on this business about the Prime Minister.'

'D.J.' were the initials of 'Diamond Jim', Quinn's code-name for a prime source in Washington who, for the past few weeks, had been supplying ultra-secret information about the deliberations of the US National Security Council. This was extremely valuable because, while the Anglo-American Intelligence links were close, there were areas where each side kept its secrets though pretending to each other that this was not the case. Ed Taylor had recently been highly amused while ascending in one of the Century House lifts to see a messenger clutching a pile of files boldly marked 'Not for Apostle', 'Apostle' being the current MI6 code-word for the United States.

Quinn did not know the identity of 'Diamond Jim' who had suddenly begun to volunteer the information out of the blue. He had been highly suspicious of the material at first but, as detail after detail proved to be true, he gratefully accepted the offerings which had to be from someone operating at the highest level of confidence in the White House, State Department or elsewhere in the Washington machine.

While no reason for this splendid service was offered by 'D.J.' it had become apparent that he was motivated by the way the Council's policy seemed to be moving towards leaving Europe to its fate in the event of a determined Soviet assault. He was clearly opposed to any appeasement of the Russians, and was warning Quinn of the appalling danger which Britain and the other NATO allies faced.

It was not uncommon for secret Intelligence to be offered in this way, the classic example being the wartime 'Oslo Report', a document dropped anonymously through the letter-box of the British Naval attaché in Oslo and containing details of German secret weapons then under development. For far too long the 'Oslo Report', which had emanated from a disenchanted German, had been regarded as a hoax and Quinn had been determined not to repeat that error.

He and Angela had pondered over 'D.J.'s' identity not only in the office but in bed, ticking off all the possibilities without reaching any conclusion beyond the obvious fact that whoever he was he certainly had courage. Inquiries in Washington were out of the question as being far too dangerous to the source.

Angela had queried the ethical niceties of encouraging 'D.J.' to betray the country that was Britain's staunchest friend, but Quinn had airily dismissed any censure on the grounds that the information was being passed to an ally which could never become an enemy. That, he believed, disposed of Angela's comparison of 'D.J.' with Klaus Fuchs, who had been jailed for fourteen years for passing atomic secrets to the Soviet Union, even though it had been a wartime ally when he had begun his traitorous service.

The Special Intelligence from Washington always arrived in a small locked leather case sent over inside the diplomatic bag, and Angela presented it to him as though it were some precious casket. 'I hope "Diamond Jim" lives up to his name again,' she said.

He picked up a long-bladed commando dagger which, to Angela's disgust, he used as a paper-knife because he knew it had been used to kill 'at least three of Britain's enemies', and slit open a white envelope sealed with wax.

' "D.J." confirms yesterday's meeting of the National Security Council,' he said, reading from a single foolscap sheet. 'What else has he got?'

There was a silence punctuated only by the bubbling of the coffee machine, which Angela turned down, and exclamations of 'Jesus Christ!' and 'God Almighty!'

'This really is something, Angela,' he said finally. 'How the hell am I going to play it? Just listen to this: "The Council decided 1) That it would not be possible to reinforce the American troops in Europe without giving the Soviets the excuse, for which they are undoubtedly seeking, to attack the NATO forces on the Central Front. Yet without very substantial reinforcement from the United States NATO would be unable to hold up the advance of the Warsaw Pact Forces for more than a few days. Resort to the standard battlefield nuclear weapons in the NATO stockpiles would be impracticable because by that time the fighting would be in and around cities like Bremen, Kassel and Munich, and the damage to West German property and the civilian casualties would be insupportable." '

'There doesn't seem to be much new in that,' Angela said.

'No, but here's the hot part: "2) There are 270,000 American troops and airmen in Europe. They cannot be withdrawn and they just cannot be left to be killed or captured." Especially in a Presidential election year,' Quinn muttered under his breath.

63

'What on earth has election year got to do with it?' Angela asked.

'It shouldn't have anything to do with it, but with hard-nosed politicians it does. Listen – "It was therefore decided that the moment a Russian attack is confirmed NATO forces will strike at the oncoming tanks and troops with precision-guided munitions fitted with enhanced radiation warheads – in other words neutron bombs. These will have the capability to strike at Soviet forces as far back as the Third Echelon – well inside Russian territory, where supplies and the later waves of tanks will be collecting. The neutron warheads will not only be far more effective against the tanks but will do relatively little collateral damage to buildings." '

'I don't understand,' Angela said. 'You always told me that Carter was bamboozled by the Russians into undertaking not to produce neutron bombs and that this President followed suit.'

'That's what we all thought but "D.J." goes on – "3) This can be achieved because the neutron weapons have been in production secretly for many months. They are already in NATO stockpiles in the guise of conventional warheads for the missiles and other precision-guided weapons already in the hands of NATO forces." '

'Good Lord, that certainly is hot,' Angela exclaimed.

'Yes, and there's more. "4) No NATO allies are to be informed of this decision until the actual moment when neutron warheads are issued to them." '

'A surprise secret weapon,' Angela commented.

'That seems to be the idea.'

'But what can you do with the information? Why is "D.J." telling you all this?'

'At last he explains all,' Quinn said, turning his eyes to the final paragraph of the typewritten, unsigned message. ' "I have been aware of this possible development since I first contacted you, when I needed to establish my good faith in case it eventuated. Now that it has there is the gravest danger that, if neutron bombs are used, the Russians may be driven to retaliate with intercontinental missile strikes against the American homeland – and against Britain too.

' "Since the whole purpose of nuclear weapons is to prevent war, surely the only sensible way of capitalizing on this neutron-bomb decision is to allow it to exert its maximum deterrent effect by letting the Russians know the dreadful carnage they face if they press ahead with their adventure. There is no safe way I can do this and, in any case, I would be unlikely to be believed. So I and millions like me are relying on you to warn the Soviet leadership at the highest level. Please act without delay. There is so little time.

' "I beg you not to make any inquiries about my identity as I have already placed myself in the danger of being branded a traitor – though not, I sincerely believe, to either the American or British people." '

'What do you make of it?' Quinn asked.

'He sounds sincere enough but, then, so many traitors do when they try to justify their treachery. I'm sure that Falconer would rate him a traitor if he could see the contents of this message.'

'No doubt he would,' Quinn conceded.

'Then you don't think you should denounce him?'

'Certainly not! Obviously he's dangerous to the United States, but being kept in the dark about American nuclear weapons policy is far more dangerous to us. Traitors to other causes are our life-blood, Angela, and we can't afford to discourage one of them.'

'But couldn't "D.J." be really a Russian sympathizer who is trying to use you to get his information into the Kremlin?'

'No, he couldn't,' Quinn said confidently. 'It would be too easy for him to make direct contact with the KGB in Washington. Anyway, you needn't worry. I'm certainly not going to put my head on a block by feeding his stuff to Moscow. I may be inclined to agree with him that it would be the best thing to do with it – as I've always told you, Soviet fear of nuclear retaliation is our only hope against the Russian military machine – but to any British court it would look like arrant treachery.'

'But if "D.J.'s" idea might do the trick, why doesn't the President simply make a public announcement about the nuclear weapons, you know, like Kennedy did over Cuba?'

'I can see exactly why he can't,' Quinn replied. 'In the first place it would brand him as a liar. He's publicly assured the Russians and the rest of the world that he wouldn't produce or deploy neutron weapons. So he can hardly announce that they've been stockpiling them for months.'

'I still think he should – even though it is election year.'

'He can't because there's a second factor. He promised to seek the West Germans' permission before deploying neutron weapons on their territory. I don't think he's done that because it would have leaked from Bonn weeks ago. He certainly hasn't told us and I've little doubt that some are in American stockpiles here. So an announcement would touch off a hell of a row in NATO, and every leftie in Europe would latch on to it to get the weapons removed. No. There couldn't possibly be an announcement.'

Angela accepted the argument but remained puzzled. 'I still find it hard to understand why the President has agreed to this step – if in fact he has. I always thought you were convinced that if the crunch came the Americans would avoid using nuclear weapons in Europe because of the danger of retaliation against New York.'

'I'm not alone in that fear, Angela. It's rife through Whitehall. But the President's in a corner because for the last decade the US has done what we've done – spent far too much on social welfare and far too little on defence. Either he has to let the Russians have an easy ride in Europe and accept heavy American casualties, or use this ace-in-the-hole.'

'I suppose you must be right,' Angela conceded.

'I'm sure *I'm* right. But is "D.J.'s" information accurate? And how the hell am I going to check it out? I suppose I could sound out Archie.'

Archie was the Director of Defence Intelligence, a recently retired admiral who had taken on the direction of all Services' Intelligence in the Ministry of Defence. Quinn collaborated well with him and they met frequently, not only on committees but at the 'Eye Club', the exclusive gatherings of those involved in Whitehall Intelligence work. But what could Archie do in the time available? Quinn asked himself. He would have to make inquiries in West Germany and security there was almost a farce, with politicians leaking their heads off and their personal assistants defecting to East Germany. No, he would have to make his own assessment of what he felt historically might be known as 'The Diamond Jim Report'.

If the information was accurate he would have to act on it in some way or other. He couldn't just sit on it. He could offload the responsibility right away by just informing the Foreign Secretary. That was what the protocol demanded. But what a hornets' nest that would split open! The Foreign Secretary was too keen to curry favour with his American counterpart to be trusted. He'd be on to the telephone to Washington in a flash and that would be the end of 'D.J.' as a source.

'It's a right bastard having this problem on my plate on top of the dreadful doubt about the Prime Minister,' he said. 'There are too many straws and not enough wind.'

He remained silent for several minutes, carefully avoiding closing his eyes, having once been told that it was damaging to concentration since it immediately shut down a large part of the brain, allowing the reveries of fantasy to intrude. The immediate idea presented by the facts was raw and risky and he would have much preferred a more sophisticated move. But time being critically short he recalled, by no means for the first time in his career, advice his boisterous father had often given him in a brogue you could cut with a knife – 'When all else fails use bloody great nails!' And any thought of his father, who had been too fond of drink to make much of his own life, never failed to recall his more frequent admonition, 'Mark's your name and that's what I expect you to be makin'.'

Suddenly Angela, who knew her master's mind, realized that light had dawned within it. The tension in his face relaxed to be replaced by a faint smile. 'You know I don't think I'm going to be needing that hot bath after all.' The significance of the remark was not lost on Angela.

'You're never going to … '

'I damn well am! We don't get many chances to kill two birds with one brick in this game. I'm going to beard the "Prince of Peace" in his den tonight.'

He picked up his red telephone. 'Get me the Cabinet Secretary please,' he asked as Number Ten answered.

As he waited he could not resist a gibe at Falconer.

'I wonder what John would think if he knew that "D.J.'s" information, which he may not know himself, travelled to me on the same Concorde that brought him to London.'

Quinn relished any opportunity to score off the CIA, but only when the motive was productive. The integrity of the Anglo-American alliance on Intelligence was paramount in his book. That was why he made such personal effort to keep the 'Uncle Vanya' contact in being, nothing and nobody being allowed to prejudice it. Britain was dependent on the Reconnaissance Intelligence provided by US orbiting satellites and other long-range surveillance techniques: 'Uncle Vanya' was the quid pro quo which kept it flowing. Satellites could tell you what war material an enemy possessed and where it was, but not what he intended to do with it. And for the all-important intentions, defectors-in-place, like 'Uncle Vanya' – and, of course, 'Diamond Jim' – were still the only reliable source.

'Sir David?' Quinn confirmed, as the familiar voice of the long-serving Cabinet Secretary came on the line. 'This is "C". I must have a few minutes alone with the Prime Minister. It's most urgent. No, David, I can't do it through you or anyone else. This is for the PM's ears only. And I mean *ears*. There's going to be nothing in writing.'

There was a pause while the Cabinet Secretary repeated his arguments against an immediate visit.

'I'm sure he's overloaded,' Quinn said sharply. 'Who isn't at the moment? But I must insist. The truth is that he could be wasting his time seeing other people without seeing me first. Let me know when I can come over to Number Ten. I'll use the garden entrance. I'll stay by the telephone until I hear from you.'

Angela refilled his coffee mug and he leaned back in his chair and sipped it, stretching out his legs so far as to display the crêpe soles of his suede half-boots, which he always called 'brothel-creepers', and fixed a cigarette into the short, amber holder, which had been a present from his former mistress.

'You know how I was complaining that the KGB gets all the executive action. Well I'm going to take some for a change,' he announced. 'You never learned Ancient Greek did you? Well there's some character in Herodotus who says, "Of all the human troubles the most hateful is to feel that you have the capacity to wield power yet no field in which to exercise it." Well, the field has suddenly presented itself.'

Angela almost had to bite her tongue to avoid asking him if

he was sure he was taking the right step, but she knew the futility of argument once Quinn's mind had been made up. He must have calculated the risks he was taking.

Quinn locked the strong-box containing the numerous messages and tapes which 'Uncle Vanya' had managed to send and put it in the office security cabinet, which had a combination lock. Then he strolled over to a corner of the room where, under an aluminium cover which nobody else was permitted to remove, a giant jigsaw puzzle, its difficulty compounded by being composed of very small pieces, was partially completed on a green baize card-table.

It was a garishly coloured picture showing one of the May Day parades in Moscow's Red Square, with the propaganda array of rockets, tanks and troops designed to give foreigners an exaggerated idea of Russia's military strength. Each time the diplomatic bag from the British Embassy in Moscow contained a contribution from 'Uncle Vanya' it was accompanied by one more piece of the puzzle. As proof of authenticity it was always a piece which fitted into the existing structure on Quinn's card-table.

He stared at it, visualizing 'Uncle Vanya's' face and wondering how much it had changed since he had seen it years before, when he himself had operated in that grey, hostile city. What would the next piece be tomorrow if 'Uncle Vanya' responded as he expected? More of the grim, forbidding wall enclosing such enormities of power? One of the onion domes of St Basil's? The red star on top of the Kremlin Tower? He noted that apart from the red star – and, of course, the weapons of destruction and the regimented crowd – there was nothing in the picture which owed anything to Communism. It had all been there before the revolution.

Chapter Six

Winifred Henderson, the Prime Minister's wife, thoroughly disliked living 'over the shop' in Downing Street. Two up and two down in one of those quiet streets behind Westminster Abbey would have been much more suited to her lower middle-class tastes. That was why she preferred to spend most of her time in the small sitting-room of the top-floor private flat. It was as far as possible from the offices and the hundred-plus staff of Number Ten which, being three houses knocked into one, was much more rambling and more populated than the public suspected from the rather unimpressive main entrance.

While she waited for her visitor that evening, she busied herself with her embroidery, a plain, primish woman with little clothes sense, disinclined to use make-up and who was passing through the menopause with little emotional disturbance. Though somewhat overweight she could not resist dipping into the box of violet creams, which was usually within reach when she sat alone during the evenings, as she so often did.

Just being a politician's wife was lonely enough: being the wife of a Prime Minister had made her almost a recluse, not that she would have minded if only Albert could have been there a little more often to keep her company. Born and reared in Overstrand, a village on the Norfolk coast, she had been used to only a neighbourly social life when she had met Albert in Cambridge and greatly disliked the large parties and banquets she could no longer entirely avoid. 'We like ourselves', was how she had first expressed her belief that a well-matched couple should be content with each other's company, and be happy in each other's silences.

There was a gentle knock on the door and a servant entered to announce the arrival of Sir Alan King-Lander, her husband's physician, who had been a close friend of Henderson's since he had read medicine at Cambridge, while the future Prime Minister had been reading history.

Sharing working-class origins, King-Lander's in Darlington, Henderson's in Liverpool, both had been ardent Socialists and, outside their studies, had been influenced politically by the same left-wing don.

'Oh, Alan, it's so good of you to come.'

'It's kind of you to ask me,' her guest replied in a deep resonant voice which had never quite lost its northern accent. 'It's good to have a convivial drink before going out to dinner. I hate arriving at a strange house without benefit of what, in my part of the world, they used to call a "sneck-lifter".'

'But at least you've already met the Ambassador and it's very informal tonight. Jane has only asked us and you, so far as I know. Frankly, I suspect that she'd rather be dining with you alone. She's taken a real shiner to you.'

King-Lander smiled and raised his arms jestingly. 'I do that to all the girls. The trouble I have with my women patients ... '

'There's many a true word spoken in jest,' Winifred said, wagging her finger. 'Seriously though, Bert will be delighted to see you. You seem to be the only person who can take him out of himself these days. He's worried stiff about the international situation, even though he pretends he's not. Do you think there's going to be a war, Alan?'

'Your husband should be able to answer that better than I can, Winifred,' King-Lander replied as he settled his heavy frame into an armchair with a brightly coloured floral cover, and helped himself to a Scotch and soda from the tray which his hostess placed beside him.

'Yes, but he never tells me anything,' Winifred complained. 'That's his trouble, I think. He bottles all his worries up inside him. I know I couldn't give him any worthwhile political advice, but I'm sure it would help him if he could just confide in somebody. What are we going to do with him, Alan?'

She looked imploringly at King-Lander who, in her eyes, was everything that a doctor should be: composed, impressive, physically attractive with his strong face and iron-grey wavy hair, with an aura of professional competence inspiring great confidence.

71

'Well, as I've told you, time and again my dear, there's nothing wrong with him. The pains he complains of always seem to be in different places. They are purely psychogenic – in the mind. There's a golden rule in my profession – common symptoms have common causes. As we get older we all have pains and the odds are that Bert's are nothing that matter. After all he's had every kind of test and he seems to be rudely normal.'

Winifred inclined her head in doubt. 'I still think he's got a heart problem. That's where the pains usually are, especially when he can't sleep at night. And you know how many pills he takes for them.'

'None of them prescribed by me,' King-Lander said firmly. 'He takes so much proprietary rubbish that it's probably causing the pain. But it's useless talking to him. He says he can't get through the day without his pills. So if Dr Bloggins' Pink Pills help to keep the wheels of Government turning, then hats off to Dr Bloggins!'

'Have a chocolate, Alan?'

'No thank you. And neither should you. What's happened to that diet we agreed about?'

'It's not working, though I'm only eating enough to keep a bird alive.'

Yes – a vulture, King-Lander thought as she reached for another violet cream.

'Sorry, Alan,' Winifred said with a little shrug. 'But I can't possibly cope with a diet while there's all this wretched tension in the house – if you can call this place a house. You'll see how strung-up he is when you see him. I'm so afraid that this trouble boiling up with Russia will be the last straw. You will take another look at his heart won't you? For my sake?'

King-Lander sighed and finished off his drink. 'I've already promised you I will, but it won't help either of you. You are asking me to look for things that aren't there. You know you remind me of the psychiatrist who was walking down Harley Street with a colleague when they passed an acquaintance who said, "Good morning". The psychiatrist looked at his friend and said, darkly, "I wonder what he meant by that?"'

As the response was no more than the wannest of smiles he poured himself another Scotch and decided that the time had come for plainer speaking. 'Winifred, if I can be frank, as an old friend, the truth is that you want Bert out of this job whether he's ill or not. You don't like being the Prime Minister's wife. You've never liked it. It's a very selfish attitude when the nation needs leadership so much. You know that there's nobody else who could keep the Labour Party together.'

'I think that's unkind,' Winifred pouted. 'It's just that I know this is an impossible job for any man, and for someone as sensitive as Bert it's a killer.'

'He worked very hard to get it,' King-Lander pointed out. 'He went into it with his eyes wide open.'

'That's true, but it's this nuclear business which has made all the difference. You know how horrified he is by the thought that millions of people might be killed by nuclear bombs. He's felt that way since he was at Cambridge. Do you remember that jingle he used to sing: "Let not the atom bomb be the final sequel/In which all men are cremated equal." '

'I certainly do. Don't you remember, Winifred, we were both together with him on the day the Americans announced that they'd dropped an atomic bomb on Hiroshima.'

'Yes, he was absolutely appalled, especially when the photographs came through.'

'I know,' King-Lander agreed. 'A lot of us felt the same. But we haven't been able to do much about it, have we? Bert's presiding over a Government which still keeps the Polaris missiles and the American nuclear bases.'

'That's why he feels such a terrible responsibility, that it will be partly his fault if anything happens. Poor dear, it's taking so much out of him. The sheer stress!'

'My dear Winifred, the danger of stress is one of the myths of modern medicine. Most of us live under far less stress than our forbears did. Oh, I agree that Bert is taking a hammering and, naturally, he looks a bit harassed but he assures me that it is not getting him down.'

'Ah, yes. But you know Bert. He would never quit, would never admit ... You will keep an eye on him won't you?'

'Of course I will. I already see him at least every other day on some excuse or other which you manage to contrive. How's the historical romance coming along?' he asked, anxious to get his companion and patient off the subject of her affliction, which he called 'displaced hypochondria' – morbid concern about somebody else's health.

'It isn't,' Winifred answered. 'I really need Bert to help me. He has all the historical facts I want in his head but he has no time to spare for me.'

King-Lander felt that she would be doing herself and the country a service if she could get off her behind and do the research in the London Library or the British Museum, but he knew that Winifred's talk about writing a historical romance was no more than a fantasy. It had originated, he assumed, in a prideful wish to emulate one of her predecessors in Number Ten, Mary Wilson, who had made a name for herself writing poetry.

As Winifred could have predicted Albert Henderson was carrying dispatch boxes, one red, one yellow, as he entered the room.

'There's just no end to the bumf,' he said, as he deposited the boxes on a table. 'And there's no way I can avoid dealing with that lot after I get back from Jane Jansen's dinner. What a life! I tell my ministers to avoid taking decisions when they are tired, but how can I do that myself when I'm working an eighty-hour week? In this job it's so important to be able to pace yourself.'

'In any job, Prime Minister,' King-Lander agreed.

'Well, how are you, Alan?' Henderson asked as he finally flopped into a chair.

'I'm fine, but Winifred still insists that you aren't'.

Henderson made a gesture of despair. He certainly look-ed trim enough, as he leaned over to pour himself a neat Scotch and replenish King-Lander's glass, and younger than his years with his slim figure, craggily handsome features and abundant wavy hair, which remained brown through judicious tinting, a deception common enough among polit-icians anxious to avoid an ageing image on television, espec-ially since its introduction into the House of Commons. This had not gone unrecorded by the Press, although he was still commonly referred to as 'the best-looking Prime Minister since Anthony Eden, Margaret Thatcher excepted.'

'Now you know you are sleeping very badly, Bert,' his wife

74

said. 'And working far too long into the night. You used to be able to eat the work and sleep like a top. It's all this extra worry ... '

King-Lander, who had been a widower for many years, had never been able to understand how Henderson, who was so forceful in politics and so tough in keeping his ministers in line, could be so patient with his wife.

'I'm sorry, Bert,' Winifred said, seeing the looks passing between the two men. 'It's just that I care about you and I don't want to be a widow.'

That selfish admission in the final phrase was typical of Winifred Henderson and had been so for as long as he had known her, King-Lander told himself. The Prime Minister's psychogenic pains could well be due to her consistently unhelpful attitude.

She hated the bustle of London and he had listened to her banging on about the joys of 'a little cottage in the country' ever since Henderson had been elected Labour MP for a South London constituency. Her dream had been to return to Norfolk, but at least Henderson had summoned up the courage to scotch that. 'Whatever happens I'm not going to Norfolk,' he had heard Henderson declare. 'That bloody wind! Straight off the Russian steppes! If anything would be likely to see me off it wouldn't be my heart, it would be that wind.' Since then she had focused her imagination on Cornwall, though Henderson had done his best to kill that by pointing out that the historical romancers had scoured the county, and that London was a far richer seam.

While some successful men had been pushed by their wives, often beyond their capabilities, Henderson had achieved eminence in spite of his. Perhaps, to spite his, King-Lander thought as he admitted, 'I'm afraid I've promised Winifred that we'll go through the motions again, Prime Minister. Tomorrow morning would suit if you could manage half an hour at my consulting rooms ... '

'OK, Alan,' Henderson sighed. 'Anything for a quiet life. Now let's talk about something else. Anything except politics and my health. Have you got a good story? We can do with a laugh. And you can tell it to the Ambassador.'

King-Lander, whose prowess as an after-dinner speaker was

exceptional, never seemed to go anywhere without some story, usually with a medical flavour.

'This is a true story which I heard only this morning about a patient of one of my colleagues at the London Clinic. For years he had done the pools without winning a penny. Then last week, in an inspired moment, he selected eight draws by picking out the towns where he had been unfaithful to his wife. He scooped the pool! Half a million pounds tax-free! Who says that virtue is its own reward?'

'I still think it is,' said Winifred who, in spite of her loneliness, had never dreamed of being unfaithful, even if only because, as she had once put it to King-Lander, who had long wondered how she had managed to produce two children, 'Sex leaves me stone-cold'.

'You can't tell that one at Jane Jansen's table,' Henderson warned. 'She's far too straight-laced. You'll have to think of another one, Alan.'

That was no problem for King-Lander. 'This one's about a doctor who was staying with a country parson, whose claim to fame was that he could immediately produce a Biblical text for any subject suggested to him and then preach a sermon on it. Over Saturday evening dinner the doctor bet the parson that he could think of a subject which would defeat him and such was the cleric's confidence that he accepted a situation in which the doctor would give him a folded paper revealing the subject as he ascended the pulpit.

'As the cleric faced his congregation and read the paper it bore the single word "Constipation"! Without hesitation the parson announced, "The text today is taken from Exodus, Chapter 24 Verse 15. And Moses took the two tablets and went up into the mountain." '

Henderson always laughed at his physician's jokes, this time so heartily that he had to wipe a tear from his eyes.

'It's not just your stories, Alan, it's the way you tell them. But I don't think you'll get away with that one at Jane's table either. She and her husband are real Puritans, Bible-punchers. She'd probably think it was blasphemous.'

'And probably correct me into the bargain,' King-Lander suggested. 'The accuracy of the story depends on which version of the Bible you read.'

'Oh, I think she'd take that all right,' Winifred said. 'She's very human and very sweet.'

'Sweet!' Henderson scoffed. 'That's not the word I'd use for her. Can you be sweet and be as tough as she is?'

'Well, she's sweet to me,' Winifred persisted. 'And I suspect she's sweet on Alan.'

At that moment the red telephone on the sideboard rang and Henderson answered it. The caller was the Cabinet Secretary with the unwelcome news that Sir Mark Quinn was insisting on an urgent meeting.

'Oh no!' Henderson reacted. 'This is the first free minute I've had all day. Tell him I'm with the doctor ... tell him anything ... I don't doubt it's urgent. Everything's bloody urgent ... '

There was a pause while the Cabinet Secretary explained that, though he did not know exactly what Quinn had on his mind, it could only be important new information about the international crisis.

'Oh all right then ... Tell him to come round in half an hour. I'll see him in the Cabinet Room.'

'I'll make it as formal as possible,' he muttered as he replaced the receiver with a bang. 'Blasted Chief Spook! Insisting on his rights! Says he has something he must tell me. Everybody has something they must tell me. And most of it I don't need to know. Least of all from that mad Irishman.'

'I take it you don't like him,' King-Lander observed.

'I can't stand him. I'd sack him if I could find a good excuse. He and his like live in a demi-monde in which they are so deceived by their fantasies that half their reports are sheer fiction. MI is supposed to stand for Military Intelligence: for me it means Mischief Incorporated! You know what a mess they caused for Anthony Eden by sending a frogman to spy on the bottom of the cruiser that brought Bulganin and Kruschev to Britain?'

'Yes. The frogman was called Crabb.'

'Well, they contemplated something even dafter. They seriously considered hiring a pickpocket who'd turned his talents into a cabaret act to pick the Russian leaders' pockets in the hope of finding documents during an after-dinner entertainment here in Number Ten!'

'I can't believe it.'

'I can believe anything about the Spooks,' Henderson insisted. 'I'm told that Quinn once ordered a miniature microphone to be inserted in the bell round the neck of a pet cat belonging to somebody he was snooping on!'

'He sounds ingenious,' King-Lander said.

'It's a pity he can't channel his ingenuity into more constructive channels. He has nothing but contempt for ordinary people. He thinks the world is largely populated by idiots. Supercilious sod ... '

'Calm yourself, Bert,' Winifred remonstrated. 'You see now what I mean, Alan. He never used to be as irritable as this. I'm sure it's bad for his blood pressure. That's something you should check thoroughly tomorrow.'

'Oh God!' Henderson murmured, holding his head in his hands.

'Have you got a headache, dear,' Winifred asked solicitously.

'No, I haven't got a headache, but you could easily nag me into one.'

'Nag? Me, nag? I'm only interested in your own good!'

'That has been the cry of the nagger down the ages,' Henderson responded, looking at King-Lander for support.

The physician's reaction was to refill his glass while Winifred sighed and reached for another chocolate.

'You'll spoil your dinner if you eat any more of those,' King-Lander remarked.

She resisted the temptation by closing the lid firmly, and suppressed her desire to tell the doctor that he risked more than a spoiled dinner by drinking so much Scotch. 'I suppose I shall have to go to the Ambassador's on my own,' she said petulantly. 'We can't both be late and Alan's got his own car.'

'I'm afraid so,' Henderson replied. 'Send the car back for me right away. I should be finished with the Chief Spook by the time it returns. That is if what he has to tell me doesn't set the Thames on fire.'

He rose wearily, picked up his dispatch boxes and prepared to move down to the Cabinet Room which, like some previous Prime Ministers, he used as an office. It might not have occurred to him consciously but any man looked impressive sitting alone at the long Cabinet table as a visitor entered.

'Make my apologies to Jane,' he called. 'See you later Alan.'

Never being one to waste a minute, Henderson took his usual central seat with his back to the marble fireplace and opened the oblong yellow box which contained the latest Intelligence intercepts from GCHQ. He hoped that its contents might afford some advance clue to the information which Quinn was coming to impart, but there was nothing more than what he had come to call 'the usual crap' – details of Soviet troop movements, which he considered to be alarmist.

Everyone knew that the Soviets carried out major exercises at this time of the year to make maximum use of good weather before 'General Winter' took command, he assured himself. Why, they were even inviting NATO observers under the usual détente arrangements to which one of his Labour predecessors, Sir Harold Wilson, had rightly been a signatory. The trouble was that far too many people saw the Russian leaders as villains, endlessly plotting the enslavement of the world. And by violent means. As King-Lander, a fellow Socialist, had put it, 'In the average British mind an anarchist had a bomb in one hand while a Bolshevik had one in both hands.' And in his experience it wasn't like that at all.

He knew most of the Russian leaders, particularly Anatoli Borisenko, the Party Secretary and President, who had entertained him at his dacha, and Konstantin Volkhov, the Premier. Most of their time was spent, just as his was, with domestic issues. And with the promotion of trade, which was so important both to the USSR and to Britain.

All they were doing with their military exercises was what their predecessors had done for years with such success – rattling their sabres to fool the West into running themselves into bankruptcy by spending too much on defence. Well he'd never fallen for that, at least no more than he had been forced to do to satisfy pressures from Washington. In Henderson's belief, the Secret Service, and Quinn in particular, was mainly to blame for promoting the Red scare in Whitehall, whence it reached the Press and the people. And in this respect he shared the view which Jane Jansen held about the CIA. Both might be essential but they did more harm than good. Half the reports they circulated 'from sources with excellent access' turned out to be inaccurate and some were concoctions.

'Ah, Sir Mark,' Henderson said somewhat testily as the Secret Service chief was shown into the long, impressive room with its chandeliers and Corinthian columns. 'I hope this really is important. Or perhaps, on second thoughts, I don't. I don't think I could stand any more shattering news at the moment.'

Quinn stood uneasily gazing at this possibly traitorous figure sitting, by democratic election, below the portrait of Robert Walpole, Britain's first Prime Minister, which hung above the fireplace. Then, invited by a gesture, he sat in the chair opposite.

'It *is* important, Prime Minister. And I am afraid that you *are* going to find it shattering.'

Henderson sighed. 'All right. Let's have it.'

'We have a source with excellent access to the deliberations of the National Security Council in Washington ... '

'Meaning, in terms which I would understand, that you have planted a spy on the most secret deliberations of our chief ally?' the Prime Minister remarked scathingly as he filled a rather small pipe.

'No, Prime Minister,' Quinn replied briskly. 'It so happens that this source volunteered his services – and let us be thankful that he did so in view of what I am about to tell you. It concerns a major new decision in the nuclear weapons field ... '

'But Sir Mark, I have the President's assurance that we are told all we need to know in that respect.'

'All the President and his advisers *decide* we need to know, Prime Minister.'

What the hell was going on behind those grey-blue eyes? Quinn wondered. Why was he stopping him from getting straight to the point? Was it to give the impression that the secret was of no special interest to him? That, of course, was precisely how Philby would have played it.

'This source reported today on a decision of the greatest moment to us taken by the National Security Council only yesterday. It was decided that if the Russians attack in Central Europe, the Americans and other NATO forces will retaliate immediately with neutron bombs which are already in position. The President has concurred.'

As Quinn paused he thought he could detect a slight

trembling of Henderson's fingers as he lit his pipe. 'I've put the whole situation down for you as an aide-memoire, Prime Minister. It's quite short.'

As Henderson read the document his face became increasingly haggard. 'But this is terrible. Just what the Americans said they wouldn't do. We've all agreed to do everything we could to hold an attack without recourse to nuclear weapons of any kind to force a pause for reflection of the dreadful consequences ... So far as these appalling neutron bombs are concerned the Americans are not supposed to have made them at all. They gave a solemn promise ... Are you satisfied that this is accurate?'

'Absolutely sure, Prime Minister. I'm afraid, as usual, I cannot reveal the source, but you can be assured it is impeccable.'

The Prime Minister thought he had heard that before but refrained from saying so. He placed the distasteful document in his yellow box along with the other secret Intelligence papers and locked it.

'Thank you, Sir Mark. As you know, I do not think the Russians are going to attack anybody. I think you Intelligence chaps misinterpret their motives. So your report may be rather academic – if it is true.'

He looked at the silent Quinn quizzically and then smiled. 'You know the Russians are highly political animals, and you need to be a politician to understand them. They'll bluster, of course, if they think it will advance them politically. But risk nuclear war after all they have achieved without it? No! It's just not on. It's not in their nature.'

Is Henderson really blind to what's happening at this moment behind the Iron Curtain? Quinn asked himself. Or did it suit his long-term purpose to pretend to be? What were his true intentions? Ah, intentions! They were always the unknown factor in the Intelligence equation. Information was easy to come by. But intentions ...

'I'm afraid I have to support the Chiefs of Staff as regards the likely intentions of the Warsaw Pact Forces,' Quinn said. 'They believe that the signs point to an attack within days. They can even say where. I know that you disagree with them, but I felt that you had to be informed of this latest development without delay.'

'You were right, of course, Sir Mark, and I am grateful to you. But tell me now that I have this information, what use is it?'

'Frankly none, for the moment, Prime Minister. To protect the source it is imperative that none of your Cabinet colleagues and none of the Chiefs of Staff are told about it.'

Henderson smiled. 'You don't think they are secure, do you? But then I suspect you think that none of us are.'

'I wouldn't say that,' Quinn lied. 'But it is an axiom of my life that the more who know a secret the surer it is to leak. The most productive source of KGB Intelligence is still the wagging tongue. And you can imagine what use the Kremlin could make of this information.'

'You know, Sir Mark, when I decided to go into politics, in the hope of creating history in preference to teaching it, I thought statesmanship was about ideals and ideas, not about who had this or that wretched bomb. I despise the hardware approach to international politics. Missiles, bombs, counter-strikes, credibility gaps, brinkmanship, the balance of terror – the jargon nauseates me. What have these dreadful things to do with creating a better life for ordinary people?'

In no mood for philosophy, Quinn kept his conversation to the point. 'It is possible that the President may tell you what I have told you on his own initiative, though I doubt that he will. If he does confirm it I would be grateful if you would let me know.'

'Hot-line conversations with the President are on a strictly private basis, Sir Mark. I too must protect my sources.'

'I do appreciate that, Prime Minister,' Quinn said refraining from mentioning that the hot-line between Washington and Moscow hardly seemed to be working. 'But the immediate circumstances are very special.'

With no intention of committing himself Henderson thought for a moment, and then said, 'These precision-guided weapons you say the Americans have stockpiled in Europe – missiles and such-like – do the Russians have them?'

'It is our belief that they have nothing so sophisticated. The Americans have sustained a big technological lead there.'

'And these neutron warheads?' Henderson asked as he knocked out his pipe, an act which Quinn interpreted as a device to avoid looking him in the eye. 'Do the Russians have them?'

'Not, apparently, in meaningful numbers. They are essentially a defensive weapon against massed tank attack and, in spite of what they say, the Soviet leaders do not really believe that NATO will ever attack them. So the pressure to produce them has not been so great.'

Henderson sucked at his empty pipe for a moment before putting it in his pocket. 'So the Warsaw Pact Forces could find themselves in for quite a shock if they attacked in mass formations expecting an easy run?'

'Undoubtedly.'

'In that case I wonder why the President doesn't warn the Soviet leaders on his hot-line to Moscow to deter them from attacking at all – if, by some quite incredible miscalculation, they should ever do so.'

'I've wondered that myself, Sir. Perhaps the President feels that at this late stage he just wouldn't be believed.'

Harbouring doubts himself about Quinn's sensational information, the Prime Minister thought the comment more than reasonable. 'You'll keep me informed if you get any further evidence on this subject from your spy, I mean your volunteer?' he asked.

'I will indeed, Sir,' Quinn said as he turned and left the room.

Was Henderson guilty or was Falconer catastrophically misinformed? Quinn pondered on the possibilities as he climbed into the back of his unobtrusive, black car discreetly parked on Horse Guards Parade and told his chauffeur-bodyguard, 'Clarges Street, please.'

Somehow in Quinn's practised estimation, Henderson had an indefinable air of guilt about him. It was the eyes. He had never liked Henderson's eyes. They looked shifty. So different from the earnest, direct gaze of the previous Prime Minister, in whom his trust had been total. If he was guilty he was a damned good actor, but then most successful politicians were, they had to be to attract and hold public and Parliamentary support. The unobtrusive, able administrator who was 'good on his arse' and got things done never reached the top. That position was reserved for the voluble orator who was 'good on his feet'.

How could a man of such achievement as Henderson have been drawn into the KGB net? From his long study of dossiers at his disposal, many containing transcripts of private conversations, some even from bedside telephone 'bugs', Quinn was convinced that in his secret life no man was totally immune to the threat of blackmail, should the KGB chance to discover a weakness and exploit it. The earlier in life the strike was made the likelier the quarry was to succumb and, once enmeshed, however trivially at first, escape became increasingly difficult as his public position improved.

From the Prime Minister's file at Century House, Quinn knew of a few sexual misdemeanours but he could hardly be said to be an ardent womanizer, attractive though he was and ample though his opportunities might be with so many young and ambitious women MPs in his party. He seemed too ambitious himself to have prejudiced his career by having a mistress, though, having seen Winifred Henderson, he would not have blamed him had he done so.

Money was a possibility that could not entirely be discounted. Like so many Socialists who acquired power by preaching the doctrine of fair shares for all, Henderson wanted an unfair share for himself and his family. 'Outside every "fat cat" is a Socialist trying to get in' was Quinn's dictum. Yet the idea that Henderson was selling secrets seemed out of character. Quinn had never liked Henderson, but could not bring himself to believe that he would ever have made himself a traitor just for cash.

Stupidity? That seemed a likelier cause. While Henderson had the common political ability of covering a moderate mind with a veneer of brightness compounded of hard work, brass nerve and ready wit, he had consistently shown lack of judgement which, in Quinn's mind, was the essence of political intelligence. So his recruitment to the Communist cause could have been completely ideological, perhaps way back when that pro-Soviet Cambridge don, who had certainly recruited others, had still been active.

Quinn looked up at the barred windows of the headquarters of 'the other firm', MI5, as his car swung along Curzon Street. What a coup for Century House if Falconer's tip proved true. Obviously, MI5 had not had a whiff of it and were certainly not going to be told. It was going to be an anxious twenty-four hours before 'Uncle Vanya' could report back – at the earliest.

Angela was ready with a tooth-chilling dry martini as Quinn's key turned in the door of her flat. She always knew when he had left the office and was on his way because the telephone started to ring. The flat, which faced the back of the building, provided quiet from the late-night traffic of Clarges Street and the 6 am thump-thump of the compressor in the garbage-collecting truck, even if a view of brick wall and concrete was the alternative. It had been chosen because, like Quinn's own apartment, there was no adjoining flat providing a shared wall where a spike-microphone, thrust into the brickwork, might eavesdrop on conversations. And the Electronics Division had fitted the three rooms, and even the two bathrooms, with anti-intruder recorders, which eliminated the necessity for crude seals on door-locks and markers in jambs.

'How did it go?' Angela asked.

'Pretty negatively, as I expected. He played it quite cleverly if he is a spy, though he did show a certain technical interest in the weapons towards the end.'

'Did you record him?'

'Of course,' Quinn answered. He withdrew a small tape-recorder from the left pocket of his jacket, which he then took off carefully to avoid damaging the fine wires leading inside the left sleeve of his pink-striped, Turnbull and Asser, shirt to the rather ornate cuff-link which concealed a miniaturized microphone.

'I must say the equipment has improved since the days when I used to do this regularly,' he said. 'But I'm not playing it back tonight, my love. I'm putting Albert Henderson out of my mind until we hear from "Uncle Vanya".'

'Yes, darling,' Angela said, suppressing a smile. By a substantial effort of will her lover might avoid talking about the Prime Minister that evening, but as for putting him out of his mind that was quite impossible for a man of his restless, ferreting temperament.

'I've booked a table at the Meridiana,' she said, referring to an Italian restaurant in Chelsea.

Mayfair restaurants like the Mirabelle, round the corner, were far too expensive for the Director-General of the Secret Intelligence Service dining out with his girl-friend, as Angela understood because she dealt with his tax and paid his bills.

For salary purposes he ranked only as a Deputy-Secretary of the Civil Service, and was paid accordingly with full rate of income tax and limited fringe benefits, even working meals with prime contacts having to be accounted for to the bureaucratic machine. Long gone were the days when the Director-General had a drawer full of money – a slush-fund which he could use as he wished.

As was their practice for security reasons, no 'shop' was talked during their meal, for directional microphones had been brought to such a pitch of technical excellence that conversation could be overheard from a quite distant table. However, Angela's prediction was confirmed after they had tried to sleep following energetic love-making.

With considerable justification Quinn regarded himself as something of a heterosexual athlete and, when asked where he had been educated, was not joking when he replied, 'Trinity and Magdalen, same as Oscar Wilde, but my habits are very different.' Normally satisfaction of his requirements left him so pleasantly exhausted that he slid easily into oblivion. That night, however, he several times shouted in his sleep in the peculiar way that told his bed-mate that he was having the horrific recurrent dream which was his particular symptom of acute anxiety.

Angela was one of very few people to whom Quinn had confessed his deepest fear, her predecessor being another. He was acutely claustrophobic, and while he could control this by avoiding enclosed spaces like lifts, pretending that he preferred the stairs for the exercise they gave him, there was nothing he could do about his dreams. In a moment of particular confidence, under the mellowing influence of wine, he had revealed how this fear of close confinement had been discovered by some bullies at an English boarding-school. Their reaction had been to shut him in an oak chest while one of them hammered on the lid with his heels. He had shrieked so loudly that the bullies repeated the treatment whenever they felt in need of enlivenment. There was one boy, whom he still remembered with intense loathing, who was usually responsible for starting the hunt for him.

Was it this searing experience, Angela wondered, which was responsible for the pleasure he undoubtedly derived from pulling off some 'dirty trick' on others? Was his satisfaction some kind of unconscious revenge? The logical consequence should have been a determination to avoid inflicting on others what had been inflicted on him, but Angela was old enough to know that this was not the way of human nature. She had seen too many instances among her friends where a son who had been harshly brought up and hated his father for it, yet treated his own children in the same manner.

Whatever its early result on Quinn's character, the trauma of the oak chest had later been reinforced during the Korean War when he was serving as a field agent operating from the British Embassy in Seoul. His only escape from the advancing Chinese during a hazardous operation had been to squeeze into the bomb bay of an American fighter-bomber leaving an evacuated airfield. The prospect of spending even half an hour in such a confined space had been so daunting that only the alternative of months in a cramped Communist interrogation cell had forced him into the aircraft's belly. From that time onwards the noise above him in his nightmares was sometimes that of hammering on wood, at others the droning whine of a jet-engine.

Throughout his service he believed that he had managed to conceal this character weakness from his colleagues, rightly suspecting that it could have affected his chances of promotion, if only because it might provide a lever to break him if ever he fell into the hands of enemy Counter-Intelligence. But those who slept with him for any length of time – and he disliked sleeping alone – eventually required some explanation of his night terrors.

On this particular night the noise was of hammering and the swirling faces of Henderson, 'Uncle Vanya', the hated Yakovlev and the shadowy, unknown features of 'Diamond Jim' intruded into the darkness of the coffin in which he had been buried alive.

It had been through Quinn's phobia that Angela had gained further insight into his character. Out of the blue he had recently received a tragic letter from the bully who had been most responsible for making his school life so miserable. Now a figure of some importance in the banking world, his letter sought forgiveness.

'My doctors have just confirmed that I shall be meeting my Maker in months, possibly in weeks, and I wish to make my peace with you, among others, whom I have offended. You may find it hard to believe, after so many years, but I have been distressed for some time – long before I became mortally ill – by the memory of the suffering I helped to inflict on you. I am hoping that, in the circumstances, you will not find it unforgivable.'

Quinn's reaction – 'I have no intention of even replying to the bastard and he can rot in hell' – brought rebuke from Angela but when he gave his reason for the refusal she knew there would be no change of mind.

'Of course I have forgiven him,' he insisted. 'But if he is such a bloody fool to think that I still hold it against him after all these years then to hell with him. I can't stand fools.'

Chapter Seven

There were few basic differences between the office of Sergei Yakovlev, the chairman of the KGB, the Komitet Gosudarstvennoi Bezopasnosti – Soviet Committee for State Security – and that of Sir Mark Quinn. Yakovlev's looked more old-fashioned, with its high ceiling, mahogany-pannelled walls and oriental carpets. The huge desk had a different shape but it, too, was piled high with folders and reports, and its occupant also regarded paper as an enemy which could only be worn down by slow attrition.

The battery of telephones was even larger than Quinn's, with direct lines to many Kremlin offices, to other Politburo and Party bosses and to the scores of KGB offices scattered throughout the vast country where the organization, the Party's main instrument of power, was responsible for keeping the people 'disciplined'.

Tall for a Russian with a flat, Slavic face, dark straight hair and somewhat bat-eared, Yakovlev was pleasant looking and, for a man in his late fifties, in good physical trim.

After a lifetime actively dedicated to the Marxist-Leninist cause, but even more so to his native land, he had recently achieved the coveted membership of the Politburo, the Communist Party's decision-making body, with the probability of still higher office. He was the first career officer of the KGB to have risen from its ranks to its political directorship, and as such was held in particular awe and respect by Counter-Intelligence services throughout the world. But he was far from happy and still further from contentment.

The higher command, and Party Secretary-General Anatoli Borisenko and Prime Minister Konstantin Volkhov in particular, were blaming him for failing to control the dissidence, the strikes and the insurrections in the satellite countries, where organizations corresponding to the KGB were supposed to take their lead from him.

At such times Zina, his secretary, who had been assigned to him ten years previously and had risen with him, was a tower of support. With her, as with nobody else, since spies from other State Departments were infiltrated even into the KGB, he felt secure in criticizing his political overlords in terms as harsh as his thoughts. She agreed wholeheartedly that leaders like Borisenko and Volkhov were criminal in the way they clung to power when so obviously overtaken by senility. They went on and on, convincing themselves that their country could not spare them. And those who had come up with them helped to keep them there, like the aged Foreign Secretary, who had even suffered a seizure in full camera view at the United Nations Assembly, and like the Defence Minister, Marshal Davorin, who, though distinguished in the war with Nazi Germany, was seventy-two.

'It's their blasted fault that so many people are so restless,' Yakovlev said as he sifted his papers. 'Our drive for influence and hegemony outside our boundaries is going magnificently. But there's no domestic change and no signs of any. Why can't these old men see that there must be changes – that our people are just not going to put up with austerity and restriction forever? Now there's this crazy idea of initiating a war in Europe to unite the people! It's lunatic!'

'Any war is lunatic,' Zina said, drawing Yakovlev one of his endless beakers of tea from a samovar, his only concession to old technology.

Born and reared in Kursk, her parents had both been killed there in a German air raid when she was small, and it had been her belief that the KGB's main concern was with preventing war which had led her into its service. A *jolie-laide*, with rather high cheek-bones, hazel eyes, and mousey hair swept severely into a bun, she did not attract men, though some years previously there had been a fiery love-affair with a foreigner, which had ended with such searing abruptness that she had never fully recovered from it. She roused no sexual interest in Yakovlev who, as a young political thruster had married the daughter of a Party boss and, while Zina knew that the marriage could hardly be said to have been happy, he was not going to risk disrupting it when he had become a public figure with such glittering possibilities.

He would not even take up the option of infidelity which he believed had long been open to him. Zina had the habit of hitching up the tired elastic of her GUM store knickers by pinching it through her dress, but that did not excite Yakovlev, who suspected that it was intended to do so. Unlike her counterpart in MI6 she did not seem made for sex, and the bedroom adjoining the office went unused, except on the rare occasions when Yakovlev spent the night there during some emergency or crucial operation.

Behind Yakovlev's desk was a huge map showing Moscow at the centre of a rather oddly shaped world, where Soviet interest had grown enormously during his political life and would expand much further, if he got his way, particularly in the eastward direction. But before then there was routine work to be done – as there always was in any struggle for promotion and power.

'Who said Intelligence work was exciting?' Yakovlev asked rhetorically, as Zina deposited a metal security-box on his desk. It was the daily KGB offering from the Resident at the Soviet Embassy in London, which had been flown out in the diplomatic bag.

He stood up, a smart but sombrely dressed figure who favoured dark grey suits, and unlocked the box with a key which he kept on a chain attached to his belt, picked out a sheaf of papers, and thumbed through them.

'Huh, if the British are really expecting us to make a move on the Central Front they are remarkably relaxed about it,' he remarked. 'There are no signs of any troop movements in Britain, no mobilization, no special reinforcements from the United States, no attempts to round up any of our subversion units there. How blind can these people be?'

'I thought you were sure that they are playing it down because they are scared of provoking us into a fight.'

'I did say that, but in this crazy game you can never be absolutely sure, particularly with the British. They are a very strange lot, the British. They never have a straightforward line. Ah, here's what I'm looking for. The latest dispatch from "John Bull".'

He slit open a sealed envelope with a miniature silver scimitar given to him as a parting present when he had ended his service in Syria, and withdrew a single sheet of paper. The message was hand-written in English which, as a result of his service in Washington and with the United Nations in New York, he was able to understand and translate with ease. Reading it with mounting interest he uttered occasional expletives under his breath. Then, needing an audience, for few secrets could be kept from Zina if she was to do her work effectively, he cried, 'Just listen to this:

' "After a meeting of the United States National Security Council earlier this week it was decided that, the moment an attack on NATO's Central Front by Warsaw Pact Forces is confirmed, the enemy" – that's us – "will be engaged with neutron weapons delivered by precision-guided missiles and shells. These will be effective right back to the Third Echelon, deep in our territory.

' "The neutron weapons have been in NATO stockpiles for many months in the guise of conventional warheads – in defiance of the Helsinki understandings and of America's stated policy. The decision is being kept secret from all NATO allies until the weapons are issued, immediately prior to action." '

He looked at Zina expectantly for her response.

'Doesn't that change everything?' she asked. 'That is if the information is reliable ... '

'Well you know who "John Bull" is don't you? It *has* to be reliable. He's the defector-in-place par excellence and he's never misled us before, though exactly how he knows this lot I don't quite understand.'

Yakovlev's interest in neutron weapons was intense as he owed his recent promotion to the stunning success of the propaganda drive against the American neutron bomb which had so impressed Borisenko and his predecessor. He reached for the red telephone among the battery of phones and other communication channels on his desk.

'See if Marshal Dominowski is in his office,' he barked.

'How am I going to play this, Zina?' he thought aloud, as he replaced the receiver. 'Perhaps we can make those old idiots see sense now. The Soviet people don't want a war with the Americans.'

He rubbed his chin pensively. 'I'm sure I can carry Dominowski with me, but Borisenko and Volkhov ... The trouble with them is that they take their advice from that old idiot Davorin who's still dreaming of his victories in the "Great Patriotic War".'

His sloping, Slavic eyes narrowed as he pictured the ancient Defence Minister giving his drivelling advice to the summit leadership, or standing in the Red Square Party line-up laden with medals. If he dropped dead, which seemed unlikely, there was someone almost as decrepit to replace him, as there was with Borisenko, Volkhov and so many others.

'Andrei Andreievitch?' Yakovlev asked almost excitedly as the red telephone rang. 'I'm so glad I caught you. I have something of the most urgent interest. Could you come across? Good! I'll have you shown up without delay.'

He asked Zina to ensure that Marshal Dominowski would not be delayed by any security checks, other than the mandatory identity-card examination at the entrance to the KGB Headquarters. Then he said, 'You know, don't you, Zina, that if Comrades Borisenko, Volkhov and Marshal Davorin get their way we shall be at war within a week?'

'Yes, it's terrible,' Zina responded, placing a fresh beaker of tea on his desk.

He sat back, sipped the tea and gazed at the ceiling. The action he had in mind carried grave personal risk, although the promise of rich reward. He would have preferred a more elegant solution but this one was ready-made and time was desperately short. Wasn't there some Russian proverb like, 'Only a fool would let the house fall down by hesitating to drive in a nail just because he can't find the screwdriver?'

He began to put down a sequence of thoughts on paper, in the red ink which only he was allowed to use, studied them, finally nodded his assent and then burned the crumpled sheet in an ashtray. He had better reason than most to know that, in the Soviet Union in particular, 'You can make a noose out of a bit of paper.'

Yakovlev looked over at Zina who was peering into a tall filing-cabinet, her heels raised out of her shoes, and decided that the time had come to break the bad news which he had learned from the Resident in the Washington Embassy early that morning. She would inevitably hear about it from someone in the Centre, as the big headquarters complex was known, and would resent not having been told by him. He loathed atmosphere in the office.

'There's something I must tell you, Zina,' he said, fiddling with his pen.

'What's that?'

'It's about Viktor Kovalsky. He's dead.'

'Dead? Viktor! How did it happen?'

'He was murdered in Washington. The CIA is putting it around that we did it, but I give you my word that we didn't. After all why should we? Why would I contemplate such a thing?'

It was a fair question. Zina had been told that it was under personal pressure from Yakovlev that Kovalsky had very reluctantly agreed to pretend to defect to the United States to establish himself, in what had become known in Intelligence parlance, as a 'mole'.

Yakovlev had discussed the project with Zina before Viktor himself had been approached. Zina was a personal friend of Kovalsky and had introduced him to his wife, Tamara. Zina had been appalled at the way Viktor had been asked to agree to be seen as a traitor and desert his wife and daughter for years, possibly forever. She knew well enough that the KGB was ruthless with its demands on its own officers just as it was with its enemies, and details of what still went on in the old Lubianka Prison, enclosed inside the headquarters complex, occasionally reached her ears. It was generally accepted in the

93

struggle for world Communism that no individual was indispensable, and in the KGB particularly every person was expendable, but for a man of Viktor's record and seniority this assignment had seemed an appalling sacrifice.

'I wouldn't ask him if it weren't of supreme importance – not just to the organization but to the whole nation,' Yakovlev had assured her.

Zina had been given no details of Kovalsky's assignment but that was normal enough, since the office was run strictly on a need-to-know basis except when it suited Yakovlev to bend the rule.

'I just don't understand why anyone should want to kill Viktor,' she said. 'The Americans wouldn't want a man with all his knowledge killed even if they knew he was a plant. They'd want to try to turn him.'

'I agree. It's all very mysterious,' Yakovlev said, as though content to leave it that way.

'Does Tamara know yet?' Zina asked.

'No, and I don't see why she should be told.'

Zina was incensed. 'Of course she must be told! That's the least you owe her. She thinks she's been deserted by a traitor. That's a terrible blow to any woman's pride. She must be told that Viktor was ordered to go and had dreadful heart-searchings before he agreed.'

Yakovlev's large brown eyes flashed their disapproval. 'Tamara cannot possibly be told he was a plant. That's the rule and you know it.'

'But now you make the rules,' Zina responded. 'In this case you must bend them.'

Always prepared to make a deal, if it suited, Yakovlev agreed. 'All right, all right. But you must break the news to her.'

'Why me?' Zina protested.

'Because you are a close friend and I'm not good at these things. Anyway it's you who's insisting she should be told … '

At that moment Zina did not like Yakovlev and the set of her lips betrayed it. But she was not surprised that the unpleasant task of informing the widow had been shifted to her. Yakovlev disliked any display of emotion. He worshipped logic and the emotional was too often linked with the irrational for his taste.

'You must make it clear to her that she is not to tell anybody else about Viktor's assignment.'

'I wouldn't dream of insulting her that way,' Zina said firmly. 'Tamara's been married to a KGB officer too long to be unaware of her duty. How shall I say he died?'

Yakovlev had already decided that. 'Say that his cover must have been broken by the CIA and they shot him when he was trying to get to the Soviet Embassy in Washington. Tell her we are doing everything we can to find out the details, and assure her that she's nothing to worry about money-wise. I'll see to that personally.'

He put his hand in his pocket, pulled out some notes and stood up, towering above his petite assistant. 'Here, take her some flowers from both of us.'

Never being one to waste time Zina put on her raincoat. Tamara Kovalsky lived in a small apartment in the Moscow suburbs, which meant a longish journey on the Metro.

Sitting in the rattling train she rehearsed what she was going to say. It was a horrid prospect, but Yakovlev had been right. It was woman's work: her work. Tamara was one of the few friends in her lonely life, for the KGB did not approve of its high-level secretaries, privy to so much information, cultivating many acquaintances. For that reason she had been allotted a larger and more comfortable apartment than her salary warranted and there she spent most of her leisure, reading and listening to music, which she taped on the machine her boss had given her to celebrate her twenty-five years in the KGB.

The more Zina thought of the circumstances of Viktor's death, and Yakovlev's reaction to it, the more it sounded like the work of the KGB rather than of the CIA. By the time she alighted from the train the unresolved question in her mind was whether Yakovlev himself had ordered it. She knew that if something had suddenly gone wrong threatening a vital operation, as Viktor's seemed to have been, her boss would not let the death of a friend stand in the way of the needs of the Service, especially if these happened to coincide with his own requirements.

It was a dreadful game that she was in. But she had no intention of getting out of it – even if it were permissible.

Marshal Dominowski looked up admiringly at the sparkling

sunshine reflected from the Kremlin domes, which had been regilded at great expense for the 1980 Olympic Games. He remembered that year only too well. There had been a suggestion in the early part of it to use the Games as a cover for a sudden strike into West Germany on the assumption that NATO would be more than usually off its guard. For, with Moscow packed with competitors and tourists from so many countries, nobody would anticipate such a move. The man who had put it forward to the Council of Defence as a serious option had been Sergei Yakovlev's predecessor at the KGB. His paper, which Dominowski, among others, had been required to consider, argued that with so many Westerners held in the Soviet capital the United States could not possibly retaliate with nuclear weapons against it. Happily, less lunatic counsel had prevailed and the KGB chief had signed his professional death warrant with his 'Project Olympic Games'.

For Dominowski, who much preferred to be with troops, Sergei Yakovlev was one of Moscow's compensations. Apart from mutual admiration of their efficiency in running their far-flung organizations, they shared a severely critical view of the way the country was being governed by an Inner Cabinet of men whose average age was sixty-nine. Given to barrack-room language, Dominowski agreed that if Communism was to progress the hierarchy must 'show more interest in that poor bastard Ivan Ivanovitch'.

The Marshal's impressive military vehicle pulled up at the entrance to the grey stone KGB complex, built round an old courtyard at Number Two, Dzerzhinsky Street, not far from the Kremlin. Apart from the guards in KGB uniform there was no sign to indicate the many functions of the organization, save for the statue of its first commander, Feliks Dzerzhinsky, so dreaded in his lifetime but to whom the Party and its ruling clique were forever in debt for forging the machinery of internal suppression.

Stepping briskly from his car, Dominowski returned the guard officer's salute, flashed his identity card and was conducted immediately to the lift for the third floor. As the 'Sword and Shield' of the Party the KGB was responsible for the continuing political reliability of the Soviet Armed Forces, through informers attached to every unit, as well as for the Intelligence needs of the Government. It seemed unlikely that Sergei would want to see him so urgently on that account.

'Sorry about the ironmongery, Sergei,' Dominowski said, indicating the array of medals across his barrel chest. 'I've just come from a strategy meeting of the Main Military Council and that old ass Davorin insists on uniforms. It enables him to show his own medals!'

'Is the operation still on?'

'Swordthrust? Yes, bigger than ever. The forces to be centred in East Germany include the 3rd Shock Army, the 20th Tank Army and the 1st, 2nd and 8th Guards Armies.'

Yakovlev gave a low whistle. 'When does it begin?'

'Midnight Saturday. By 0400 hours on Sunday morning the first tanks and helicopters are due to cross the West German border.'

'Hoping, no doubt, that, being a weekend and during the holiday season, NATO will be half depleted and half asleep.'

'They were when we took Czechoslovakia. The First Echelon should be well on its way to Hamburg, Hanover and Kassel before they can do much about it.'

Yakovlev shook his head in sad disbelief as Dominowski continued.

'By Day Five most of West Germany is to be occupied with most of Holland and most of Austria. A halt will then be called, if not before, with the claim that the danger of a German revenge attack on the Soviet Union has finally been removed. Provided the West then formally accepts the reality of German reunification under our control, our forces will then withdraw from Holland. Austria is to remain a matter for negotiation.'

'Do you think that is the way it will go?' Yakovlev asked. 'All that in six days?'

Dominowski sat back in his chair, folded his arms and stretched out his legs. 'I've had to advise the Military Council that I do. Everything is in our favour, as you know from your own reports. The West are politically paralysed and are doing nothing. But it's still a gamble. We can't be absolutely sure that the Americans will lack the resolve to retaliate against our cities with their long-range nuclear missiles.'

'Any gamble with millions of our citizens lives is totally irresponsible,' Yakovlev said.

'I agree, Sergei. I'm opposed to the whole project because it's so unnecessary. The so-called fear of an attack by West Germany and NATO is a fiction – an excuse for another "Great Patriotic War" to solve problems that would either solve themselves in time or should be tackled by other means.'

'Including all the unrest?'

'Of course. None of the generals, apart from Davorin, are being fooled by this bullshit put out by Moscow Radio and *Pravda*. NATO is *not* going to attack us and never will attack us. Those plans for the invasion by NATO, which are supposed to have fallen into our hands, are fakes. Nor is there the slightest evidence that the United States is going to sign a military pact with Peking. So my colleagues are just as opposed as I am to losing tanks and troops which we may well need soon for a showdown with China.'

'And who can be sure that the Chinese won't seize the opportunity to strike at our rear if we get bogged down in Europe?' Yakovlev asked.

'That's another gamble. It's always been the prime principle of our strategy that we must never have to fight on two fronts, but we'll just have to do whatever Borisenko decides without protest. That's our job, I'm afraid.'

'Well, Andrei, it's like you've always said, the Party's control over the Army is too tight. Initiative is stifled. But everything may not be as much in the Red Army's favour as you think. That's why I called you over. Take a look at this. You might have to reconsider the whole position.'

He passed the Marshal the original document from 'John Bull' together with his Russian translation of it. Dominowski was deeply shocked by what he read.

'But can you be sure that this is accurate, Sergei?'

'Look, Andrei Andreievitch, this is so important that to convince you I will break a golden rule and tell you the source in absolute secrecy. This information originates from the British Prime Minister!'

The Marshal looked flabbergasted. 'Is he one of us?'

'He helps us,' Yakovlev said guardedly.

Sensing doubt as well as astonishment in Dominowski's mind Yakovlev rose and, after consulting his pocket diary, twisted the combination lock dial on a filing-cabinet, withdrew two thick folders, each labelled 'John Bull', and placed them in front of the Marshal.

'These are the reports, with dates and translations, which we have received from that source. Take a look.'

'May I?'

'You may, but I would never show them to anybody else.'

Dominowski turned a few pages, sampling the subject matter, closed the folders and commented, 'Astonishing, Sergei. Astonishing. But if America's allies are not being told about these neutron-bomb deliveries how does the British Prime Minister know about them?'

'I confess I have no idea. But he has supplied us before with American information he should not have known. Maybe the President made an exception of him on the special relationship basis. He is also friendly with the American Ambassador in London, according to our sources there. I shall be checking the situation out in West Germany but meantime, as time is so short, do you agree that if the information is correct it changes everything?'

'Absolutely,' the Marshal replied without hesitation. 'The success of "Swordthrust" depends almost entirely on the preponderance of our massed tanks. In the near-certainty that the NATO forces will try to hold us without recourse to nuclear weapons we plan to operate on a frontal width of 1000 yards. A hundred neutron bombs used with precision could blunt the attack almost to destruction. They could also prevent the concentration of our support forces.'

Yakovlev saw with satisfaction that Dominowski was deeply disturbed at the damage which might now be inflicted on his beloved tank units.

'Marshal, it may take some time to confirm or repudiate this information. Meanwhile, do you agree that because it might be true it is our duty to see Comrade Borisenko to warn him that the situation may not be as favourable as we thought?'

'I certainly do, Comrade.'

'Then you will come with me and lend your great authority?'

'I will.'

The Marshal offered his hand. 'Something always turns up for Russia,' he said with a faint smile. 'Maybe this is it.'

'I hope you are right. Somehow these old men must be stopped from plunging the nation into war before it is absolutely necessary. You know I'm beginning to suspect that they want to see some great leap forward in their lifetime and they know they haven't much left.'

'Or, they are suffering from senile dementia,' Dominowski suggested. 'Perhaps that's why most old men make the mistake of treating those younger with contempt. It's bad enough having to listen to bloody old fools like Davorin talking such balls. What really infuriates me is that we are required to believe them. Lenin never allowed ideology to take precedence over reality.'

So the Marshal, too, was smarting from the contempt to which he himself had been subjected over the preceding weeks, Yakovlev realized. That was good. Their immediate interests were the same. If events turned out as he was hoping, he would remember the help Andrei Andreievitch had given him.

Sensing a trace of a satisfied smile playing round Yakovlev's lips Dominowski asked, half in jest, 'This room isn't bugged is it?'

'Not when you are in it, Marshal,' Yakovlev lied. 'Let's drink to the success of our venture which could save so much suffering.'

He poured two vodkas.

'To peace, Andrei Andreievitch!'

'To peace, Sergei!'

They consumed the spirit at a gulp, then Dominowski put on his red-banded hat and held out his hand. 'I will hear from you when you have fixed an appointment with the Secretary-General?'

'Right.'

As he turned to leave he noticed a chess-table in one corner of the room. On it stood a fine Chinese set arranged in a half-completed game.

'Playing with that nice secretary of yours?' the Marshal asked.

'No. Zina doesn't play chess.'

Dominowski looked at the state of the game. 'It looks as though the red king will shortly be checkmated.'

Yakovlev did not reply but fervently hoped so.

Chapter Eight

On the first floor of the main American Embassy block in Grosvenor Square, which housed the large CIA contingent, with its 'analysts', who worked closely with British Intelligence, and its few active agents who operated independently, the mission chief, Ed Taylor, was at work in his office. He was putting the finishing touches to a routine report about to be transmitted to Langley Headquarters when his secretary announced that the Ambassador wished to see him urgently. He thought for a moment then said, 'Tell her I'm out and I'll call her back soonest.'

He picked up the telephone and called Falconer who, as he expected, was reading quietly on his bed in his room at the Grosvenor House Hotel, round the corner in Park Lane.

'Any idea what Her Excellency might want?' Falconer asked.

'Haven't a clue. This is the first time she's acknowledged my existence. Could it be about you?'

'Sure could, if she's found out I'm here. I suppose she could have got wind of it from one of the State Department boys who liaise with Langley. Anyway you'd better find out. We do need to know. A frontal approach, Ed.'

Taylor had spotted Jane Jansen entering and leaving the Embassy on several occasions, and was familiar with her photographs which had appeared almost daily in the *Washington Post* during her running battle with the CIA, together with those of her Senator husband. To the left-wing liberals, Marxists and others making political use of the Jansens they had become known as the 'White Knight' and the 'White Lady' – mostly because of their silver hair, and their zeal for human-rights' crusades. Pictures of them hand-in-hand at the time of the 'White Lady's' ambassadorial appointment had appeared nationwide with tear-jerking captions about the sacrifice being made on behalf of their country by this ideal all-American couple.

As she shook hands with Taylor, he had to acknowledge that her photographs had not flattered her. Though somewhat severe, she was a good-looking woman for her doubtful age, her figure being youthful, with its rather small bosom, slim legs and regularly coiffured hair which, since her departure from Washington, had been restyled with a blue rinse.

She removed the spectacles she used only for reading and motioned Taylor to be seated. She remained at her large desk, impressively backed by the flag of the United States and her ambassadorial standard. Usually when speaking to visitors she sat on the elegant settee in the tastefully furnished office. It was clear that this meeting was intended to be formal and brief.

'I won't beat about the bush, Mr Taylor. You know my views about your organization and they haven't changed. On the contrary. I have been informed that Mr Falconer, that dreadful man, is in London. Can you tell me what he is doing on my territory?'

'He is here on a private visit. He's going to see the Derby – he breeds racehorses, you know. And he's also saying goodbye to his old associates in the British Intelligence Service. He's retiring shortly.'

'Well, that's the best news I've heard in a long time, Mr Taylor. But are you certain that's why he's here? Personally, I wouldn't believe a word that man says. I only hope he's not up to his old tricks of spying on our friends. That seems to be his speciality. Spying on friendly countries is not just wrong, it's immoral.'

'There's no question of that, Ambassador ... '

'There'd better not be,' Mrs Jansen interrupted rudely. 'I'm not having him or anybody else fouling up our relations with the British Government, and particularly with my friend the Prime Minister.'

'I assure you there's no question of that, Ambassador.'

'I sincerely hope not, but you fellows have a long record of fouling up diplomatic relations. Anyway, so far as Mr Falconer is concerned I shall be making my own inquiries. I have my own resources, you know. Tell Mr Falconer that when you see him.'

She made it clear that the interview was at an end and

102

Taylor withdrew rather awkwardly from the presence.

Instead of returning to his office, he scurried round to Falconer's hotel. As he entered the room, Falconer rose from his bed, put a bookmark in the paperback racing novel he had bought at the hotel book-stall and carefully placed his pillow over the telephone.

'Boy, you're certainly right about that woman being a bitch,' Taylor said as soon as he was seated. 'And what a gabbler. You get no chance to talk when she's in flood.'

'Yeah,' Falconer replied sourly, 'she's the opposite of that guy Winthrop Aldrich. When he was Ambassador here they used to say that his mouth was always shut but his flies were always open.'

As Taylor recounted his conversation with Mrs Jansen, word for word, Falconer grew increasingly concerned.

'You know she might squawk her suspicions to Henderson,' he said, rubbing his chin. 'If she does and he takes fright it could foul up the entire operation.'

Taylor, who knew the value of preserving silence when it suited, was startled by the words 'entire operation'. Was there something more to Falconer's visit than he knew? If so, it was useless to question a clam like John.

'If she finds out the real purpose of my visit – the Henderson situation, I mean – she could even blow something in the Press,' Falconer said. 'You know what a publicity hound she is, and she'd go to any lengths to ditch me. I wonder how the hell she found out I was here.'

'By the way,' Taylor said, almost casually as he prepared to leave, 'I've found out who "Uncle Vanya" is.'

'Who?' Falconer asked with extreme interest.

'It's a guy called Rakitin. He's the personal assistant in Borisenko's office, a trusted old time-server.'

Falconer whistled. 'No wonder he's such a hell of a source. Who told you?'

'Angela Strickland. She made a slip of the tongue while I was in Quinn's office waiting for him.'

'Ah, I told you she might be productive.'

'Yeah. We were talking about "Uncle Vanya" and suddenly she used the name Rakitin. I checked out on him and that's who he is. I felt rather sorry for Angela. She obviously realized she had made a boob.'

Felt sorry for her! What was a guy like this doing in the Intelligence game? Falconer thought. 'Well more fool Mark O'Toole for letting her know it,' he said. 'It never pays to confide in women, Ed. Have you fed it back to Langley yet?'

'No. I thought I'd tell you first.'

'Good boy! Leave it to me, Ed. I'll feed it into the machine when I get back to Langley. I'll make sure that they know it's from you.'

'OK' Taylor agreed. 'Quinn has certainly pulled a fast one on Yakovlev getting a defector-in-place in the most sensitive office in the Kremlin.'

'Yeah, I guess Comrade Sergei would be for the high jump if Borisenko found out.'

'Tell me, John,' Taylor inquired, smoothing back his hair, 'why does Mark detest Yakovlev so much? I know he's Enemy Number One, but there's usually some respect for a worthy opponent and Quinn's hackles rise the moment his name's mentioned.'

'Oh it's very interesting,' Falconer said, settling himself full-length on the bed. 'Their professional paths crossed in a way which Quinn has never been able to forgive. The British Ambassador in Moscow – I forget his name, it was some years ago – had been set up by Yakovlev, who was then a field officer. His outfit had recruited a prostitute and infiltrated her into the Ambassador's residence as a chambermaid.

'Quinn had a cover job on the Ambassador's staff then and he had recruited another Russian woman on the domestic staff of the Residence to work for him. This woman spotted the ambassador and the chambermaid hard at it and the upshot was that, after Quinn reported the episode, the ambassador was prematurely retired.

'Yakovlev was so furious, stupidly for him, I think, that he insisted on taking revenge. Poor Mark O'Toole was tricked into arriving at a restaurant in a quiet part of Moscow believing that some new defector would be there. The KGB pounced on him, beat him up and then accused him of trafficking in drugs. They whipped him into the Lubianka, planted dope and a great wad of roubles and American dollars on him, and held him incommunicado for several days. Yakovlev spotted that he was claustrophobic so he stuck him in the smallest cell he'd got. Something like a doghouse that he couldn't stand up in. Poor Mark O'Toole was just about screaming.'

'Gee, no wonder Mark hates him.'

'Yeah. Yakovlev had discovered his character weakness.'

Falconer could not resist a chuckle as Taylor asked, 'How did they get him out?'

'Under diplomatic immunity. The Russians finally handed him over but they made him *persona non grata* – with publicity.'

'With publicity!' Taylor echoed. 'Who wouldn't be sore?'

Being thrown out of a target country was a professional hazard for any undercover agent. When it was done with publicity his cover was blown for operating in any other.

'Fortunately for Quinn his superiors weren't too upset about it.' Falconer continued. 'He'd done a good job getting that fool of an ambassador out and they knew he'd been victimized. And he'd given nothing away under pressure. In fact, being restricted to a desk job in London did him a world of good. From then on his rise was meteoric, but he's never forgiven Yakovlev for framing him and putting him in that doghouse.'

It was later that evening when they walked towards the Café Royal Grill for dinner that they first realized they were being followed. Taylor, who was intensely interested in the history of London, believed that the only way to get to know a city was to walk its streets. To Falconer, a countryman, pavements were pavements wherever he was, but he humoured his companion, remarking that, at least, it would be good for Taylor's figure.

'This is the Old Watling Street, a Roman road that used to go straight down to a ford over the Thames at Westminster,' Taylor explained as they strolled down Park Lane. 'But when London Bridge was built they diverted the traffic that way.'

Though Falconer appeared to be walking quite slowly his stride was so long that Taylor was having difficulty keeping up with him – it seemed as though everything about him was deceptive. As they turned into Piccadilly, Taylor noticed that two men, whom he had seen chatting by the lifts in Grosvenor House, were close behind them. He paused at a shop window to show Falconer some amusing montage pictures made of old watch parts and other mechanical components. The two men also stopped, seemingly to discuss something happening in the park on the other side of the road. When Taylor stopped again, pretending to explain something about the In-and-Out Club, the two strangers slowed down their pace.

'Let's split at the Green Park Underground Station and see who the tail's on, you or me,' Taylor suggested.

They both entered the tube station followed by the men and when Taylor dived up into Stratton Street through a side exit, the two men remained talking while Falconer fiddled for change by a ticket machine. Minutes later, when Taylor reappeared with a newspaper he had bought, the shadowers were still there.

'It's me all right,' said Falconer who was enjoying the encounter. 'What do you think they are? KGB? Do they usually tail you here?'

'Occasionally,' Taylor murmured. 'But obviously if they know you are in London they are going to be more interested in you. Well, we can soon find out if they are KGB. Follow me.'

Taylor led the way in leisurely fashion under the road and up the stairs on to the south side of Piccadilly and walked down towards Piccadilly Circus, eventually turning right down one of the arcades into Jermyn Street. They stopped momentarily to look into the window of a famous cheese shop, then reached Eagle Place, a short thoroughfare leading back to Piccadilly containing a telephone kiosk. Waiting until there was nobody else in Eagle Place Taylor dialled 999 and called, 'Police! There's a dangerous looking package dumped by the telephone box in Eagle Place.' He hung up before he could be questioned.

A police patrol car was there within two minutes, its siren wailing as it speeded down the bus lane against the normal traffic flow from Piccadilly Circus, where it had been stationed. Taylor and Falconer stood at the Piccadilly end of Eagle Place watching the two men who were still standing in Jermyn Street. The arrival of the police had no effect on the 'tailers' who continued to look into a shop window.

'That makes it pretty sure they are not KGB,' Taylor said. 'They usually get the hell out of it quick when they see a CIA man summon the police.'

They wandered across the road towards the Café Royal to

claim their table in the Grill Room, which Taylor had chosen because of its historical associations with Oscar Wilde, Shaw, Arnold Bennett and other writers. The two men who continued to follow them went into the bar and ordered drinks.

'What do you make of them?' Falconer asked, after they had been conducted to their banquette seats in the glittering Grill Room by the smiling Italian manager.

'They must be Brits. Private eyes hired by Her Excellency?' Taylor hazarded. 'If so they are not very good. Unless, of course, they are a deterrent tail,' he added, meaning watchers who deliberately let their quarry know they are being followed to scare them out of achieving their purpose.

'In that case they could be MI5 or Special Branch put on to us by the Prime Minister?' Falconer suggested. 'Let's ask Mark Quinn about it. He may be able to find out something.'

Falconer judged that Taylor had performed rather ably on that limited and routine course. But did he have balls enough for the big challenge? Or was he one of those over-sensitive, too highly strung geldings who would refuse at a really dangerous fence?

The following morning, the first Wednesday in June and therefore Derby Day, was cloudless. While hundreds of men were laying out their grey tails and toppers and thousands, who would soon be streaming to Epsom by rail, were seeking out their binoculars, Quinn was looking disconsolately out of his office window at the glorious sunshine bathing the river. He would have hated to go to the Derby and, in truth, there was nowhere he would rather be than in his office, sifting through the mass of telegrams and intercepts which had accumulated through the night. Indeed, how anybody in their right minds could pretend to enjoy themselves when war seemed so imminent he could not understand. Still, what the hell! There was nothing they or he could do to stop it. The politicians had seen to that with their complacency and bland assurances.

He allowed himself the luxury of a few more moments of feeling that he was unfairly chained to his desk, then sat at it to continue his scrutiny of the latest information. He was looking for signs that 'sleepers' among the hard-line Communists and professional subversives might be rousing themselves in response to orders from the KGB, which had long sustained them both in Britain and West Germany. Any movement by them would be a sure indication that a Soviet attack was imminent. There was none.

'Things are looking grimmer and grimmer,' Quinn remarked to Angela. 'Satellite pictures confirm that Warsaw Pact Forces are still massing far back into Western Russia as well as in Poland, Czechoslovakia and East Germany. Their so-called "Exercise Swordthrust" is scheduled to start in four days time. Some exercise! Estimates talk of 30,000 tanks being mobilized!'

'And we seem to be doing nothing.'

'*We* are doing all we possibly can,' Quinn said crisply. 'It's the bloody fool politicians who are doing nothing. Hiding their heads in the sand as usual. And the NATO generals seem just as stupid. They know what's happening yet a dozen of them have accepted invitations to "observe" the exercise. You know what will happen? They'll be dead or in the bag as soon as "Swordthrust" switches for real.'

'Maybe the politicians have ordered them to accept the invitation as evidence of good faith,' Angela suggested.

'That wouldn't surprise me,' Quinn said, making a note to find out if this were so. 'How the hell anybody ever fell for that part of the Helsinki Agreement I'll never understand, especially after the blatant way the exercise subterfuge was used to take Czechoslovakia by surprise in 1968. You weren't here then, Angela, but we repeatedly warned the Foreign Office – and Number Ten – that the huge build-up on the borders of Czechoslovakia was not an exercise but mobilization for an attack. The Foreign Office refused to believe it.'

'Are they fools, villains or both?' Angela inquired.

'You may well ask. Whatever they are they still think they are dealing with gentlemen. Some of the Russian generals may be gentlemen, but they'll still do whatever those ruthless old bastards in the Politburo tell them. They daren't do anything else.'

He picked up a piece of paper and held it rather far in front of him, being vain enough to be still delaying the inevitability of spectacles. 'Ah, here's the report from the private detective on the Prime Minister's movements yesterday. He's a good chap that!'

He pursed his lips as he perused it. 'Hm, can't see anybody here who could be the courier ... But there must be one. Henderson couldn't be such a fool as to contact any Soviet Bloc agent directly.'

Being aware of the incredible weaknesses and stupidities of so many men in high places through reading their dossiers, Angela was not so sure. 'He might have no alternative if the KGB is turning the heat on him.'

Quinn shook his head and scowled. He did not like being contradicted even when seeking counsel. 'What time did you ask John Falconer to call?' he asked.

'He's due any time now. You asked me to telephone him as soon as you had seen the bag from Moscow.'

'Good. I'm looking forward to his reaction. Is Ed Taylor coming with him?'

'I gather not ... '

'Just as well. There are some things he shouldn't know.'

'But don't you think Falconer will tell him?'

'No way,' Quinn said decisevely. 'The essence of tact lies in keeping your mouth shut, and Falconer is noted for it. Need to know, my dear! Need to know!'

Angela continued to busy herself cutting out ministerial answers to Parliamentary questions from Hansard and looking more than usually attractive as the sun streamed through the high window onto her hair. It was her duty to spot any statements which might have relevance to Intelligence affairs and to paste them in a special book. In the rush of recent events she had fallen behind with the task. Quinn had requested a thorough search of the last three weeks' issues, suspecting that some of the extreme left MPs might have been required by Soviet Intelligence to ask questions devised to produce answers of use to Moscow in the current crisis.

As her scissors snipped away crisply Quinn could not help asking, 'What happens to all the discarded Hansards?'

'They go through the shredders. Everything does. That's your instruction,' Angela replied without looking up.

'Pity,' Quinn grunted. 'They should all be used for fuelling the central heating. It would be a fitting end for them.'

'How come?' Angela asked, realizing that her master

109

wished to make one of his sarcastic comments and would not like to be deprived of the opportunity.

'Because it would be re-cycling hot air.'

Falconer's arrival was announced on the intercom and Angela showed him in.

'Morning, John,' Quinn said briskly. 'I've got news for you. Your hunch about the PM was dead right. I fed him some disinformation and, sure enough, I've just had it played back to me from Moscow. Almost verbatim!'

' "Uncle Vanya" didn't lose much time did he?' Falconer said with a satisfied smile.

'He never does. And he even sent his usual Russian joke.' Quinn picked up 'Uncle Vanya's' message and read, ' "Could a horse gallop from Leningrad to Moscow? Answer – No, because it would be eaten on the way." Another jibe at the chronic meat shortage. Not up to his usual standard but the rest of the message is spot on.'

'As a matter of interest, Mark, what did you feed Henderson that made him react so swiftly?'

'Oh, it had to be something really hot and I came up with a beauty. I told him that I had secured information, which I had confirmed, that your National Security Council had taken a firm decision to use precision-guided neutron weapons immediately the Russians approached the West German frontier in force, and that these were already stockpiled in position. I larded it up with some convincing collateral Intelligence ... '

It seemed that Falconer could scarcely believe his ears. 'For Christ's sake, Mark, that's not disinformation. It's true. The Council took exactly that decision four days ago.'

Quinn affected a look of intense surprise. 'But my dear fellow, how was I supposed to know that? I assure you that it's an absolute coincidence. Or is it? I suppose it could be parallel thinking. Perhaps in my mind I worked out what your chaps might be likely to do ... '

'Wasn't it irresponsible in the extreme to feed anything as sensitive as that into Moscow? Christ knows what the reaction in Washington will be if they get wind of it there.'

Quinn shrugged. 'I didn't feed it in. The Prime Minister did. But what the hell was I to do, John? We'd agreed that action was crucially urgent and the idea just presented itself.

It was a case of having to fight fire with fire. In any event, it seemed to me that the information – disinformation, I should say – might make the Russians think twice about attacking. So it couldn't do much harm. You know, John, I thought our purpose – yours and mine – was to prevent war. If we can put the fear of God up the Kremlin what harm's done?'

'Well, for a start, Mark, if this gets back to Washington they'll think I leaked it to you. Very few people knew about it. At this stage even the NATO commanders think that the weapons in their stockpiles are ordinary tactical nukes which were sent back to the States for the usual routine maintenance and then returned.'

'Come to that, John, why didn't you tell me? Then I wouldn't have used it. I think we were entitled to know about such an important decision. After all, we are the meat in the sandwich.'

'Oh come off it, Mark!' Falconer exclaimed, almost angrily. 'You know very well there are some secrets we have to keep from each other. And in this case there were pressing reasons. In the first place how could we tell you when we were sure that your Prime Minister was working for the other side?'

'Well it's no good crying over spilled secrets.' Quinn asserted. 'Our priority now is what we should do about Henderson.'

'Have you any idea how he gets his information to Moscow so quickly?'

'None. I got the report of his movements from his private detective this morning. It covers every minute. There's nobody he saw who's a possible starter.'

Quinn passed the list of contacts to Falconer who ran his eye down it.

'I suppose we'll have to eliminate Her Excellency, Mrs Jane Jansen,' he said. 'I don't mind telling you that I had her past pushed through a fine sieve when she was attacking us. If there had been anything at all the Press would have had it, pronto. Ed had an informer at her dinner last night – one of the Embassy servants – but he had nothing relevant to report.'

'Maybe they were able to talk privately when the servant wasn't there,' Quinn suggested.

Falconer shook his head. 'No, he planted temporary bugs

111

all over the place and had a pocket recorder. He got the lot. The conversation couldn't have been more prosaic.'

'There's no telephone evidence either,' Quinn said. 'Yet there just has to be a courier.'

Falconer paused and stared at Quinn through his thick lenses. 'There is a runner on this list you may not have considered. Someone Henderson spends a lot of time with.'

'Who's that?'

'His doctor.'

'Sir Alan King-Lander! But that's impossible. He's a most distinguished physician ... with a worldwide reputation ... '

'What else do you know about him?' Falconer asked.

Quinn gave a rather helpless shrug. 'I know next to nothing, though I suppose we have something on file. I know he's a close personal friend of the PM, but I'm never invited to functions at Number Ten so I've had no opportunity to meet him.'

'Exactly! So you could have a blind spot about him, Mark. He'd make the perfect courier wouldn't he? Henderson sees him in the absolute confidentiality of the doctor-patient relationship. Then anyone can go to visit him at his consulting-rooms under the same conditions without raising suspicion. Has he ever been positively vetted?'

'I'd be sure he hasn't,' said Quinn, who was somewhat thrown by the suggestion. 'It's never occurred to anyone, so far as I know, to PV any Prime Minister's doctor. If it was anybody's job it would be MI5's, and that shower in Curzon Street wouldn't be telling us about it. But why should he be regarded as an official subject to vetting any more than the PM's other close friends. He doesn't see papers ... '

'*Shouldn't* see papers,' Falconer corrected. 'You are not going to like this, Mark, but we've had King-Lander under heavy surveillance for some time.'

'The hell you have! To what degree?'

'The full treatment. We've bugged his consulting-rooms. The National Security Agency did it for us,' he said, referring to the American Intelligence-gathering organization so noted for its reluctance to reveal its functions in Britain, or elsewhere, that its initials were alleged to stand for Never Say Anything. 'They are our experts here on electronic surveillance and I didn't want to embarrass Ed by bringing our mission into it. It would have worried him stiff. You know how sensitive the Agency is here after all that row about spying on your Trade Unions. Anyway Ed doesn't really have the facilities.'

'Too bad,' Quinn said sardonically.

'It wasn't very difficult,' Falconer continued, ignoring the barbed comment. 'They induced one of the American drug companies to send the doctor a rather elaborate desk diary, which is more elaborate than it looks, and we followed up by getting one of our operatives referred to him for a second opinion. He managed to plant a back-up bug on the bottom bar of his dressing-screen!'

'Belt and braces!' Quinn observed.

'Yes, they've worked well. Belt and braces always do.'

'Have you anything definite yet?' Quinn asked.

'Nothing positive but some very significant negative responses. I'll explain what I mean later. Meanwhile I can assure you that King-Lander is not quite what he seems. For a start that's not the name with which he was christened. He was Adolf Gländer with an umlaut over the "a". He changed his name for professional reasons – to give it more authority. It seems that in your country a hyphen helps.'

'It does.'

'His parents emigrated from Leipzig before the war. They weren't political refugees and they weren't Jewish. The father was a locomotive engineer and was offered a good job in Darlington. Adolf, their only child, won scholarships to the grammar school there, and then to Cambridge. He was very bright and a tremendous worker. He's never looked back. He deserves his eminence.'

'You *have* checked out on him haven't you, John? Has he any relatives behind the Iron Curtain?'

'Distant, but they do exist.'

'And his politics?'

'Confirmed Socialist, not a Communist, but likes the goodies of life. A bon viveur.'

'Is that all you have?' Quinn asked, suspecting that Falconer was holding back the prime information.

'No. King-Lander's a widower and he is susceptible to the ladies. He visited Moscow twice for international medical conferences, and was set up by the KGB.'

'The usual compromising photographs?' Quinn inquired.

'Yeah. I feel sorry for him because he had no idea then that he would ever become a Prime Minister's doctor. So why shouldn't he have amused himself?'

'Another of the KBG's long shots!' Quinn commented. 'They have so many that some are bound to come up. But the number of intelligent men who fall for the sex frame-up never ceases to amaze me. When did they start putting the heat on him?'

'The first time he visited Moscow with Henderson. He yielded so easily to them that I suspect he'd crack if you interrogated him.'

'Interrogate him!' Quinn said. 'I wouldn't dare touch him.'

'Well you may change your mind when you've seen the situation for yourself. Or rather heard it. We have a small room opposite his consulting-rooms in Harley Street, hired in the name of a phoney acupuncture specialist. I think you'll enjoy listening to what goes on.'

'When can we do that?' Quinn asked eagerly.

'I happen to know that this evening should be propitious. Sir Alan has an interesting patient coming to see him, a rather frequent one – a woman.'

'I can't wait, John ... '

'Good, but we'll have to be careful. Ed and I are being tailed around London, and we're fairly sure that it's not by our friends from the KGB. Could it be MI5?'

Quinn smiled deprecatingly. 'Anything's possible with that lot. I suppose it could also be Special Branch ... '

'Well, whoever it is we'll have to take precautions. Can you pick me up by car outside the Dominion Theatre in Tottenham Court Road at 5.30 pm? Ed says its opposite a tall building called Centre Point. If they are tailing me I'll have hoped to have shaken them off by then.'

'I'll be there,' Quinn said.

'By the way, Mark,' Falconer added, almost as an aside as he prepared to leave, 'I'm afraid we won't be handing that KGB defector over to you.'

'Kovalsky? Why not?'

'He's dead. Murdered. Here's a cutting about it from the *Washington Post.*'

Under the small headline, 'Unknown man found shot',

Quinn read a brief account of how a middle-aged white man shot in the chest and head had been found in a downtown Washington hotel. The bullets had been fired from a nine millimetre calibre pistol. No clues to his identity had been found and nobody had come forward with information about him, though he was known to have had one friend who had booked him into the hotel. Checks of his fingerprints against the files of the FBI had proved negative, so his remains, labelled 'John Doe', had been transferred to the morgue for eventual cremation if checks with Missing Persons Bureaus also failed ...

'How did you let it happen?' Quinn asked uncharitably.

'Some foul-up by the case officer. I'm having him sorted out. It's a damn nuisance. Kovalsky was really valuable. The fact that the KGB went to such lengths shows that.'

'You're sure it was the KGB, John?'

'Who else could it be? Robbery was no motive. He still had money on him. And remember it was the second attempt.'

Quinn nodded, though he was not impressed. 'Well let's hope he'd already spilled all his material.'

'I'm sure he had,' Falconer said emphatically. 'You couldn't stop him talking.'

'M'm, I suppose we could take his murder as further evidence that his information about the Prime Minister was right.'

'I'd certainly interpret it that way, Mark. I don't have to tell you that I don't want anybody else knowing that we've bugged the Prime Minister's physician. And that applies particularly to Mrs Jane Jansen. She and King-Lander are more than friendly, by the way.'

'Is that right? Do you think she might have put the dogs on you?'

'It's not impossible,' Falconer replied. 'She certainly knows I'm here and she's being very nosey about it.'

He looked at his watch. 'It's time I was off. I'm going to see the Derby for the first time. Anything I can back for you? Are you a betting man?'

'In every big race I always back Jock Strap,' Quinn replied with a flicker of a smile.

'Jock Strap? Surely there's no such horse.'

'That's right. I don't like private activities over which I

115

have no control. It's too much like my daily work. And I don't like losing money to bookmakers.'

'Well let's hope I don't. See you on the dot at 5.30.'

As soon as Falconer had left the room Quinn picked up his green telephone. 'Take the tail off those two Americans,' he ordered. 'It's blown.'

As Quinn set up the machine and earphones to translate the 'Uncle Vanya' tape, which he always regarded as being too precious and too secret to be handled by anyone else, Angela asked quietly, 'Why did you ask me to leak "Uncle Vanya's" identity to Ed Taylor?'

'Reasons, my dear. Reasons,' he replied. 'I never do anything without good reason. Like the reason I am now going to the washroom is all that caffeine in your coffee.'

As soon as he had left the room Angela put one of the earphones to her ear, let the tape run for a few seconds, then wound it back. She did not understand Russian but she was quite certain that the voice on the tape was not that of an old man, as she knew Rakitin to be.

Chapter Nine

On that same June morning, which was as brilliant in Moscow as in London, Anatoli Borisenko, General Secretary of the Communist Party of the Soviet Union and Chairman of the Praesidium, posts which made him virtual dictator, was feeling the physical limitations of his seventy-two years. However, he was in no mood to admit them. He had always been a glutton for effort and, apart from his routine bleats about the weight of paper-work, was pushing himself without complaint so that none should see that his appetite either for hard work or power had declined. That is none save Rakitin, his personal assistant. To hide his true condition from him would have entailed more energy than it was worth, and it

116

did not matter for his trust in Rakitin, who had been with him so long, was absolute.

After a brief bout of chronic bronchitic coughing, which invariably blued up his sagging, hang-dog features, Borisenko patted his chest and breathed deeply and wheezily.

'Have you taken your tablets, Comrade Secretary-General?' Rakitin asked.

'Is it time for them again?'

'I'm afraid so. The doctor says it's most important that you don't miss them.'

The Secretary-General tapped out two tablets from a bottle with distaste, hating to admit that he needed them, and swallowed them with a gulp of water, exaggerating the sag of the striated skin below his once pugnacious chin.

'You look after me very well, Rakitin,' he said gratefully. 'I'm afraid age has too many penalties. Life's very unfair when you think of it. One strives so hard through youth and middle age and then just when you should be entitled to sit back and enjoy the fruits of your efforts, your health begins to fail.'

'I can't see you ever sitting back,' Rakitin said, rather unctuously.

'Ah, but in all honesty I'd dearly like to retire to my dacha in the birchwoods. I've had enough of the Kremlin.'

'But we couldn't afford to lose your services now with all this trouble ... '

Borisenko nodded sadly. 'There's always been something to stop me. Now it's all this terrible unrest and this dreadful danger that the Germans will take advantage of it to attack us. You know how they've always hated us and hankered after revenge – ever since we defeated them in the "Great Patriotic War".'

Rakitin, an emaciated time-server who had fought with Borisenko at Stalingrad and then right on to the capture of Berlin, knew it well enough, but also knew that the risk of an attack from that quarter was nil.

'Is there still more evidence that they are preparing to attack us?' he asked.

'There is indeed,' Borisenko said putting his hairy hand on a pile of papers, which, as Rakitin knew, had been manufactured by the propaganda machine. 'Marshal Davorin is certain of it from his sources and you know what faith I place in him. He has secured actual plans for the invasion from a source at NATO Headquarters. The time for the next phase of the historic clash between Capitalism and Socialism is upon us, Rakitin. Sadly I have difficulty in getting some of our younger comrades to see it. Unlike them, however, I am not prepared to risk seeing everything I have helped to build up destroyed again. In the circumstances, Rakitin, you are right. It would be a disaster for our country if I quit now. Marshal Dominowski's due shortly, isn't he?'

'Yes, Comrade Secretary-General. With Comrade Yakovlev. I expect they are waiting in the ante-room.'

Borisenko's face looked even bleaker at the sound of Yakovlev's name. This was the man he had selected for future stardom by appointing him head of the KGB and to membership of the Politburo, and it was not working out to his satisfaction at all. Having been granted one of the major seats of power he was pushing his own ideas.

'Loyalty, Rakitin! Where is it to be found these days? Not among the young.'

'No, Secretary-General.'

'So let them wait. It'll do them good. You know I don't want to see either of them but they are insisting on their infernal rights. Yakovlev says he has something crucial to tell me. Somebody always has something crucial to tell me ...'

He picked up his pen and continued to sign documents for several minutes. 'You'd better show them in now. Stay out of the room, but I'll leave the intercom on so that you can tape what they say.'

As Dominowski and Yakovlev entered the brightly lit room, which was filled with sunshine and artificial light from the many chandeliers, the Secretary-General continued to write for a few moments without acknowledging them. Then he screwed the top onto his fountain pen rather laboriously, sat back in his chair and observed, 'Ah, Comrades. The situation in the provinces doesn't improve does it? All these demonstrations and strikes. Riots, one might call some of them. What has happened to the internal discipline? We are very disappointed in the KGB's performance. Very disappointed.'

Yakovlev, who like the Marshal was still standing, bit his

118

lip but took the criticism patiently, having expected it. Giants could still be frightening at close range even if they happened to be old, and he felt the roof of his mouth going dry.

'What's this special news you have for me?' Borisenko asked, motioning them to be seated.

Yakovlev passed him a slip of paper. 'This is information from an absolutely reliable source. The Marshal agrees with me that it changes the entire military situation. That's why I asked him to come with me.'

Borisenko's bushy eyebrows rose in response to this remarkable statement and as he read the document his face reddened with annoyance.

'You will see that the Americans have broken their promise not to develop or deploy neutron weapons,' Yakovlev explained.

'None of this would surprise me,' Borisenko said, letting the paper fall on the desk with some distaste. 'If it were true. Have you checked it? Confirmed it? Secured any collateral evidence?'

'There has been no time yet,' Yakovlev said. 'We have agents with access to information about NATO nuclear stores, but it will be some time before we could expect any answers ... '

' "Some time" will be too late,' Borisenko snapped. 'The Neo-Nazis and the American Imperialists will have attacked us by then and we shall have to defend ourselves. Who else knows about this document?'

'Only the Marshal. I needed his technical advice.'

The Secretary-General looked at them both through narrowed eyes, already convinced that they were seeing too much of each other and wondering why. 'Keep it that way,' he ordered. 'I propose to take no notice of this scrap of paper unless you secure definite confirmation. You realize, don't you Comrade Yakovlev, that if your information is true your department must be grossly inefficient. Neutron weapons – the barbaric, capitalist bombs – stockpiled for months and you only find out about it now when we are about to be attacked! However, I am inclined to believe it may be a hoax by the enemy, that you Intelligence people have it all wrong.'

'There is no way it could be a hoax,' Yakovlev protested.

'It's from a source at the highest possible level, a source which has given us invaluable service ... '

'At the highest possible level,' Borisenko echoed scathingly. 'I suppose you mean the President of the United States!'

'Not quite. But the next best person.'

'Oh! And exactly who is this great source?'

Yakovlev was surprised by the question. Normally Borisenko kept himself aloof from the minutiae of KGB operations, as had most of his predecessors.

'You know our sources have to be sacred, but the circumstances are so critical that I will make an exception to convince you. It is the British Prime Minister, Albert Henderson.'

The set of Borisenko's face as he stared in amazement with his mouth half open told Yakovlev that his disclosure had been a blunder.

'The British Prime Minister! You mean to say that you had the temerity to recruit him? And without my authorization! That is a gross interference in political matters beyond your competence.'

Yakovlev swallowed hard. 'We did not recruit him, Secretary-General. His information is volunteered through an intermediary. We have no direct contact ... '

'I should think not,' Borisenko fumed.

The news had completely confirmed his belief that he had made an error of judgement in appointing Yakovlev. He was too young and too inexperienced to handle the responsibility.

'Now look here Comrade Yakovlev, certain decisions have been taken and certain dispositions made which cannot be changed now. We must forestall another Capitalist invasion of the Socialist Motherland. Even if your information is correct, it's come too late.'

' "Exercise Swordthrust" goes ahead as planned then in spite of this new dimension?' Dominowski asked, breaking his silence.

'Certainly Comrade Marshal. You've already agreed to it.'

'I did, Secretary-General, but that was before we had this new information ... '

'Now look, Marshal,' Borisenko interrupted with mounting irritation. 'For years we have listened to you demanding more tanks, more guns. Our people have made great sacrifices to give them to you. They are not just toys to be paraded on Red Square. We expect you to use them when the time comes to speed the triumph of Socialism and that time is upon us.'

'I agree with you that we have tank supremacy, Secretary-General. And we are grateful to you for what you have done to achieve it. But I must be absolutely honest. If this information is correct we face enormous losses in tanks – the "cutting edge" of our forces – and worse still, in tank crews. Even if it is not true we must be prudent and take precautions in case it might be. That means we must disperse our ground forces. We cannot attack in mass formations as we intended. In fact all our projection forces are now at risk.'

Borisenko thrust out his chin aggressively. 'You don't need to lecture me on elementary tactics, Marshal. You seem to forget that I was a commander in the siege of Stalingrad when you were still at school.'

'I do not forget it,' Dominowski replied. 'I am just anxious that we do not make the mistake which the Nazis made there, and at so many other places. But this is a new dimension. It is my advice as Commander-in-Chief of the Warsaw Pact Forces that "Swordthrust" must be delayed, at least until we have time to change our dispositions. You want us to advance at a minimum of thirty kilometres a day. That is Marshal Davorin's figure. So … '

Borisenko rapped on his desk impatiently. 'So make what changes you can. Improvise, Marshal! Improvise as we commanders did in the "Great Patriotic War ".'

'It's much more difficult today, General Secretary,' Dominowski said almost sharply. 'Intricate technological problems requiring close study are posed by modern weapons like this new threat which Comrade Yakovlev has discovered.'

'And how much time would our scientists need to catch up with this new threat, as you call it?'

'It might take two years,' Dominowski replied lamely.

'Two years! And you were the one who led us to assume that if there was to be a first nuclear strike it would be by the Warsaw Pact Forces! Where should we be now if we had said we could not fight the Germans for two years in 1941 because they had a technological advantage?'

Yakovlev saw with some concern that Dominowski was in danger of losing his temper. 'Whatever the other Chiefs of

Staff may tell you, Secretary-General, I know that, apart from Marshal Davorin, they agree with me that we are not yet ready to take on NATO with an absolute certainty of winning, even without this latest news ... '

'Oh!' Borisenko exclaimed, pretending to reach for the telephone. 'And would you like me to call them in, Marshal? Like you, they have repeatedly assured me that we have overhauled the United States in every field of the arms race, including the heavy nuclear missiles neither side is ever likely to use. Anyway, the opinion of Marshal Davorin carries more weight with me than any of your reservations.'

The Marshal shook his head and decided to try another tack. 'There's the Third World reaction too, Secretary-General. We have several situations in Africa and the Middle East ready to fall into our hands like ripe plums without risking our forces ... '

'They'll be riper still once the Third World has watched us push the Americans out of Europe and blacked their eye in battle. Anyway, what the hell do we care about the Third World? Look at Egypt. We gave them millions in arms and aid and what did we get in return? Kicked out of the country!'

Both visitors could see that they had no chance of changing the old man's mind, but Dominowski felt bound to raise a matter of personal honour which had worried him for weeks.

'We've invited very senior NATO commanders to attend "Swordthrust" as observers under the terms of the Helsinki Agreement. What happens to them when "Swordthrust" becomes an attack?'

'They'll be prisoners of war, won't they? Treat them as a bonus. I don't understand you, Marshal. You agreed to the principle of using the Exercise as a deception to gain surprise. So why this sudden surge of conscience about a few enemy officers? The trouble with you young commanders is that you are getting soft and far too cosy with the other side.'

The clenching of Dominowski's fists at this modest slur on his loyalty was not lost on Borisenko.

'Have no fear, Marshal,' he said in a more conciliatory tone. 'You are going to win. In six days, as planned, and with very few losses. The Capitalists won't even try to reinforce when they see the speed of your advance. Why would they want to provide us with more prisoners of war? The simple truth is that the West has been putting its faith in diplomacy and they've blundered. You know, Marshal, I'm beginning to think I have more faith in you and your men than you have yourself.'

Dominowski's broad shoulders heaved a shrug of resignation. 'When may we expect the final decision on the time when "Swordthrust" is to be converted into an operation?' he asked.

Sensing that the Marshal had been completely overborne Yakovlev coughed nervously then said, 'It is my duty to point out, Comrade Secretary-General, that our Intelligence sources can still produce no evidence to support the contention that NATO or the West Germans alone intend to attack the Warsaw Pact Forces or harass them in any way.'

'I have to agree with that as far as purely Military Intelligence from the GRU is concerned,' Dominowski said. 'It is our belief that the Americans will not attack in Europe and that the Germans will not move – indeed, cannot move – without them.'

'Famous last words, Marshal! Famous last words! Let the nation be thankful that the Party has other sources of more accurate Intelligence and more experienced people like Marshal Davorin to analyse it,' Borisenko said, his face blueing with unrestrained anger. 'Comrade Yakovlev, in view of your consistently unhelpful attitude it would be better for all of us if you did not attend the meeting when our final decision as regards "Swordthrust" is taken. We can't afford to waste time going over old ground. You can be assured that, if I feel it necessary, I will put your view to the rest of the Politburo members who may be present.'

'Am I being suspended from the Politburo, Secretary-General?' Yakovlev asked.

Surveying him with some contempt Borisenko replied, 'Shall we say that it is my personal request that you do not attend until further notice. I think it would be better if history can see that we were not swayed from our duty to the Socialist Motherland by technical pressures which may turn out to be purely hypothetical. As Chairman of the Praesidium I am effectively Supreme Commander of the Soviet Forces. The generals must do as I decide. That will be all, Comrades.'

Dominowski and Yakovlev left the room in silence and Rakitin re-entered.

'You taped all that traitorous talk, I hope,' Borisenko said.

'Indeed I did.'

'Get me a copy. I want to play it over to Premier Volkhov. The last place I want any dissidents is in the Politburo. I have treated Yakovlev like a son and this is the gratitude I get. What did you make of that neutron-bomb business?'

Rakitin shrugged. 'I suppose it could be true, knowing the Americans. If it is they could kill a lot more of our soldiers than we expected.'

'No doubt,' Borisenko said tersely. 'But we have a great preponderance of soldiers compared with the enemy and no war is ever won without casualties and a willingness to accept them – least of all by this country.'

He sat back feeling slightly breathless. The past half an hour had been harassing but worth every minute. Yakovlev had put his head on the block and, by association, Dominowski, too. It was a pity about the Marshal. He had a fine record but he seemed to have gone soft. And there was no place for vacillators in the Soviet hierarchy.

'It's time for your pills again, Comrade Secretary-General,' Rakitin said. 'Your visitors upset you.'

Borisenko screwed up his face. 'They brought unwelcome news didn't they. It would have upset anyone.'

Borisenko took two tablets from the phial but did not have time to take them. 'I fear I must go somewhere else first,' he explained, pushing back his chair. He steadied himself on his desk then picked up the stout walking-stick propped beside him, but never seen in public, and shuffled laboriously towards the door, looking even older and more crumpled than his years.

On leaving the building, Yakovlev and Dominowski talked briefly beside their black Zils limousines, well out of earshot of their chauffeurs. Neither needed to tell the other that their days in office were numbered, though Borisenko would be unable to move until the current crisis was past. Marshal Dominowski was too popular with his troops for the Secretary-General to risk a decline in morale, which his dismissal would engender. And someone with experience had to be in control of the KGB, which had sizeable armed forces of its own, during a major military operation, when Intelligence and the efficient action of subversion and sabotage units would be vital.

'Do you think that old idiot is deluded?' the Marshal asked. 'Do you think that he really believes his own propaganda about the NATO attack and the secret American pact with China? Is that what age and power can do to you if you stay in office too long? He never stops talking about the criminal American weapons that threaten détente, and here he is preparing to attack the Americans! He has to be mad!'

Yakovlev smiled grimly. 'They say that power corrupts your judgement, so the longer you stay in power the greater its effect. But whether he is deluded or not the problem is the same. That decrepit old sod, who can hardly walk, is going to lead us into a totally unnecessary war. He'll keep the Politburo in complete ignorance of what we have told him.'

The Marshal shook his head as though still disbelieving that this was possible. 'Men like that, living in the past, are incapable of understanding the impact of modern sophisticated weapons. He and that ass Davorin are still thinking in terms of peasants armed with rifles and cavalry charges.'

'And when they do eventually retire or die in office they'll be replaced by people just as old and just as hidebound. You know the candidates.'

Dominowski nodded dispiritedly. 'Yes, it's a hopeless prospect.'

Watching the Marshal's reactions closely, Yakovlev pressed home his argument. 'More old dodderers who won't be able to see that the German position will fall into our hands through subversion anyway, without any need to fight. Our penetration of the West German political machine is deep and wide and we have almost 1,000 subversion units set up in the Federal Republic. Nearly 20,000 agents all working to order and with increasing effect.'

'So why the hell should we risk damage to our war machine when we may need every tank and every gun to stem the hordes of China?' Dominowski asked.

They stared at each other silently for a few moments as though reading each others' thoughts.

'Let us meet again later today, somewhere privately,' Yakovlev suggested. 'We mustn't be seen talking here too long.'

The Marshal nodded and waved to Yakovlev as his chauffeur drove away towards the Borovitzky Gate in the high Kremlin wall. His first action would be to check with the GRU, the Forces' own Intelligence gathering machine, to see whether they could possibly corroborate Yakovlev's information.

Chapter Ten

John Falconer did not hire topper and tails for his visit to Epsom although he did treat himself to a green trilby hat of distinctive style from Lock's, the famous hatter in St James's Street, and also sported a red rose in his buttonhole. Ed Taylor had offered to keep him company but Falconer made it clear that he would rather be alone to study the form seriously and to watch a stallion which he fancied for his stud in Virginia. He wanted Taylor to be handy at the end of a telephone.

He genuinely loved the atmosphere of the racetrack with its colour, its crowd drawn from every social level, and its very special blend of noise. But he was not there purely for pleasure.

Nobody he knew recognized him as he watched the paddock parade, but he had spotted Jane Jansen and her guests, Albert and Winifred Henderson in one of the boxes. He knew Henderson had no particular interest in racing and, seeing that the Prime Minister seemed to be enjoying being photographed by the Pressmen, he assumed that this was part of his political act of looking relaxed in spite of the gloomy warnings in the newspapers.

Surely the British were the only people who could stage such a show of nonchalance at such a time of danger, Falconer thought. It reminded him of that British sea dog who insisted on playing bowls with the Armada on the doorstep. Well, maybe their attitude would turn out to be justified, he mused, as he walked away from the paddock.

He made no effort to avoid the tipster, a short wiry man in breeches and bowler hat who might have been a jockey at some stage. As usual, most of the tipster's attempts to foist a sealed envelope containing a racing certainty on prospective clients were repulsed, but Falconer did not spurn him.

'On the turf and under the turf,' the tipster said in a hoarse voice to which, without hesitation, Falconer replied, 'All men are equal.'

The tipster, who had been looking for a tall man wearing a green trilby and red rose, smiled and proferred an envelope from his inside pocket for which Falconer gave him a pound. It contained a single, small sheet of paper bearing the advice:

Domino (nap)
n.b. Collateral
Urgent Need (outsider).

Had the tipster read the message it would have meant that Domino was a racing certainty, the next best being Collateral while Urgent Need was a good outside chance. There were, however, no such horses running that day and to Falconer it all meant something very different. Domino meant a soldier in whom he could now place full confidence, and n.b. stood for neutron bomb about which the sender urgently needed outside collateral evidence.

At the bottom of the page was a short coded message consisting of a few letters and numbers. Falconer noted them, reached into his jacket pocket for a black leather wallet and opened it close to his chest as though consulting something written inside. It was in fact, a pocket chess set with flat, plastic pieces in slots in the same positions as those on the chess-table in his Washington apartment. The coded message was his opponent's next move.

Falconer smiled. The move not only made sense and therefore authenticated the message but was typical of the man who had sent it. He took out a small notebook, removed its slim propelling-pencil and said to the tipster, 'I'll give your friend some advice in return.' He wrote:

Cheltenham 1.30
April Nights
n.b. Milk Run
Ramstein
Cheltenham 5.00
Sembach
Rhein Main
Zweibrucken

For good measure he added a further tip which read: 'For future meetings watch Rakitin. Suggest a double with Quinn.'

After opening the black wallet again and studying the chess pieces he jotted down his responding move below the 'tips' as proof of authenticity. Then he heavily underlined the initial letter C in both references to Cheltenham, tore the page from his notebook, folded it and gave it to the tipster who had an envelope ready. The tipster sealed the envelope with a practised flick of his tongue, placed it in his inside pocket then, with a smile and a little salute, disappeared into the crowd, where he went through the motions of trying to sell two more envelopes before quitting the course.

Falconer watched the Derby in which he had genuine interest, placing a small bet which he lost. Then, after standing as near to Mrs Jansen's box as he could, in the hope that she might see and recognize him, he made his way from the colourful scene to the chauffeured car which Taylor had provided. He had noted that while Mrs Henderson seemed to be enjoying the occasion, particularly the strawberries and cream, Henderson was either bored stiff or extremely worried. He had need to be worried. The next twenty-four hours was going to be crucial.

Falconer had gone through the motions of shaking off any 'dogs', though none was apparent, before he arrived one minute before time at the entrance to the Dominion Theatre. He had alighted from his car at Morden Underground Station, left the train at Waterloo, then doubled back onto a following train which took him to Tottenham Court Road.

Quinn's car was dead on time and, though there was still no sign of pursuers, Falconer insisted on taking a circuitous route, involving doubling back several times, to the surveillance room which the US National Security Agency had hired in Harley Street, the medical Mecca which saw more Rolls Royces to the acre than any other area of London. The car paused for several minutes a few doors higher up the street while Falconer and Quinn looked out not only at passers-by but at nearby windows, paying special attention to the slightest movement of curtains. There was none, but they took the precaution of entering the building separately.

Quinn was led up the narrow stairs to one of the many rooms into which the once-private house had been split to accommodate the maximum number of doctors, dentists and other practitioners prepared to pay a ludicrous rent per cubic foot for the cachet of a Harley Street address. Cramped quarters, even attics, were dignified by the name 'surgery' or 'consulting-room', just as some of the pokiest rooms in London occupied by lawyers were known as 'chambers'.

One window of the narrow, low-ceilinged room rented by the NSA overlooked the rather elaborate consulting-rooms of Sir Alan King-Lander on the opposite side of the street, and was invaluable for checking on the identity of patients, and others who might be posing as patients, entering the building. The main feature of the room, however, was a table where a pleasant-looking, young American wearing earphones was listening intently to a black box of electronic gadgetry linked with a tape-recorder. There was also a camera for the occasional operation of which a middle-aged American, who also served as a window-spotter, was responsible.

'These are my colleagues,' Falconer said.

'Hi,' said the young man, while the older stranger nodded affably. Quinn was used to colleagues who remained nameless when there was no need to know their identities.

'Anything happening?' Falconer asked.

'He's got a patient there,' the man with the earphones replied. 'A real one. Some guy with a heart problem. The interesting one is still in the waiting-room.'

Across the road, in the suite befitting his eminent position, King-Lander was sitting at a beautiful walnut desk having examined the patient, who was dressing behind a green, silk screen. Quinn picked up the proferred set of earphones and heard the physician say, 'I think that should help you. Fix an appointment with my receptionist to see me again in about ten days time. And, of course, don't hesitate to telephone me if you feel any worse, particularly if you get any chest pains.'

'Thank you, Sir Alan,' the patient replied. 'You are always so reassuring. I feel more relieved already ... '

'He certainly has an effective bedside manner,' Quinn murmured.

'He's better still with women,' the young American observed. 'You won't believe it but there's one old doll, who arrives in a Rolls Royce, who's so crackers that she believes it's raining inside his office and puts her umbrella up. I heard him talking about her to another doctor who called on him. Guess what he does to humour her – he puts on a raincoat!'

'Ah, brilliant psychology!' Quinn remarked. 'No wonder Henderson confides in him. But I wonder if he'd make that effort for a poor patient.'

The receptionist was heard to announce, 'Mrs Czapek, Sir Alan,' at which point, after a sign from the electronics operator, Falconer also donned earphones.

'Ah, Mrs Czapek,' King-Lander was heard to say in a rather less than welcoming voice. 'Do sit down.'

There was a slight pause and from then on the eavesdroppers could hear nothing but a continuous crackle.

'There you are, Mark,' Falconer said triumphantly as he took off the earphones. 'White noise! Nothing but white noise! It happens every time that woman calls. There's no doubt what causes it. The KGB has fitted his room with an anti-bugging device. He has only ever bothered to switch it on when two people have visited him – this Mrs Czapek and the Prime Minister.'

'And who is Mrs Czapek?' Quinn asked.

'She's the wife of one of the so-called Second Secretaries at the Czech Embassy here. He's a high-ranking Intelligence officer.'

'So, she's the courier for the information which the Prime Minister passes to King-Lander.'

'Right! And, no doubt, she brings him any instructions. What a set-up! The PM can visit his doctor alone without raising any suspicion, and so can she. She's perfectly entitled to use a British doctor, and who would have the resources to keep every Soviet Bloc diplomat's wife under surveillance?'

'Who indeed?' murmured Quinn, who knew that MI5, the organization responsible for countering the activities of foreign agents in Britain was grossly understaffed. Because of financial restrictions, which even the Thatcher administrations had done little to relax for fear of being accused of setting up a police state, it numbered no more than 2000 including typists.

'I must say that this is an elegant set-up John,' Quinn remarked, waving his hand towards the consulting-room across the road. 'Really very elegant. The information can be in the Soviet Embassy within the hour, and on its way to Moscow in the next diplomatic bag.'

The eavesdroppers were unable to see King-Lander hand Mrs Czapek a small envelope which she put into her handbag. Had they done so it need not have been anything more than a private prescription.

'It's clear again,' the young American announced. 'He's switched off.'

Quinn put one of the head-set receivers to his ear and heard the physician call, 'Next patient please,' over his intercom.

'Well, Mark, are you convinced?' Falconer asked.

'Absolutely. I must congratulate you on an excellent job.'

'So what now?'

'I'll have to interrogate him, and because of the circumstances I'll have to do it personally. We'll get nowhere without a confession.'

'And where will you get with one?' Falconer asked.

Quinn smiled mysteriously. 'I think I can see daylight.'

Seeing that Quinn was not going to be forthcoming, Falconer rubbed his chin and said, 'I'd prefer it if you could hold up the interrogation until tomorrow ... '

'No problem, John. It'll take that long to set it up. But why the no-rush?'

'Oh it's just to do with a hunch I have.'

'John, you know I always back your hunches!'

'And, as you said, you never back losers,' Falconer replied with a grin. 'Here's something that might help you. Summaries of a few relevant conversations, not just from here.'

131

Falconer handed over several folded foolscap sheets which he had taken from his inside pocket. Quinn gave them a cursory inspection and was surprised to see that some of the recordings, at least of Winifred Henderson's dialogue, must have been made in Number Ten Downing Street.

Quinn and Falconer were preparing to leave separately when the window-watcher suddenly cried, 'Hey, just take a look at this!'

They moved over to the window just in time to see Her Excellency, the American Ambassador step out of the Embassy limousine and walk into the building housing King-Lander's consulting-rooms. They both picked up their earphones in anticipation and did not have long to wait. On hearing the identity of his visitor King-Lander instructed his receptionist to show her in.

'Alan, darling, I just had to see you ... ' they heard Mrs Jansen exclaim in a tone suggesting that the visit was in no way professional.

'Look, Jane, I told you that you mustn't come here. There's no way you can become a patient of mine, or be seen to be one. I'd be struck off the Register.'

Falconer glanced quizzically at Quinn who indicated that he would explain King-Lander's fear later.

'But I'm not a patient, I ... ' they heard Mrs Jansen say.

'It's still dangerous just to come here in case people see you. Your face is well-known now.'

'Perhaps, darling, but nobody knows about our relationship,' Mrs Jansen said pleadingly. 'I haven't been able to get you on the telephone. Your receptionist keeps putting me off. There isn't anything wrong is there? I just had to know.'

'Excuse me, Jane,' the eavesdroppers heard King-Lander say. 'It's hot in here. I must switch on the air-conditioning.'

Then there was nothing but white noise.

'God Almighty! What a turn up for the book,' Falconer exclaimed. 'What do you make of it, Mark? Do you think she could be part of the act?'

'She's certainly gone a bundle on King-Lander. That's why he was so worried when she turned up at his consulting-rooms. You can be hauled up before a medical tribunal for jumping into bed with your patients in this country, and they've obviously been at it. Presumably, he met her through the PM.'

'That's right. He was at the dinner Mrs Jansen put on for the Hendersons the other night. But they'd met before then at Number Ten. This has real possibilities.'

Quinn could not get out of the box of a room quickly enough, and Falconer was figuratively rubbing his hands as they descended the stairs. 'The "White Lady," indeed! I wonder what the "White Knight" would say if he knew. Or the *Washington Post*.'

'You're not thinking of leaking it, John?' Quinn asked with some concern.

'Not at this stage.'

'Later, perhaps?'

'Who knows? We'll have to see if it would pay dividends.'

To Quinn the situation was complicated enough, especially with the danger of war gathering momentum every minute. 'Far be it from me to give you advice, John, but it never pays to let private rancour intrude into a professional problem.'

Falconer gave him a sharp glance but refrained from mouthing the immediate thought which the remark had generated concerning Quinn's hatred of the Prime Minister.

Quinn was wondering whether Mrs Jansen's arrival was as complete a surprise to Falconer as he made it out to be. With someone so contriving he could never be sure. Then a further complication occurred to him.

'Supposing King-Lander tells her we've been bugging him after I have given him the works and it becomes obvious that we have?'

Falconer looked horrified. 'If you mention that the CIA has been involved in any way all hell could be let loose. That bitch is damned astute at generating publicity for herself. I don't think that she can be trusted with anything that might appeal to the newspapers.'

Quinn smiled and patted Falconer's shoulder as they delayed their separate exit into Harley Street.

'Don't worry, John. I'll make it clear to King-Lander that the effort was entirely British. And she could, in fact, be a bonus. I see some interesting advantages.'

'Such as?'

'For a start I can make it clear to King-Lander that if he tells her anything we'll blow something in the American papers that will make her look guilty of more than adultery. And if she finds out anything about the Henderson business from her own resources we can lean on her with that tape-recording you've just made. It could be doctored to sound a lot nastier than it is.'

And an even bolder project had occurred to him. If MI5 could make a blue film of the private sex-life of a Middle East ambassador, how about the United States Ambassador as a candidate? Anything useful, that might be bartered to the CIA one day for some special favour, was worth considering.

Chapter Eleven

Secretary-General Borisenko was in a suitably sour mood for the task he had to perform that morning. Even the faithful Rakitin had felt the rough side of his tongue as he busied himself about the office. No doubt, thought Rakitin, the Secretary-General had slept badly, either through worry or because of his chest pains. And, of course, he was too frail to take the exercise which would help to ensure sound sleep.

Rakitin brightened as the heavy mahogany doors opened to admit the stooped and even frailer figure of Premier Volkhov, who was no longer able to walk without the support of a stout cane.

'Ah, Konstantin,' Borisenko said, putting down his pen. 'Thank you for coming. I want you to be here when I deal with these two dissidents.'

Rakitin settled the Premier in a chair, then padded softly from the room.

'Yakovlev doesn't surprise me,' Volkhov said, blowing his nose noisily. 'As you know I always thought that fellow Kovalsky would have been a better choice if you were intent on promoting a young "flier". But I just can't understand Dominowski. Everything is poised to carry him to glory and he remains reluctant.'

'It's Yakovlev's fault,' Borisenko snapped. 'Those two have been spending too much time together and they are a dangerous combination. The KGB and the shock troops of the Red Army! Very dangerous indeed, Konstantin!'

'You think it's as bad as that?'

'I certainly do. I've had them watched. It's too late to do anything about them at this juncture, except for giving them their orders. But they will have to be dismissed the moment that victory is assured.'

'I'm sure that Marshal Dominowski will do his duty, Anatoli,' Volkhov averred in a cracked voice.

'I agree. Once battle is joined there will be none better, none braver, none more determined. But Glavpur has reported that he disapproves of our commissars. He thinks that our political representatives are interfering in matters which should be left entirely to the Army.'

'Does he indeed!' Volkhov exclaimed with a frown of disapproval.

'He does. And I'm quite shattered that a man of his capability, courage and honesty should have allowed himself to be swayed by this fear that the Americans will use nuclear weapons first. We've always faced that possibility and made ample allowances for it. We have more than 50,000 tanks, Konstantin. We can afford to lose a few hundred of them and still defeat the Imperialists.'

Rakitin knocked and entered the room to announce the arrival of Dominowski and Yakovlev who had come straight from another meeting in the Kremlin.

Borisenko was in no humour for niceties. 'I have to tell you that owing to the need to inflict a major blow to American morale and to secure our Western front for the coming conflict with China, it has been decided irrevocably – I repeat irrevocably – that "Exercise Swordthrust" will be converted with all speed to the subjection and occupation of the Federal Republic of Germany. West German and American agents are stirring up trouble throughout the Socialist countries and these enemies of the people must be taught a lesson once and for all.'

135

Volkhov, who was looking intently at the Marshal with his chin resting on his hands, which in turn were supported by his stick, gave his assent. 'It is the Politburo's view that success can be taken for granted. We are relying on you, Marshal, as our great tank expert, to give us a quick victory. Six days is the requirement. Then we can offer the Americans a quick peace and proceed with the reunification of Germany, removing the Neo-Nazi danger forever.'

'You can be sure that I will do my best for the country, and for the Party,' Dominowski responded solemnly. 'It is my duty to point out, however, that the new nuclear threat ... '

'It is the opinion of a majority of the Politburo that the Americans will not resort to nuclear weapons, either to defend German territory or to recover it,' Volkhov said peremptorily. 'Marshal Davorin, who has great experience, is convinced of it.'

Dominowski refrained from stating that Davorin's experience of nuclear problems was superficial but Yakovlev, who could also see that technical argument was useless, was determined to put some further information on the record. He unfastened the straps of his bulging briefcase and removed a document.

'I must report that we now have collateral evidence to support the information I gave you about the nuclear intentions of the United States.'

'Let's have it,' Borisenko said impatiently.

Yakovlev read from the document which was based on a coded message in racing terms forwarded to him in the diplomatic bag from the Soviet Embassy in London.

'During April there was a nightly delivery – what the Americans call a "milk run" – of neutron bombs by C.130 Hercules aircraft to the US Air Force base at Ramstein in West Germany. There were also deliveries by C.500 Galaxy transports to the US Air bases at Sembach, Rhein Main and Zweibrucken.'

'Aren't transport flights to these air bases pretty routine?' Borisenko asked.

'Yes. But not in such numbers, Secretary-General.'

'And what evidence have you that the planes were carrying nuclear weapons and neutron bombs in particular?'

Yakovlev hesitated then answered, rather weakly, 'We have

136

sources inside some of these bases and their first reports strongly indicate that the main cargoes could have been neutron bombs. And the flights fit with the information we received from that summit source I disclosed to you.'

'Flights of fancy, perhaps,' Volkhov suggested. 'No, Comrade, the Politburo has made its decision and, as you well know, that is immutable. I assure you we considered every eventuality ... '

'Not quite, Comrade Premier,' Yakovlev said lifting the flap of his briefcase again. 'There is a further factor you have not yet considered.'

He whipped out a Stechkin machine-pistol, levelled it at Borisenko and fired a brief burst into his chest. Volkhov gallantly attempted to defend himself by drawing a sword from his thick cane, but Yakovlev cut him down with another burst, while the Marshal looked on impassively.

Rakitin, who rushed into the room, was horrified by the sight of the two bodies streaming blood: Borisenko slumped at his desk, Volkhov twitching feebly on the floor. Yakovlev motioned him into a corner with his pistol while he drafted a few lines on Borisenko's notepaper.

'Come here, Comrade Rakitin,' he commanded.

Rakitin cowered but Dominowski assured him that he had nothing to fear, so long as he did exactly what he was told.

'Here is a statement announcing that, while working at his desk, Comrade Secretary-General Borisenko, who had been in failing health for some time, suffered a fatal heart-attack. In going to assist him Comrade Premier Volkhov, who was visiting the Secretary-General's office and whose lameness from arthritis had been increasing recently, fell and suffered a skull fracture from which he has since died.'

He thrust the paper into Rakitin's unwilling hand. 'Now make sure that this gets on to Moscow Radio without delay. You know the drill for doing that well enough. There is an officer of mine waiting to conduct you to wherever you need to go, and to bring you back. On no account are you to enlarge on the statement. If you are asked you are to say that you were not on hand when the deaths occurred. You came into the office and found the Secretary-General dead and the Premier dying. There was no time to summon medical help.

And there must be no mention whatever of the Marshal or myself. Is that understood?'

'But will this be believed?' Rakitin stammered, holding out the statement in tremulous fingers.

'It will be believed where it matters. And it's more credible than the official clap-trap that NATO was about to attack East Germany!'

Dominowski adopted a rather more friendly tone. 'You'll find the Kremlin ringed with tanks, Comrade. Also the radio station and other key points. It's the usual precaution when the State is deprived of its leader. After all, we don't want any palace revolutions here!'

'No,' said Yakovlev. 'And we don't want agents of the Imperialist West and counter-revolutionaries taking advantage of the State's misfortune. The people will understand that. To provide immediate leadership I shall be taking over as Party Secretary and the Marshal is to be the Minister of Defence.'

As Rakitin left in confused bewilderment with the KGB officer guard, who had accompanied his Chief and Dominowski through the corridors, locking each door behind them, Dominowski asked, 'Isn't it a risk letting him go? He was very faithful to Borisenko, you know ... '

Yakovlev smiled and shook his head. 'There's no risk. He wasn't faithful to anybody, but he has one or two vital functions to perform. Then we can execute him legally. Rakitin's a traitor. He's been working for British Intelligence.'

Dominowski was staggered. 'I can't believe it. Rakitin!'

'You'll believe it when I show you the evidence.'

'Of course, I take your word for it, Sergei. It's just that one doesn't know who you can trust these days. How long have you known that he was a spy?'

'Only a little while. It suited us to let him carry on. It will still suit us for a few more hours.'

Dominowski looked puzzled but Yakovlev had no intention of enlightening him further. Instead he moved towards Borisenko's desk, lifted the body and dumped it on the floor. Then having made sure there was no blood on the chair he sat down at a corner of the desk.

'We must draft a statement about a period of mourning,

Andrei Andreievitch,' he said. 'There'll have to be a lying-in-state, then they can both be cremated and their ashes interred in the Kremlin wall with suitable inscriptions.'

He looked over at the bodies. 'There are no signs of violence about the head, so the mourners won't see anything they shouldn't. They were both good men, you know. They just clung on to power too long.'

The Marshal nodded sadly. 'I suppose those arrests we agreed on are already under way?' he asked.

Yakovlev looked at his watch. 'Most of the Politburo will be in protective custody within twenty minutes. They'll be treated gently and with respect. Then we can convince the old ones that they should resign – for their own good and for the country's.'

'I shall certainly be relieved to see the back of Davorin,' Dominowski said. 'Then he can dream about his old battles in his dacha instead of round the conference table.'

'Yes, it is essential that you lose no time in asserting your authority as Defence Minister.'

Yakovlev clasped his hands behind his neck. 'I think we can congratulate ourselves, Andrei Andreievitch, that we have both served our country well today.'

'I'm sure we have,' Dominowski said. 'It would have been monstrous to allow those two old men to plunge us into a war. When I heard your collateral evidence about the neutron bomb deliveries I was no longer in any doubt and then the GRU came up with supporting evidence of its own – as a matter of routine, of course. I didn't ask them.'

'Not likely,' Yakovlev thought.

'Not only our tanks, but our command centres, supply depots, even some of our nuclear stockpiles would have been at risk. But we'd never have convinced them, Sergei. No, you are absolutely right. There was no other way, with so many of their relatives and friends in commanding positions.'

'Your first job will be to deal with "Swordthrust",' Yakovlev said. 'You can make an announcement postponing it for a few weeks as part of the national mourning. After all, as Party Secretary, Borisenko was effectively Chief of the Armed Forces.'

'Then it can go ahead later as a normal exercise?'

139

'Of course,' Yakovlev said. 'You have no doubts about what we have done have you?'

'Not after I heard your collateral evidence … '

'No, Andrei Andreievitch, I was thinking of something else which I thought we both understood. It was us or them. We should have been disgraced – or worse.'

'Yes, Sergei,' the Marshal said sombrely. 'It was us or them. I did realize that. But what is more important is that we have prevented something which would have cost thousands of soldiers' lives. Let us continue to arrange things so that victories fall to us without a fight.'

'Except for China,' Yakovlev corrected.

'Of course. Except for China. But that should present no great problem now.'

'Our immediate problem is disposing of these bodies,' Yakovlev said, rising from his chair. 'But I have made arrangements for that.' He picked up a telephone and barked an order. As he and Dominowski marched out of the room they passed three KGB officers carrying swabs and bowls.

Chapter Twelve

Quinn and Angela were in festive mood when Falconer and Ed Taylor arrived at Century House. They were drinking champagne and Angela poured two more glasses for the expected guests.

'We were just celebrating the coup in Moscow,' Quinn explained. 'Here's to what's left of "Exercise Swordthrust". You've heard that it's been postponed.'

'I sure have,' Falconer said. He did not like champagne, rating it as 'a woman's drink', but took a glass to be sociable and raised it in salute. 'How do you construe the events, Mark? What's your appreciation?'

'I don't have to make one. I know the facts. "Uncle Vanya"

has come up with the details. Borisenko and Volkhov were both murdered by your old friend Sergei Yakovlev, with Marshal Dominowski lending moral – and military – support. They've taken over and are firmly established in an otherwise bloodless coup.'

'I suspected as much,' Falconer responded. 'I had no idea that Marshal Dominowski was involved, but it was obvious that Sergei couldn't have moved without some Red Army insurance.'

'You think that the war is off, then?' asked Taylor, who was anxious for the return of his wife and children from America, and was unaware of the full facts.

'Certainly for a year or two while the new leadership consolidates its position. "Uncle Vanya" has made it clear all along that both Yakovlev and Dominowski were opposed to the war in Europe. They claim – I repeat claim – that it is no longer possible to impose Communism at bayonet point, at least in Europe.'

'And elsewhere?'

'That's a different matter, especially if they can go on getting somebody else to wield the bayonets.'

'Well let's drink to the health of "Uncle Vanya",' Falconer proposed, raising his glass.

'Yes, I suspect he's going to need it, poor devil,' Quinn commented. 'He's been associated with Borisenko for so long that he must be among those now under arrest. So I suppose we've had his last message. In fact, I'm astonished that since he knew that Yakovlev had shot both Borisenko and Volkhov he was given the time to send any message to me.'

'Perhaps Yakovlev wanted you to know,' Angela suggested, twisting a swizzle-stick in her champagne.

Falconer gave her a quick glance, as though surprised by this appreciative remark, then asked, 'Perhaps you can now tell us who "Uncle Vanya" is if he's no longer of use.'

'It was Rakitin, Borisenko's personal assistant.'

'The guy who found them both dead, according to the radio statement,' Taylor said with affected surprise.

'That's him.'

'Then he certainly is a loss,' said Falconer sadly. 'How the hell did you manage to suborn him?'

'Ah, John, as you said, there are some secrets we just have

141

to keep from each other, but I don't doubt that Rakitin is spilling all to the KGB right now – if he's still alive. Your old friend Yakovlev, or his thugs, will have thought up some nice, refined way of exploiting some weakness or another, if it's only his advanced age.'

Suddenly feeling sick, Angela busied herself opening another bottle of champagne, taking care that the cork emerged with no more than a whisper, and refilled the glasses. Quinn kept his eye on Taylor, looking for any facial display of interest in Rakitin's likely fate.

'Now we've got a breathing space it's up to the politicians to make good use of it,' Quinn said. 'To strengthen NATO without further delay.'

'You mean that Yakovlev will be as tough as the others when it suits him?' Taylor asked.

'Of course. Perhaps tougher. He's a dyed-in-the-wool Communist, and a right bastard in every other way. He believes that Soviet domination of the world is inevitable and highly desirable, and he will go to any lengths to achieve it. It was only over methods and timing that he fell out with Borisenko.'

'You're dead right there, Mark,' Falconer said. 'And, meanwhile, I'll bet you there will be a pretty ruthless carve-up of the dissidents under the pretext of preventing counter-revolution. But I have my reasons for feeling sure that there will be no frontal attack in Europe while Dominowski remains Defence Minister.'

'And what are they?' Quinn asked expectantly.

Falconer smiled broadly at Angela. 'Ah Mark, as you rightly said, there are some secrets we just have to keep from each other. Do you still intend to go ahead with interrogating King-Lander?'

'Of course. I've fixed an appointment for this afternoon as a certain Mr Webb whose family doctor fears he may have a serious blood disorder.'

'You think it is still necessary?'

Quinn looked puzzled. 'Well, don't you? The war may be off, though we have to check that the Warsaw Pact Forces really are being stood down – but we still have a dangerous spy in Number Ten Downing Street.'

Falconer somehow did not look as though he thought it

mattered any more. He contented himself with saying, 'Well, I leave it to you. But you won't let him know how you caught him? About the disinformation, I mean?'

'Of course not. I'm going to play the daft lad. I'm rather good at it.'

Falconer, who was truly brilliant at what he called 'playing the dope' and had given quite a performance of it that morning, gave a gesture of doubtful assent.

'I'll give you a full report tomorrow, John,' Quinn promised. 'I think I will be able to wrap things up. Then perhaps we'll broach another bottle of champagne.'

When the Americans had gone Quinn sat back in his chair and stared at the ceiling.

'What did you make of Falconer's suggestion that it might not be necessary to do anything about King-Lander and the PM now? What's changed in that direction to make him think that?'

Angela had already been giving the question thought. 'Perhaps he reckons that, with war averted, Henderson and King-Lander can't do much harm now. So it may be better just to try to keep them under control rather than let them know they've been caught, with all the complications that would entail.'

'But how could we control the Prime Minister? How could we deny secret information to him? We've done that before with junior ministers but Henderson's no fool. He'd spot it immediately if reports and intercepts were being withheld from him. No, my sweet, there was something else revolving in that tortuous mind. Maybe shopping the PM wasn't the only reason for his visit to London. I shall have to give it some computer time.'

He tore off a sheet of paper from a jotting pad and began to write down the events which had occurred since Falconer's arrival.

Whatever the result of his deliberations there was no way he was going to allow that 'dangerous bastard Henderson' off the hook.

Chapter Thirteen

To King-Lander's proficient receptionist Mr Webb looked uncommonly fit for a man believed to be suffering from polycythaemia. Experience had taught her, however, that appearances could be very deceptive. Perhaps his restlessness was a symptom, for he insisted on standing by the window of the waiting-room, presumably in a day-dream, as there was nothing of interest across the street, so far as she could see. But, as with most activities in Mr Webb's life, there was definite purpose in his preoccupation with the other side of Harley Street. He was watching for a certain movement of the curtains in a small, high window which would tell him that Sir Alan had switched on the anti-bugging device in his consulting-room. There had been no such signal when the receptionist jolted him out of apparent reverie by announcing brightly, 'Sir Alan will see you now.'

It was going to be an unusual consultation for Harley Street, with the patient asking the searching questions and the doctor being given the bad news.

'Please sit down, Mr Webb,' King-Lander said quietly to his new patient as the receptionist ushered him in. Immaculately dressed in the old professional style – black coat, pin-stripe trousers and handmade white shirt with a stiff collar – he evidently eschewed the white jacket in his consulting-rooms. These were elegantly furnished, with a splendid break-front bookcase containing his medical books being the dominating piece. He picked up the confidential letter which had been sent to him ostensibly by the patient's private doctor, and re-read it.

'Your doctor has kindly referred you to me, Mr Webb. He insisted that it was urgent so I think that first ... '

Quinn pulled his chair a little closer to the doctor's desk and interrupted him. 'I should tell you right away, Sir Alan, that my name is not Webb. I am Sir Mark Quinn, the Director-General of the Secret Intelligence Service. These are my credentials.'

He reached into his inside pocket and showed his Century-House pass. King-Lander gave it a cursory glance and said, 'I see. Your identity is so secret that you have to use an alias. I fully understand, but presumably the symptoms ascribed to "Mr Webb" are really yours.'

This was a cool customer indeed, Quinn thought as he looked at him squarely and said, 'I am afraid you do not understand, Sir Alan. I am here for professional, not medical, reasons. As for aliases I am not alone in needing those, am I? I know, for example, that certain people know you as "John Bull".'

King-Lander, whose complexion was pink at any time, blushed profusely. 'I don't understand, Sir Mark. If this is ... '

'Perhaps you will understand if I tell you that we know all about that electric switch you use when certain patients come to see you. Mrs Czapek, for instance.'

'Mrs Czapek?' King-Lander echoed.

'Yes, the lady from the Czechoslovak Embassy. The one to whom you give the messages for delivery elsewhere.'

'What has she been saying?'

'Quite a lot, I am afraid, Sir Alan. I know that smoking is not normally permitted in doctors' surgeries but I think that you might like a cigarette.'

Quinn offered the doctor a cigarette from his case and lit one himself, noting that his quarry's hands were trembling as he lit his.

'Whatever made you do it, Sir Alan? A man in your position!'

'Do what?'

'Oh, come on now! You know what I am talking about – your relationship with Soviet Bloc Intelligence.'

The physician did not reply but stared in front of him as though confused.

Was he going to be clever enough to stay dumb, Quinn wondered. That was the danger. Without a confession he would be powerless. 'Look, Sir Alan,' he said affably. 'If you help me I can help you. I can help you very much. We want to deal with this unpleasant business without any scandal, without any publicity. But you must appreciate that in my job I have to know the truth.'

'You said that you knew it already.'

'That's true,' Quinn said hastily. 'But I need you to confirm it if I am to be helpful to you. And nobody else can help you, Sir Alan, nobody at all.'

King-Lander hesitated while he tapped the ash from his cigarette. 'It's very difficult,' he said. 'Others are involved.'

'Like the Prime Minister?' Quinn suggested blandly. 'I do have great sympathy for your position, you know. The conflict of loyalties. The terrible pressure ... '

King-Lander gave a deep sigh. 'I mustn't say anything that could incriminate anybody else.'

Adopting a more deliberate tone Quinn leaned forward and said, 'Sir Alan, you do not appear to have grasped the situation you are in. Either you tell me in confidence or you will face interrogation by the police and cross-examination in open court. Then anybody you may be trying to protect will be denounced publicly with appalling consequences for all of us.'

King-Lander stubbed out his cigarette and exhaled the last of the smoke with a heavy sigh. 'It's almost a relief to be able to tell somebody about it. I've always hated doing it. I have no interest in the Russians. I loathe everything they stand for.'

'I'm sure you do, Sir Alan. And I can assure you that they have no interest in you beyond using you. Tell me how it all began.'

'I made a fool of myself with a girl on a visit to Moscow where I was giving a paper at an international conference on haematology. I say a girl. She was a mature woman, a quite well-known doctor herself.'

'A Russian?'

'Yes, from the Institute of Haematology in Kiev. She spoke excellent English and we were staying in the same hotel, the National. She asked me to her room to show me some of her research results ... '

Quinn sighed. Oh God, he thought. A variant of the 'come up and see my etchings' routine. It was amazing how people continued to fall for it.

'I know what it's like to be lonely in Moscow, Sir Alan,' he said. 'I was stationed there for two years. Did they take photographs.'

146

'Yes. I realise I should have known better, but we'd both had a few drinks. And she was attractive.' He summoned a faint smile and added, 'There was something strangely exciting about the fact that she was a Russian. And that rather old-fashioned underwear ... '

Quinn smiled with him. He, too, was turned on by such things. 'You understand now that the woman was taking orders from the KGB.'

'I suppose she was. I never saw her again after I left Moscow, although she's still active medically. I see her name in the international literature.'

'I'm not saying she was a phoney doctor,' Quinn said. 'The KGB would press the Patriarch Archbishop of Moscow into the Service if they could. When did they show you the photographs? The KGB I mean.'

'On my first visit to Moscow with the Prime Minister. He's not allowed to travel abroad without his doctor.'

'And they threatened to show them around?'

'Yes, like they did with that MP some years ago. They showed me how they had destroyed his career.'

Quinn nodded, recalling the incident in which compromising pictures of the MP taken with a Russian woman in Moscow had been circulated to leading politicians, to other public figures and to the Press.

'Did you tell Henderson when they approached you in Moscow?'

'No. It would have put him in an impossible position. He would have had to dismiss me.'

'But couldn't you have called their bluff by resigning as the PM's doctor, and then reported the matter privately to the security authorities?'

King-Lander looked down at his desk, obviously in deeper embarrassment.

'The Russians had some information which frightened me more. They showed me evidence of an affair I once had, very foolishly, with one of my women patients. She was a well-known woman married to a big industrialist. They knew all about it. If their information had reached the General Medical Council there would have been a terrible scandal, and I should have been ruined.'

'They had been busy, hadn't they?' Quinn remarked,

realizing that King-Lander was far from being the strong, self-disciplined character he seemed.

'Now, Sir Alan, your relationship with the Prime Minister interests me very much. I know you are very old friends. I take it that Moscow's requirement was for you to act as some sort of courier between him and the KGB.'

'That sort of thing. They wanted me to tell them everything that the Prime Minister confided in me.'

'And he confided in you a great deal?'

'Yes. He sought my opinions – as a counterweight to the official advice from the civil servants, whom he did not entirely trust. He had nobody else.'

'And I take it that he knew exactly what you were doing with the information.'

'I wouldn't say that,' King-Lander demurred. 'I'd put it the other way round – that, had he been aware of what I was doing, he wouldn't have objected to the Russians knowing some of the things I told them.'

'Like that latest information you gave them about the American neutron bombs, Sir Alan? Information which I gave the Prime Minister in the strictest secrecy.'

King-Lander nodded wearily. 'Things like that. It was the kind of information which the Prime Minister probably felt the Soviet leadership should know in the interests of preserving peace.'

Peace! Quinn could just hear Henderson and King-Lander in their privacy bandying about that most precious concept, which the Communists had seized upon and prostituted to promote Russian Imperialism. He decided that the time had come for a more aggressive approach. 'You said *if* the Prime Minister had known what you were doing. I put it to you that he knew exactly what you were doing.'

'I very much doubt that, Sir Mark. You had better ask him that question yourself. I can't breach the confidentiality between myself and the Prime Minister. He is my patient, apart from being my friend.'

'That's rich,' Quinn scoffed. 'You cannot breach the confidentiality with me but you've been doing it daily with the KGB! I had better tell you flatly, Sir Alan, that you could both be tried for treason for what you have done.'

King-Lander shook his head emphatically. 'Me, yes. But

148

not Albert Henderson. There's nothing treasonable about him. He's a good Brit. His politics may not appeal to you, but ... '

'I have no politics,' Quinn snapped. 'They are a luxury denied to me by my job.'

'Well I can still assure you that if the Prime Minister ever suspected that information was getting to the Russians through me – and I'm not saying he did – he would have regarded it as part of his secret diplomacy, part of his determination to prevent war and keep détente going in the interests of the nation.'

'Which nation?' Quinn asked, with a hint of a sneer.

'The British, of course.'

Quinn had dealt with several spies who had genuinely deluded themselves. Were King-Lander and Henderson two more? Surely they were too intelligent for that. No. Henderson's role must have been deliberately traitorous. All those leaks of technical information. They couldn't just have been imparted to King-Lander in friendly conversation. The doctor must be covering up for his old friend. Still, it was academic anyway if things went the way he intended.

'What will happen to me?' King-Lander asked miserably. 'Are you going to arrest me now that I have confessed.'

'Most certainly not,' Quinn said as though offended by the suggestion. 'I have no powers of arrest. We should have to involve the police to do that. No, Sir Alan, you have been helpful and you'll find that I am a man of my word – provided you continue to co-operate. I must tell you that what I have in mind will involve a certain amount of deceit, although less than you've been practising during the past few months.'

'Tell me.'

'It must be obvious to you that the Prime Minister can no longer continue in office or even in Parliament ... '

'Why ever not?' King-Lander interrupted. 'It's not his fault if I've betrayed him.'

'Because, my dear Sir Alan, at best he's guilty of very serious breaches of security through confiding in you, whether he knew you were a spy or not.'

'But that's not the situation as I understand it, Sir Mark. The Prime Minister, or any other senior minister for that matter, has the power to authorize himself to disclose secret information, publicly if he wishes. I do not think you could make an Official Secrets Act charge stick against the Prime Minister for confiding in private to me.'

The bastard is well briefed isn't he, Quinn thought. He hadn't landed his big fish yet.

Quinn's eyes narrowed, accentuating their gimlet quality, as he said, 'Look, Sir Alan, if you force my hand so that I have to turn you over to the police, Henderson will at least have to be called as a witness and his resignation will then be automatic. There will also be a public scandal which would be extremely harmful to Anglo-American relations and to British prestige generally.'

'So?'

'So you'll have to tell him that it's imperative that he resigns for medical reasons – genuine reasons which you have discovered, and which threaten him with premature death if he continues in office.'

King-Lander looked horrified. 'But he's perfectly fit … '

'That may be, but it is your task to convince him that he is not. It's the only way out for both of you. I promise you that if you succeed the public will never know anything about your treachery, or his.'

To Quinn's surprise the promise appeared to have done nothing to relax the grim set of the physician's features so, making use of information which Falconer had passed to him on the foolscap sheets, he continued, 'As I understand it the Prime Minister is forever undergoing medical tests because his wife suspects that he has heart trouble.'

'Yes, but there are no grounds for those fears.'

'Nevertheless, you have to tell him, with all your powers of persuasion, that his wife's fears have been justified after all. That if he continues bearing the great burden of his office he could be dead in three months.'

King-Lander shook his head firmly. 'I can't do it, Sir Mark. It would be a terrible thing to do to an innocent man, and it would be most unethical professionally. I just can't do it, whatever happens to me.'

'Sir Alan, what could happen to you could be twenty years in prison. Whatever the Prime Minister might dream up to make himself immune to prosecution would not apply to you.

Come now, haven't you often lied to a patient who was mortally ill by assuring him that he was not?'

'Of course. All doctors have. One must never deprive a patient of hope.'

'Then what's wrong about doing the reverse to save a patient from international disgrace? Without it the Prime Minister has no hope. His political death will be instaneous if the true facts become known.'

To Quinn's surprise King-Lander did not seem to be impressed.

'I thought you had already made it clear that the true facts are not going to become known.'

'Then you have misunderstood me,' Quinn said hastily, wondering whether his fish were slipping away after all. 'What I said was that we must do all we can – you and I – to prevent such a calamity. Unless we act I have to make it clear that the matter will not be entirely in our hands.'

King-Lander looked quizzically at Quinn who had decided that the time had come to play a card he would have preferred to withhold.

'The American CIA, the Central Intelligence Agency, could find out about all this. It may not share our inhibitions. Neither may the President, who would have to be told about Henderson. So we have to move fast. When is the first opportunity at which you could give the Prime Minister his sad news?'

'I could do it tonight, I suppose,' King-Lander said with an air of resignation which convinced Quinn that he had triumphed. 'I have the results of his latest overhaul. His cardiogram and so on.'

He reached wearily into a drawer and extracted an envelope. 'They are all here. But they are perfectly normal for a man of his age.'

'Never mind,' Quinn said disarmingly. 'The Prime Minister's not the only one of your patients who's not really ill is he? There's Mrs Czapek, isn't there. What do you tell your receptionist about her?'

'She thinks she's suffering from chronic anaemia.'

'Right, you lied about her so you can lie about the Prime Minister.'

Sensing that his subject might need one final push he

added, 'There is something else we know about you, Sir Alan. Your sordid little affair with Mrs Jansen.'

'But you wouldn't make use of that!'

'I wouldn't want to, Sir Alan. But others might. The CIA has no love for Mrs Jansen or for her husband, the so-called "White Knight". On the contrary.'

King-Lander looked dazed with disbelief. 'All right,' he said. 'But I shall do it with great reluctance. And no doubt with great regret. Whatever you may think of Henderson he is a good man at heart. He'll be a sad loss to the nation when it needs leadership so badly.'

'I think the country will be a lot better off without a man who spills secrets around like confetti. And I'm sure that would be the view of the great majority of his supporters if they knew what he had done.'

'What if he insists on a second opinion?' King-Lander asked.

'That can be arranged. Leave it to us.'

'But, Sir Mark, I should then be asked to produce his records and the results of the last tests.'

'Then send them to us. We can replace them with something different. We have access to people who can do that. We have previous experience in that direction, Sir Alan. An inverted T-wave on the electrocardiogram is among the changes required, if I remember the term rightly.'

The physician was so horrified at the possible faking of someone's medical records that he could not resist commenting, 'My God! The things that go on ... '

'Indeed, Sir Alan,' Quinn responded earnestly. 'But the difference between our behaviour and yours is that our intentions are for the well-being of the British nation. And it's intentions that matter.'

'In that case I must tell you, once again, that Albert Henderson's intentions were always good. No doubt he was sometimes mistaken, as we all are. But he has done a great deal for East-West relations.'

'Some would say too much. And what did it amount to on the night? It's only by the grace of God that we are not going to be at war – nuclear war – with the Soviets within the next few days!'

'But the Prime Minister would take some credit for that.

He never believed that the Russians would attack us, in the next few days or at any other time.'

'Then he was deluded. I can assure you that if Borisenko and Volkhov had not died so conveniently this country was to have been subjected to a most savage air attack. So perhaps it could be argued that Henderson is mentally unfit to continue in office. But it's the heart situation you must latch on to. That's what will frighten him most – and frighten his wife. If you tell her she's been right all along she'll be better than any second opinion.'

King-Lander looked so glum that Quinn felt that the moment warranted a more cheering note. 'Once you have convinced him that he must resign your troubles and his should be over. As soon as he ceases to be in receipt of secret information the KGB will lose all interest in both of you.'

'You don't think they will take revenge on me?'

'Absolutely no chance. Neither they nor we waste any time on dead microphones. And we shall arrange to let them know that is what you are from now on. Talking of microphones does the KGB have this place bugged?'

'I have no idea, Sir Mark. I've often thought they might.'

'They did come and fit that anti-bugging equipment – what I believe you call the "air-conditioner" – which you switch on sometimes?'

'Yes. I let them in one evening when my receptionist wasn't here. I didn't stay with them. They showed me where the switch would be and I left them to it.'

'Well then you can be sure that they did fit bugs as well, Sir Alan. Permanent bugs run off the mains. I suppose they asked you to switch off the anti-bugging device except when you had special visitors?'

'Yes. Except when the Prime Minister came and Mrs Czapek. They said it was necessary to save the batteries.'

Quinn laughed. 'Don't you believe it, Sir Alan. It was so that they could listen in to all the rest of the conversations in this room – just in case you might be playing any tricks on them, or let slip some other information that might strengthen their hold on you.'

King-Lander was plainly frightened. 'But they might be listening now ... '

'I have no doubt they are,' Quinn said. 'And I certainly

153

hope they are. The sooner they know their game's been blown back in Moscow the better. It would be wise to switch on your "air conditioner" now, Sir Alan.'

King-Lander obliged while Quinn noted the position of the switch.

'Don't worry any more, Sir Alan,' he said reassuringly. 'We'll come and sweep the rooms and dismantle their apparatus. My experts will be quite interested to see it.'

He had not conducted such an interrogation for years, normally leaving such a task to his specialists, and he had thoroughly enjoyed it. He had secured all he needed and there was the mischievous satisfaction of letting the KGB and the hated Yakovlev know that their top source was being eliminated by a deception far more sophisticated than the crude frame-up to which he had been subjected in Moscow.

Quinn knew that Yakovlev could make no capital out of his knowledge in his new sensitive position. There would be no attempt to warn Henderson in such a politically explosive situation. His interest now would be concentrated on Henderson's successor – examining what pressures might be exerted to encourage the Parliamentary Labour Party to adopt a more full-blooded left-winger.

'You seem to have it all tied up, Sir Mark,' King-Lander conceded. 'But what about Parliament and the British public. Will they be fooled?'

'My dear chap that's the easiest part of all. There's plenty of precedents for Prime Ministerial resignations on the grounds of ill-health and, frankly, the country would have been a damned sight better off if there had been more. Downing Street gives no medical details. But I'll see to it that something is leaked to the lobby correspondents at Westminster to convince them that the PM has a serious heart problem. They'll buy it and it'll be splashed all over the "Yellow Pages".'

'My name for the newspapers,' Quinn explained. 'I'm not enamoured of them. They make my life too difficult.'

'But what happens if Henderson goes on living a full life into old age?'

'Well, the age of miracles isn't past, is it doctor?'

King-Lander forced a smile in the final realization that

154

Quinn was offering him a deal he was in no position to refuse, and which he hardly merited.

'All right, Sir Mark. I'll go along with you. But, in return, you do guarantee that nobody will ever know of my lapse?'

'Your lapses,' Quinn corrected. 'I do guarantee that, except of course for the few people in my department who *have* to know by the very nature of their work. I'll be absolutely honest with you. This conversation has been taped. I would have stopped you using that switch had you attempted to do so.'

'It never occurred to me.'

Quinn fixed him with a stare as though not entirely sure of him. 'My point in telling you that everything about you is on secret record is to convince you and anybody else who might be listening that if I happened to be run down by a car or suffered some other fatal "accident" it wouldn't help you.'

'But they wouldn't do anything like that … '

'*They* would do anything, Sir Alan. The KGB assassination squads are not mythical. They killed an important defector in Washington only the other day. And perhaps you remember the poison pellets planted by a prod from an umbrella. You must take my advice and have no further contact with your former "friends".'

'What if I'm approached by Mrs Czapek?'

'You won't be. I'm arranging things so that Mr Czapek and his hard-bitten wife will be recalled to Prague within the week. Should anyone else try to contact you telephone me immediately at this number. You must ring me anyway to let me know the result of your meeting with the Prime Minister.'

He passed over a slip of paper. 'If I am not there they will know where to contact me. I won't insult you by asking for your passport. If you were to disappear abroad there would be no escape for Henderson. We should have to devise some other way of removing him which might not be so painless. So you are a hostage for his continuing good health which, after all, is what a doctor should be.'

The Secret Intelligence Service was no longer in the assassination business at any level, at least not on the mainland of Britain, but Quinn could see no harm in letting King-Lander believe that it might be.

Quinn rose, finally confident that both his fish were safely in the landing-net.

'Cheer up, Sir Alan. There'll be a Resignation Honours List. You could go to the Lords. Lord King-Lander! It would sound very good and we wouldn't oppose it. It would help to preserve the appearances. The Prime Minister might even join you. The load there wouldn't put a strain on anybody's heart!'

Looking exhausted King-Lander could summon nothing more than a lame smile.

'You can switch off your "air-conditioner" now,' Quinn said as he took his leave.

Chapter Fourteen

Rakitin had not needed to go far to fulfil that first demand from his new leader. No further than his own office in the Kremlin, where he had simply telephoned the Chief Executive of the State Broadcasting Services to present his person for instructions, as he had done so often in the past.

The executive arrived within minutes, already aware, from the tanks and troops in the streets, that something serious was happening. Rakitin was in a state of distress but the executive attributed this to natural emotion as he raced away with the typewritten bulletin. No sooner had he left than, to Rakitin's relief, the KGB officer in charge smilingly announced that he was free to go home.

'Don't bother to clear up your papers, Comrade. You can do that some other time.'

Shattered by the day's events, Rakitin was taken to his flat by his usual driver who bade him farewell, having been told that his services were being withdrawn.

'Somebody else will be calling for you, Comrade Rakitin,' the driver said, pretending not to notice the proffered hand.

'No doubt,' Rakitin muttered, as he entered the gaunt concrete apartment block.

His wife was not surprised to see him in a state of agitation, for she had already heard the snap announcement of Borisenko's death on the radio. He seemed too numbed to give her any more detail, but he could not sit and relax, as she insisted he should, rising from his armchair from time to time to peer through the curtained windows.

'Sit down, dear. There's nothing to see out there. You are in a state of shock. You must relax ... '

She was right, so far as Rakitin could see. There was nobody watching out there. And later that evening when he took his dog for the usual walk he felt sure that he was not being followed. By 11 pm he was in bed, beginning to believe that honourable retirement might be the only penalty he faced.

Soon after 1 am, however, he was roused by continuous ringing of the doorbell. His wife opened the door to find three strangers who had been sent to collect her husband in a hurry. She was used to having her sleep disturbed by a ringing bell. Rakitin had often been telephoned at night when Borisenko needed some information, or his presence back at the Kremlin, for some urgent reason. But these intruders, so lacking in respect for such a senior government servant, looked and behaved as one would expect of KGB muscle-men.

'It's all right, my dear,' Rakitin assured her as he pulled on his clothes. 'There must be something they need at the office. I'll soon be back.'

The roughness with which he was bundled into the waiting car and the speed with which it moved, ignoring traffic lights, quickly convinced him that he was not going to his office and he was not surprised when the destination proved to be Number Two, Dzerzhinsky Street. No explanation was offered when he was conducted towards an interrogation room, nor for the presence of his two young grandchildren who were sitting sleepily on a bench in the corridor with a KGB man on either side of them.

His efforts to talk to them were forbidden by the muscle-men, who thrust him through the door where an interrogator, specially selected for certain qualities, awaited him. Rakitin swallowed hard as the door closed behind him. His grand-children were his weakness.

157

The interrogator had digested his instructions from the Kremlin, which were brief and very straightforward – to secure a confession in the shortest possible time, details being of no importance.

Rakitin went through the motions of denying any treachery, any links with any foreign Intelligence Service, or any break with Party-line thought, but by daybreak he had signed the necessary confession, accepting the assurance that his family would not be harassed or harmed. When members of the British Embassy staff known to be MI6 men were named at random Rakitin admitted having been in touch with each of them.

He was kept waiting alone in the semi-dark interrogation room while his tormentor reported on the outcome to the most important office in the Kremlin, where a woman took the message and relayed the next instruction. Rakitin was then handed over to a uniformed KGB captain, who drove him with an escort to a wired-in enclosure some twenty kilometres outside Moscow. Soon after daybreak he was summarily shot.

Securing some names for Rakitin's MI6 contacts had been purely routine. No action was to be taken against them. The last thing that the new administration wanted was any diplomatic incident with Britain or any other nation while it was consolidating itself. The new brooms faced too much domestic sweeping to wish to concern themselves with disturbing dirt in any foreign corridors.

Rakitin's rapid liquidation had removed the only dangerous witness to the murder of Borisenko and Volkhov. A small paragraph reporting his execution for unspecified 'crimes against the State', with no mention whatever of espionage, would be enough to demoralize Yakovlev's old enemy, Quinn, by letting him know that his private hot-line into the Kremlin has been severed.

Secretary-General of the Communist Party of the Soviet Union, Sergei Yakovlev, had no qualms about sitting at the desk where he had assassinated his predecessor, especially in view of the precautions he had taken to ensure that he would not suffer a similar fate, precautions in which, because of his KGB service, he was expert.

In replacing those who had owed their preferment to Borisenko and Volkhov he had plans for proceeding slowly so that he could not be legitimately accused of conducting a Stalinite purge. His first move had been to bring in an age limit for serving officers, which pleased Dominowski, who had no further ambitions, and to indicate to those politicians on the Politburo that service there after the age of sixty-five would no longer be acceptable. This had led to quick public expressions of gratitude from the older Politburo members that at last they were being allowed to retire, though privately they would be going with bad grace. But Yakovlev was being careful not to deprive them in retirement of their perquisites, which would soon disappear through natural wastage, meaning in their case natural death, or to indicate that they were in any kind of disgrace.

In this soft approach he was at some pains, privately and publicly, to avoid discrediting Borisenko, claiming to his Politburo colleagues and to the Russian people that he was the late leader's choice as successor, in spite of recent minor differences. That was why he had ruled against the customary, lengthy interrogation of Rakitin, which would have exposed Borisenko as being witless enough to have harboured a spy in his private office.

He had decided, too, that he would have to soft-pedal on the innovations in domestic policy – like the improved supply of consumer goods which the old régime had failed to consider seriously, much less implement. Changes would be necessary but some months would be needed to consolidate his situation and, regrettably, that would require some firm repression of dissident factions – a temporary measure to discourage counter-revolutionaries, of course. Promises of liberalization on 'human rights', whatever they might mean, would be made at a later date.

Yakovlev's first personal requirement had been for an assistant whom he could trust completely for, in view of Rakitin's incredible betrayal, loyalty was of greater concern than competence. There would always be some faction or some individual, eaten with envy and ambition, plotting to topple him. A disloyal personal assistant who might be bribed or suborned, even by his successor at the KGB, though he was being chosen with the utmost care, could be extremely dangerous in providing the requisite political ammunition through access to private documents and conversations.

His choice, therefore, fell naturally on Zina to whom he had been able to confide, not only the secret information an assistant had to know to do the job, but his private fears.

'I'm not sure that I should take it,' she said to his complete astonishment when he told her that she would be joining him in the Kremlin.

'Why ever not? I thought you'd be delighted.'

'I'm certainly flattered,' Zina replied, fingering the beads she invariably wore. 'I don't have to tell you that there's nobody I would rather work for than you. But there is something you should know.'

'Yes?'

'I knew that you were going to kill Comrade Borisenko before you did it.'

Yakovlev looked at her sternly, and with some concern, as nobody had had the temerity to express that widely held suspicion to him.

'I saw that your machine-pistol was missing from your drawer, so I looked in your briefcase and saw it there,' Zina continued. 'I also overheard your conversations with Marshal Dominowski about organizing tanks and troops at key points.'

'I assume that you realize now how necessary it was,' Yakovlev said, knowing that denials were pointless.

'I suppose so, but I want you to know that there was a moment when I felt it was my duty to warn Comrade Borisenko and I nearly did.'

'Oh! And what stopped you?' Yakovlev asked. He was beginning to think that it would be wise to withdraw his offer.

'I was in a terrible position. I admired Comrade Borisenko so much before he became senile – I know you were right that he was senile – but that seemed to make it worse. I mean that a helpless old man should be shot down. You know how I hate violence.'

'Don't think I enjoyed it,' Yakovlev countered. 'But that helpless old man and his cronies were about to plunge the whole of our nation into violent war. Somebody had to stop him. I was able to and it was my duty.'

Zina's face showed how torn she had been. 'I know you

were right the way things have turned out, but I wanted you to understand that I did have doubts. There was a conflict between my loyalty to you, my boss, and to Comrade Borisenko, my leader. You didn't know it but for a moment I, a woman alone in your office, could have changed the fate of the world just be lifting the telephone.'

It sounded melodramatic but Yakovlev appreciated that it was true. 'Why didn't you make the call?'

'What a question!' Zina said. 'Only a man could ask it. I was terrified until you got back safely. You may not have noticed it but I padded out your briefcase with some extra papers to make the pistol less noticeable.'

Yakovlev shook his head despairingly. 'I'll never under-stand women. I never have and I never will.'

'You've never understood me. You've always taken my loyalty, for granted. That's why I had to confess my doubts to you. You see I have been thinking about poor old Comrade Rakitin. He once loved Comrade Borisenko, yet he turned against him when he believed he was doing something that was ruinous to the country.'

'And you think that one day you might do something like that?' Yakovlev asked.

'I nearly did, didn't I? Or, at least, I think I nearly did.'

Yakovlev, whose professional life had been spent trying to delve into people's characters, rose from his chair and put his arm round Zina's shoulders, the first sign of physical affection he had ever displayed.

'Zina, my dear, what you have told me is the best proof I could possibly have of your loyalty and your trust in me. You will be doing me a great service if you will join me. Your boss and your leader will now be one and the same. And after all,' he added, feeling that the situation was becoming a little too tense, 'who else can make tea as well as you do?'

Zina smiled inwardly, for there was an intriguing secret about her tea-making, then said, 'There is one thing I would like to know before I make up my mind. The truth about Viktor Kovalsky's death. Was he killed by us – by you, in fact?'

Yakovlev folded his arms and sat on the edge of the desk. 'I give you my word that he was not,' he said categorically. 'He was killed by the CIA.'

'But did you know they would kill him when you sent him out?'

Yakovlev was clearly embarrassed. 'I have to admit that I thought it possible. He was part of the events which have prevented war and saved so many lives.'

'So you were at least party to his death.'

'In a way, I suppose. Viktor was a soldier in an undercover war and I sent him into action because I knew that, whatever happened, he would never really defect. He died for his country.'

'I just don't understand what part he could have played,' Zina said.

'I'm not in a position to explain. I may one day. But you can take it from me that his role was essential. Any soldier has to be expendable and he knew that.'

Zina seemed to be as satisfied as she was ever likely to be on the subject.

'Will you join me then?' Yakovlev asked.

'Do you really need me?'

'Yes I need you.'

'Then I'll come.'

Yakovlev put his arms round her and kissed her on the cheek.

'Secretary-General, we must be careful,' Zina exclaimed, looking apprehensively at the heavy door.

Yakovlev released her and laughed. 'Not now, Zina! Not now! Now we can do anything we like.'

Chapter Fifteen

By late afternoon King-Lander had made up his mind. He had briefly considered the obvious alternative – that he should kill himself – but, as he realized Quinn must have surmised, he was a survivor. Instead he had chosen what he knew to be a truly cowardly way. He decided to telephone Winifred first and tell her the news in the hope that, in defiance of his instructions, she would be unable to resist informing her husband. He felt it would then be easier for him to lie to the friend he so much admired.

'Winifred, I need your support. I don't know how we are going to tell Bert but your fears have been entirely justified. I've been wrong. He *has* got a heart problem.'

'Oh dear, is it serious?'

'Serious enough if he doesn't take a long rest, and a permanent one from politics.'

He could almost detect a note of delight, or at least relief, in her voice as she asked, 'Shall I tell him?'

'No, Winifred, you mustn't. I should tell him first. That's my duty. I'll make an excuse to call in and see him this evening. Is that possible?'

'Yes. He'll be free for a few minutes around 6.30 pm. Then we have to dress for dinner ... '

There was a pause as the implications began to sink home. 'Perhaps we'll have to cancel it now,' she said. 'I don't suppose Bert will feel like eating.'

'You'll have to cancel a lot of things, Winifred. I'll be round soon after six unless I hear from you. We should have a brief chat first.'

King-Lander was not surprised to receive a telephone call from Downing Street within the hour. It was the Prime Minister.

163

'What the hell's all this, Alan? I thought you told me there was nothing wrong.'

'I'm sorry, Bert, but I was badly mistaken. Medicine is far from being an exact science, you know, and the dangerous symptoms have just shown up on the last tests.'

' 'You say "dangerous"?'

'Yes. I'm afraid that's right, and I'd rather not talk about it on the telephone. Let me call and see you at six-thirty.'

'All right, but why the hell did you tell Winifred before telling me? She's doing her nut. Saying I've got to resign today, cancel tonight's dinner ... '

'I'm sorry, Bert. I shouldn't have told her but you know how emotional she is. I needed to prepare her for the shock. I told her not to tell you anything. I suppose she was too upset. I assure you that my intentions were for the best.' He almost added, 'And it's intentions that matter', as he heard a grunt and the telephone went dead.

Replacing the receiver with a sigh, King-Lander realized that Henderson would be fighting all the way to ignore the medical advice. With Winifred in the know he at least had a strong ally.

Soon after six, King-Lander presented himself at the front door of Number Ten, where the duty policeman who recognized him as a regular visitor pressed the bell to request entry. As he climbed the main staircase he passed, on the wall to his left, the array of portraits and photographs of Britain's former Prime Ministers. Henderson's, which was at the top of the stairs, would soon be moving down one place, if the unpleasant mission he faced proved successful.

Whose photograph would be there in three weeks time when the ballot for a new Labour leader had been completed? he wondered. Someone far less fitted for the post than Bert! Of that King-Lander was sure. What a tragedy!

With two hours to mull over the possibilities, Henderson had decided that he would rather die in harness than spend the rest of his life in a cottage with Winifred. That prospect was too daunting. Helping his wife with the historical romance she had been talking about for years but never started! God Almighty! Better to collapse in the Cabinet Room than rot in

164

some wretched backwater, pandering to cabbages and chickens. Besides, who was there with his skill and experience to lead the Party, or the country for that matter? Torn apart, through the continued entry of Left-wing extremists and Communists posing as Socialists, the Party needed a manipulator of his capability to hold together at all. The possible successors were either committed to the Right or Left. And there was all that controversial legislation in the pipeline. No! His departure at such a critical time would be a national disaster.

With his mind made up he was in almost buoyant mood. He tidied the papers on the desk in his first-floor study, which overlooked St James's Park and had been re-decorated first by the Wilsons and then, in more elegant taste by Edward Heath, and left to join his wife and King-Lander in the upstairs flat.

'Now what's all this nonsense, Alan?' he asked breezily.

'I'm afraid it's not nonsense, Prime Minister. I must be absolutely frank with you, and I may as well say it in front of Winifred. If you do not retire from political life without delay you could be dead in three months. Your cardiogram shows an inverted T-wave, and there are other symptoms which indicate that, unless you unburden yourself of all stress, you could suffer a massive coronary thrombosis at any time.'

The doctor's demeanour shocked Henderson into temporary silence. His face was blanched and his hands tightly clasped as Winifred said quietly, 'You see, Bert, it is really serious.'

'But I can't quit now,' Henderson complained. 'I'm the only one who can cement our relations with the new Soviet leadership. I'm the only one who's met Yakovlev. All this guff in the newspapers about him being a villain because he was head of the KGB must be alienating him. He's not a bad man. And he's just my age group. I could do business with him.'

'Someone else would have to do it if you did die suddenly,' King-Lander pointed out sympathetically. 'Nobody's indispensable, Bert, and too many good men have driven themselves into early graves believing that they were.'

'And you are indispensable to me, dear,' Winifred said, touching his hand.

'But a few more weeks or months would make no difference, and then ... '

'I'm afraid they could make all the difference,' King-Lander warned. 'There could be some sudden political crisis and you've already admitted that you have been working an eighty-hour week.'

'But I'm young enough to cope ... '

King-Lander shook his head. 'The fifties are now the most dangerous decade for coronary disease. And the younger you are the more serious an attack is likely to be. One would expect the reverse, but sadly that is not so.'

Winifred reached across and put her hand on her husband's knee. 'Oh Bert, please see sense and do as Alan advises. He's your friend as well as your doctor. It's for the good of all of us. For me and for the children. You don't want to leave them fatherless when they need you most and look like doing so well at University.'

'There's also the country to consider,' King-Lander ventured.

'The country! What do you mean?'

'I mean that in your condition it would be irresponsible for you to continue in office. Others have done it, including some of your predecessors against their doctors' advice. And remember Roosevelt at Yalta. The results have been catastrophic.'

'Oh, God!' Henderson muttered under his breath. It must be far more serious than he had imagined. King-Lander was being much more adamant than he had expected.

'I can get you a second opinion,' King-Lander proposed. 'But I can assure you it would do no good. The symptoms are too clear-cut – including of course those chest pains you've experienced for so long. You have to face the facts, Bert. Not just the facts of life, the facts of death.'

From Henderson's gesture he could see that he was not interested in a second opinion, such was his confidence in his friend's ability. King-Lander decided to firm up the diagnosis.

'My advice is that you should resign without delay and then take Winifred on a holiday – somewhere you can relax. Just one more Cabinet meeting to announce the news to your colleagues. Then off you go to the sun. I'll come with you if

166

you like. We could play some gentle golf – that's not contra-indicated provided you don't overdo it.'

Henderson was not encouraged. 'And when we return? What then?'

'Settle down somewhere quiet and write your memoirs. You've a great story to tell. All about your work for peace.'

'Oh yes, dear,' Winifred enthused. 'We could write together. You your memoirs, me my historical romances.'

Oh God! Historical romances! It was plural now was it? Henderson thought. 'I need to be alone,' he announced peremptorily. 'I won't be long. You stay with Winifred, Alan.'

He left and walked down the stairs slowly towards the Cabinet Room on the ground floor, passing two servants on the way as though unaware of them.

'Do you think he'll be all right?' King-Lander asked with some concern.

'Oh yes,' Winifred replied. 'He just wants to cry. He cries at the drop of a hat when he's alone or with me, but never in front of anybody else.'

The Cabinet Room, the pinnacle and power-house of Henderson's ambitions, seemed bigger than usual and as he sat down in solitude in his usual seat he felt smaller. He sought, through habit, for his pipe but then replaced it in his pocket and holding his head in his hands allowed the tears to flow.

God, life was unfair, he told himself. He had striven so hard through so many lean years to snatch the Party leadership and eventually the Premiership. Now he was being deprived of it all. And through no fault of his own. The thought of leaving Downing Street and all it signified was shattering. He had everything to offer – youthfulness, exper-ience and the constructive attitude to international relations of which East-West cordiality was infinitely the most impor-tant, with each side physically capable, for the first time in history, of literally destroying civilization and poisoning the world.

The events of the past few days had convinced him that he had been right and the so-called 'mandarins' of Whitehall, like that mad Irishman Quinn, had been utterly wrong. The Russians wanted peace and the way to peace was undoubtedly through East-West trade, as Harold Wilson had seen; as *he* had seen. Now all his plans had collapsed just because of some squiggle on a heart chart.

All he could see in the immediate future was a dreadful, unedifying squabble over the vacant leadership with a pack of envious and over-ambitious nonentities, who owed their positions to him, behaving like hyenas round some carrion carcase.

Damn it and blast it! A breakdown of his health was the one thing he had not foreseen. Sure he had belly-ached privately about the grind of an eighty-hour week but that was no more than a legitimate grouse. He could eat the bloody work! And see that his ministers worked just as hard! He looked round the table visualizing the familiar faces and wondering how they would react when they heard the news.

Ah, there was no justice. Suddenly to be plunged from the peak of power and patronage to the abyss of impotence. From being the first man in the land to being a nobody. Would he be remembered? Had he done enough to be remembered? No. His main objectives were still in the planning stage. Anyway, peoples everywhere never remembered the men of peace. They liked their heroes to be men of war.

Who remembered Walpole, the man on the wall behind him? But in Henderson's view Walpole had been a great creative politician; the first to realize that the House of Commons could be a power-base; the first to develop a Cabinet of senior ministers with himself in the prime position.

He wiped his eyes and felt again for his pipe. As he filled it from a rather battered pouch he looked up and down the long tapered table which was the shape of a huge coffin. Appropriate, he thought with bitter reflection, as was the ticking of the mantelpiece clock, which seemed unusually loud.

He looked at the sunbeams streaming through the windows and lighting up the motes of dust which, in spite of the almost clinical cleanliness of the room, were dancing in the moving air. Some of them seemed to have tails like tiny crotchets. Spelling out his swan-song?

Such morbid thoughts were out of character for him. It would be so much better, so much more manly, to go down fighting, to drop dead perhaps in the chair in which he was

168

sitting. But he knew he should not delude himself. He had always been short on physical courage and it was no good pretending that he wasn't afraid of death.

Poor Alan! It must have been terribly difficult for him. To have to admit that he had been so wrong! To have to convey the appalling news to such an old friend. Alan must be right. He was one of the finest physicians in the land. Perhaps he had been slow in spotting the diagnosis because of the very fact that he was dealing with the Prime Minister. Henderson remembered that this seemed to have happened to King George the Sixth. The early symptoms of mortal illness had been there but the doctors could not bring themselves to see the obvious because they could not believe it could happen to the King.

Oh yes, Alan was right, blast it. Those persistent chest pains! He could even feel a dull ache now. There could be recompenses. He could write his memoirs. Make some money, explain to the world what he had intended to do had fate been kinder. Then, after a rest, take on some consultancies, some committee work. But only in London. There was going to be no cottage in the backwoods. No sitting round the fireside cooped up with Winifred day after boring day. *That* could be a killer. No, if he couldn't be Prime Minister he couldn't be nothing.

He would have to make a special appointment to see the Queen. She would have to be told first. There would be some sympathy there; they had always got on well together, rather to her surprise. Then there would have to be a resignation statement to be preceded by an announcement to the Cabinet. Again he wondered how they would react. A few would be genuinely sorry. He could name them. But there were others, like the Chancellor of the Exchequer and the Foreign Secretary, who wouldn't be able to believe their luck. Older men who had given up all hope of the Premiership when such a young Party leader had been elected. They would be the most effusive with their sympathy, and the least sincere. Severing relations with them would be almost a consolation.

And there was another private consolation. As even the wretched Press had now realized there would be no possibility of war with Russia in the immediately foreseeable future.

So he would be leaving a stable situation so far as that counter-productive scare was concerned. A pity he could claim no credit for it. But then nobody could. Nobody outside Russia could exert any control over coups in the Kremlin. He thought briefly about the secret report on Yakovlev's coup which Quinn had sent him. He didn't accept it all, but there could be no doubt that Borisenko and Volkhov had been assassinated. Well, it was a purely domestic matter in which no other nation should or could have interfered. But how he hated violence!

As he composed himself to return to the flat he felt deeply grateful that he had always been able to live and function politically in a country where leaders were elected in a truly democratic manner and could only be dismissed in the same way.

Such agonies of remorse afflicted King-Lander for what he had done to Henderson that he dismissed the idea of a holiday in the sun or anywhere else. It would be bad enough having to see him professionally, prescribing treatment and even phoney drugs of which he had no need, without having to face him for days at a stretch. He was in no doubt about how he should have resolved the situation. He should have killed himself. Now, somehow, he had to live with his conscience. There was only one effective treatment – to immerse himself in work. To accept every patient, every hospital round, every speaking engagement.

As Quinn had predicted the KGB left him alone. Mrs Czapek had deliberately been made aware that she was under surveillance, and when the Resident KGB officer in Kensington Palace Gardens had received the transcript of Quinn's consulting-room confrontation of King-Lander, which had indeed been overheard by Soviet eavesdroppers, he had contacted Moscow with a most urgent request for further instruction. No new political head of the KGB had yet been appointed, but the Chief at the Centre was able to contact his old boss, Yakovlev, who ordered an immediate end to further dealings with King-Lander. Now that he was in political command he wanted no KGB interference with his opposite number in Britain, or in any other country. That situation now held more potential embarrassment than it was worth.

So all the Soviet Bloc agents and so-called diplomats, who had been involved in the surveillance and 'protection' of King-Lander, were called in by the Resident to a hurried conference inside the cantilevered, wire-meshed, bug-proof room in the basement of the Soviet Embassy in Number Thirteen, Kensington Palace Gardens. They were told that the operation was dead until further order, but each was required to submit a final report for attachment to the King-Lander-Henderson dossier in Moscow. The documents transmitted in the diplomatic bag included photographs of the Prime Minister's physician and Her Excellency, the American Ambassador, in circumstances which could hardly be said to be compromising but could be misconstrued. The Resident was a thorough operator. They might prove of use one day.

As evidence of his good faith towards Quinn, King-Lander ignored the anti-bugging switch. He had little doubt that security men somewhere had him under close surveillance. They might even be following him about, as indeed they were for a time, but he could detect no evidence of it.

It was midday in a busy morning of consultations in Harley Street, but he had to make time and room for what he hoped would be his final meeting with 'Mr Webb'. Quinn needed a first-hand account of the medical showdown with the Prime Minister, though he had already been alerted by telephone of its apparent success. King-Lander was relieved to find the Secret Service Chief in a most affable mood. Gone was the veiled threat or the slightest hint of censure. Indeed, congratulation for a difficult assignment expertly handled was on his lips.

'There is still one aspect of this sad affair which is not completely satisfactory for my peace of mind,' Quinn said. 'Tell me, Sir Alan, now that it is all over, do you think that Henderson knew that you were passing the information he gave you to the Soviet Union?'

'What do your own sources tell you?' King-Lander ventured to ask.

'I'll be honest with you, as you've been straight with me. They indicate that the Prime Minister did know. That the espionage – for that is what it was – was a joint effort, a conspiracy. But I would like to know your view.'

To Quinn the expression on King-Lander's face was of honest doubt.

'I just don't know, Sir Mark. Honestly I don't. I can tell you that we never discussed the possibility of deliberate leaks. He never hinted that he knew of my unfortunate connection with the KGB. And he never gave me information with any instruction or suggestion to pass it on.'

'Then why are you in doubt?'

'Because he went out of his way to tell me so many secret things. I thought it possible that he had learned of my predicament and was making use of it. You see he never told me anything that didn't further his crusade for peace with Russia.'

'And you never thought of enlightening him yourself? To warn him of your predicament so that he wouldn't tell you these dangerous things?'

'How could I?' King-Lander asked. 'For all I knew he might have had me arrested.'

Quinn bit his lip, revealing that the questioning had not worked out to his satisfaction. 'Well, thank you very much, Sir Alan. Provided the Prime Minister goes ahead and resigns without much delay I see no reason why I should trouble you again. Normally, in a case like yours, a long interrogation is necessary. But as you have been so co-operative we can forgo that. I bid you good morning.'

He was not prepared to shake hands with a traitor.

As he walked through the waiting-room he was amused rather than surprised to see a person, whose face he knew but whom he had never met, sitting there impatiently. It was Mrs Jane Jansen.

'Poor King-Lander,' he thought. 'I'll bet she's giving him a rough time.'

When Mrs Jansen was announced King-Lander was shocked on two counts. He had hoped, if forlornly, that he had seen the last of her and was concerned that she might have recognized 'Mr Webb'.

'Alan, I'm absolutely appalled by your letter,' she announced as she swept in, impeccably groomed and elegant in black. 'What have I done to be treated like this?'

She opened her handbag, took out the letter and a handkerchief indicating that there might be tears.

'Oh dear,' King-Lander responded rather helplessly, as he stood, staring dejectedly at the carpet. 'It was the easiest way out for both of us, Jane. It's just that, well, I've been thinking things over and it's not possible for us to go on.'

'Why ever not?' she asked, almost sharply.

'There's your position to think of as well as mine. And your husband's. You are a very public figure here now and if these damned gossip writers see us together ... '

Mrs Jansen was most unimpressed. 'I don't give a damn about the gossip writers.' Then, changing her tone, and with an imploring look, she said, 'I thought I'd made it as plain to you as a woman can that I'm in love with you and that you are all I care about. Don't you understand, Alan? I'm prepared to give up my job and my marriage for you. Nobody could make more sacrifice, though, as you know, my marriage hasn't amounted to much for years.'

'The public doesn't know that.'

'No, but I don't mind if it does know. I never thought I would be able to say that but it's true ... '

Wondering whether this startling confession, which went much further than any of their pillow avowals, was more than a wile of a woman used to getting her own way, King-Lander sighed hopelessly. 'I'm sorry, Jane, but you really mustn't give up your life's work for me. I know it's a cliché but I really am not worth it and, frankly, I have to tell you that I wouldn't give up my work for you.'

'I wouldn't expect you to,' she replied quietly, while unfolding her handkerchief. 'Men don't feel like women do – not any I've met. But, Alan, darling, doesn't the fact that I am prepared to resign the ambassadorship – tonight if you like – mean anything to you? Do you want me to go down on my knees to you?'

'Of course not, my dear. I'm very flattered. I've never been so flattered. But you mustn't do it.'

He noted that Jane had turned in her seat so that he was faced with her profile, her best feature, which was a picture of near-tearful misery, staring ahead and inviting him to put his arms around her consolingly, if not lovingly. Was her display of despair, so alien to her sharp professional composure, genuine? It could be. In private she was passionately responsive to affection. But it might be no more than the act of a clever and determined woman unused to being defeated and merely anxious to keep their cosy relationship in being. In either case, surely she must know that he would not allow her to destroy her career at her time of life.

Hardened to the emotions of others, as his profession had taught him to be, King-Lander felt that any gambit was justified to resolve a situation which, for him, had never been more than another intriguing affair with a woman of spirit and achievement and which, in his sudden crisis, had become dangerous and enervating. 'Certain things have happened since we met ... ' he faltered. 'Things I can't explain. Anyway, there's no way that we could get married ... '

'Is there another woman then?' Mrs Jansen asked sharply.

King-Lander had been expecting the question and decided to take advantage of it. 'In a way there is,' he lied. 'I don't suppose I shall ever marry her either but I couldn't in fairness marry anyone else.'

'Fairness! That's rich after the way you fooled me,' she snapped, quickly recovering her composure and returning the handkerchief to her bag. 'OK then, let's forget about marriage. Let us just go on seeing each other, like we have been. It's second best for me but I'll settle for it.'

With relief at this prompt return of Jane's usual pragmatism, King-Lander compromised. 'Let me think about it, Jane. I'm rather confused. I've been going through a very difficult time. But please promise me one thing.'

'What?'

'That you won't come to these consulting rooms again. It's terribly unsettling for me. I can't deal properly with my patients if I'm emotionally upset.'

'But you refused to answer my telephone calls. I left messages for you at your apartment and at your club. You didn't respond. And I was damned if I was going to write to you after the way we've been with each other. Treat me in a civilized manner and I won't be driven to come here.'

'I'm sorry, Jane. It was cowardly of me but I just couldn't take any more stress. Promise me you won't come here again. Please.'

She looked at his face, which was drawn and paler than usual. 'You certainly don't look well. What's been the trouble?'

174

'You'll understand, shortly. There'll be an announcement, but there's nothing I can tell you now.'

Confident that she had fulfilled her purpose, she opened her compact to repair the non-existent ravages to her make-up. 'All right, Alan. I promise I won't come here again. But I'm tearing your letter up as though I'd never seen it.'

She did just that and deposited the bits of paper on King-Lander's desk.

'Au revoir, Alan, darling. I expect to be hearing from you later today. I've kept the evening free.'

King-Lander stood up, forced a smile and allowed her to kiss him. 'By the way,' he asked, 'that man who went out just before you came in. Did you recognize him?'

'That rather attractive man with the silvery hair? No. Who was he?'

'Oh, just a man from Whitehall. I thought you might have known him.'

He closed the door behind her, then slumped into his chair, puffing out his cheeks, as though exhausted by an uphill climb.

The young American in the surveillance flat opposite took the cassette of the conversation to Falconer's hotel to hand in personally, as requested, but he felt that his haste was hardly justified. There seemed to be little that was in any way incriminating.

That, too, was Falconer's view as he played back the tape while lying on his bed. King-Lander had made no attempt to use Mrs Jansen's infatuation to get himself off any hooks. Clearly he seemed to be playing it straight. A pity though that he wouldn't be able to get his hands on the fragments of that letter! It would have made useful collateral together with the tape if ever there was need to shop the 'White Lady' – or stop the 'White Knight' in his tracks.

Chapter Sixteen

Late that night the newspaper offices in Fleet Street and its offshoots were in turmoil. The news-agency tapes were tapping out accounts of a report in the *Washington Post* to the effect that the British Prime Minister, Albert Henderson, was about to announce his resignation for medical reasons. Sir Alan King-Lander was named in the report as being involved in the drama leading to the sudden decision.

Telephone calls made by Fleet Street journalists, roused from their beds by irate night news editors, produced an immediate response from an equally sleepy Downing Street Press Officer that the idea was preposterous. But a few minutes later, after reaching the Prime Minister on the night telephone, the same Press Officer was replacing his angry denial with a curt 'No comment'.

To the editors this meant only one thing – that the report must be true and that their political writers and lobby correspondents had been scooped, monumentally, by the American paper. No name had appeared on the *Washington Post* report, so it seemed possible that the information had leaked from the White House, on the assumption, wrongly as it transpired, that Henderson had privately warned the President of his imminent departure from the political scene. On the other hand, the editors realized that it could have leaked in London, the absence of the name of the London correspondent being a deliberate gambit to cover the source.

The latter was also Falconer's view when he was woken by a telephone call from Ed Taylor who had been alerted by CIA Headquarters at Langley.

'I sense the devious hand of our friend O'Toole,' he said, using that device to avoid mentioning Quinn's name on the telephone.

'But why would he want it leaked?' Taylor asked ingenuously.

'To speed the parting guest,' Falconer replied, still speaking in riddles. 'He can't stand him and he's not having him changing his mind if he can help it. What worries me, Ed, is that there might be more to come.'

'But that wouldn't be in O'Toole's interest.'

'Not in his department's interest,' Falconer corrected. 'But the pressures of his own private vendetta may override those. Now that he's got the bit between his teeth he may not be content just to unseat him.'

Falconer's assessment was astute, as usual. Quinn had indeed alerted the *Washington Post,* but not directly. He never had any direct contact with the Press, and held them in some contempt for the way their probings and criticisms of his department infringed the secrecy essential to its work. 'If journalists had their way they'd make me go around in a car with the number-plate "MI6",' he claimed.

Fearing that Henderson might vacillate, he had thought of channelling a leak to two British lobby correspondents through different intermediaries. However, he decided that one American outlet would be safer because it could forestall any Whitehall witch-hunt to discover the origin of the information.

A retired MI6 man who spent much of his time in West End clubs, keeping his ears open for Whitehall and Foreign Office gossip, was asked to call at Quinn's flat in Cadogan Gardens for a drink. He did occasional services for his old firm and one of these was cultivating contacts among the foreign correspondents to whom interesting items of information were occasionally passed when it suited Quinn's purpose. As a result of the brief discussion in Quinn's flat the resident correspondent for the *Washington Post* in London was given one of the scoops of his life, and he handled it with discretion. He did not, for instance, try to secure confirmation from Downing Street, which could have resulted in an announcement or a leak to British newsmen, thereby destroying the charm of exclusivity.

Falconer was mistaken, however, in suspecting that the *Washington Post* would be given any follow-up story. Quinn would have been delighted to blacken Henderson publicly, as proof particular of the KGB and Communist penetration of the Labour Party to the very summit but, in the interests of the department and of the nation, that was a temptation which he had to resist.

Henderson's reaction, on being awakened with such unwelcome news, had been to telephone King-Lander to accuse him of leaking the information through gossiping with Jane Jansen. The physician naturally denied the charge with some vehemence, but Henderson was not entirely satisfied once he had admitted that he had spent part of that day with the garrulous lady from Grosvenor Square. King-Lander's parting suggestion was that Winifred had been gossiping with Jane on the telephone, but this was roundly denied by Winifred to a degree which almost ended in tears on the pillow.

'I wonder if this bloody place could be bugged,' Henderson had remarked as he extinguished the light and prepared to sleep again.

Winifred shuddered at the thought. 'I'm glad we're getting out of it,' she murmured through the sheets, a tactless comment which did not help to calm her husband into slumber.

There could be no delaying an announcement now, Henderson realized as he lay wide awake in the darkness. What an infernal nuisance the Press was! The Cabinet would have to be told next morning, after the Queen, of course. Then the senior civil servants and ambassadors. Then the Press, and finally the public through a television appearance. He would make the most of that though he saw one snag. He would have to go through the Party motions of commending his successor, whoever he might prove to be.

Chapter Seventeen

The Chapel of Saint Edward the Confessor in Westminster Abbey was all that Falconer had expected after Taylor's description of it. Since his arrival in London, Taylor had become so entranced by the encapsulated history in the Abbey's stones, tombs and inscriptions that he had become something of an authority. So on Falconer's last day in London, prior to his farewell visit to Century House, he had inveigled him there.

As they meandered through the maze of tombs, chapels and dark corners, Falconer's immediate reaction had been to remark, 'Excellent place for making a contact or even for a dead letter-box. I wonder if the KGB use it much?'

The look on Taylor's face told him that some rather more historical response would have been more appropriate, so Falconer asked, 'Why "the Confessor"? Was he always confessing his sins? Or did people come and confess to him?'

'I'm sure he did a lot of confessing, John, but "Confessor" was a title for a saint who didn't have the privilege of being martyred. It's a tribute to your inquiring mind that of all the people I have brought here you are the first to ask what it means.'

Falconer smiled his gratitude for the compliment but thought, I bet you didn't let any of them get away without telling them.

As they walked slowly from the Abbey towards the Houses of Parliament, with Falconer occasionally looking round to check that they were not being followed, there was a screech of brakes and a thud as an elderly woman stepping unwarily on to the pedestrian crossing was struck down. It was Taylor's reaction to rush forwards to join those already laying the injured woman on the pavement, but Falconer pulled him back.

'Let's go round the other way, Ed. She's bleeding and I hate the sight of blood. She looks as though she might be dead.'

To Taylor this was a new glimpse into the character of a man who consciously revealed little of his nature, which was more contradictory than he had imagined. His phobia for blood and guts harked back to an horrific childhood experience when Dan, his butler, had shown him how to blow up a bullfrog with a straw until it burst.

They walked the whole way round Parliament Square and crossed Whitehall stopping to look at the evening paper placards announcing, 'Henderson to resign!' 'Bert to Quit Riddle'. Taylor bought both papers but there was no official statement, and Henderson was still declining to comment.

'There isn't any chance that he'll change his mind is there?' Taylor asked.

'None whatever. But I'd laugh myself sick if he did. Just to see Quinn's face! And to spike the *Washington Post!*'

They crossed the Embankment on to Westminster Bridge, where Taylor inevitably began to explain that when the first bridge had been built there in 1740 the City merchants, who had a monopoly through London Bridge, were furious about the trade it attracted to the West.

Falconer listened patiently, though his mind was on other matters. Then about halfway across, at the third lamp standard with its triple iron lanterns, he halted and placed an oblong gift-wrapped parcel he was carrying carefully on the parapet. He looked downstream at a chain of barges moving easily against the normal current on the flooding tide, while Taylor stared up at the gilded roundel below the lanterns and was immediately enthralled.

'Gee I've never noticed that monogram of Victoria and Albert before ... '

'Look, Ed,' Falconer interrupted. 'There are a few things I should explain to you before we meet Quinn. It's safe to talk here. Anyway I don't think we are being followed today.'

'Go ahead. I haven't mentioned it but I must say I'm a bit bemused by events.'

'I'm sorry about that, but this was a case where secrecy was absolutely of the essence. I still can't put you fully in the picture, but there were some points on which I had to lie to you so I feel I owe you some explanation. I trust that you will keep what I tell you entirely to yourself.'

'Sure thing,' Taylor replied. He did not feel badly about being deceived because it was routine practice in the Intelligence game. As he filled his pipe in anticipation of what might be a lengthy denouement, Falconer continued.

'First, that information about the neutron bombs I told you about. The National Security Council took no such decision. We have no neutron bombs ready for use in Europe. The components have never been assembled. Such as they are they are still all States-side.'

No straightforward deception ever surprised Taylor for whom muddying the truth was part of his daily life. 'Then it was darned clever of Quinn to have thought of it as his disinformation on Henderson.'

'Like hell it was,' Falconer scoffed, stabilizing his hat a little more firmly against the upstream breeze. 'It had been fed to him from a source of his own inside the Council.'

'Quinn had an Intelligence source inside the National Security Council?' Taylor exclaimed in astonished disbelief.

'He sure did. Someone by the code-name, "Diamond Jim". But we soon had "Jim" under control, and we saw to it that he fed dear Mark O'Toole some very accurate and sensitive information which he could check out from other sources. So when the neutron-bomb stuff came up Quinn just had to believe it.'

'And you wanted him to leak it to Moscow through the Prime Minister?'

Falconer looked at Taylor fixedly and his mouth broadened into a smile. 'Quinn reacted exactly as I had predicted. In this game, Ed, you need to understand the minds of your friends as well as your enemies! I knew that Quinn hated Henderson and everything he stood for. I reckoned that he would make the utmost use of the information.'

'Even though, so far as he knew, it would help Yakovlev, whom he hates?'

'Yes. There was a balance of hates,' Falconer said, using his cupped hands like tipping scales. 'It happens often enough in our business. I guess Quinn hates Henderson more.'

Taylor's admiration for Quinn as an operator was declining fast. 'But it was incredibly irresponsible of him,' he said.

'Quinn didn't look at it that way. I knew he was so sold on the deterrent effect of nuclear weapons that he was convinced that it could do nothing but good to let the Russians know. I don't blame him, Ed, especially as "Diamond Jim" was pressing him to do just that. After all, Britain would have been right in the thick of it if there had been a war. And we seemed to be doing nothing to help them.'

'They weren't doing much to help themselves,' Taylor remarked. 'I can't really see why you had to involve Quinn at all, John. Couldn't you have fed the neutron bomb disinformation into the KGB machine direct?'

Falconer shook his head decisively. 'There was no adequate channel. It was vital that the information should be believed in Moscow. So it had to be fed in to the KGB through a level as high as the British Prime Minister. Without Red Army support Yakovlev could achieve nothing. So Dominowski had to be convinced that the weapons really existed. And to do that Yakovlev had to be in a position to show him hard evidence – evidence which he believed himself. Dominowski is nobody's fool and he was bound to check the information out through his own sources.'

'The GRU?'

'Of course. We were able to discover that the Chief Defence attaché in the Soviet Embassy in London, a GRU professional, suddenly started asking questions about Henderson. And he learned enough to report back that the British Prime Minister was indeed a KGB agent.'

The reply convinced Taylor that Falconer had certainly not come to London just to deal with the Henderson problem. The big game had been to prevent a war and to do it by disposing of Borisenko, Volkhov's death being probably no more than an accidental bonus. And the nub of the ruse had been the deliberate channelling of the neutron bomb disinformation to Yakovlev himself. It was staggering but, right under his nose, there must have been a full-blown operation in which he had even played a bit part without knowing it.

The probability that the CIA had actively co-operated with its arch-enemy, the KGB, to get rid of the Soviet leadership seemed incredible, even to someone like himself who had worked in Counter-Intelligence in the past, but that was what Falconer seemed to be telling him. Suddenly he could see why such an operation would have piquant appeal for the Counter-Intelligence Chief. Assassination was totally forbidden to the CIA since the Congressional showdown but there was no ban on encouraging the KGB to do it!

'Did you have direct contact with your old friend Yakovlev?' Taylor asked artlessly, appearing to look at the back of a building he knew well, the Defence Ministry with its secret radio tower on its roof. 'I know that in your department there has to be some sort of on-going dialogue with the other side ... '

Falconer remained silent for a few moments, his hands clapped on the parapet, his eyes on the buttress dividing the current below, his mind wondering whether his immediate objective outweighed the risk of enlightening his colleague to an unnecessary extent. He decided that it did. Indeed, it would help him to make an important judgement.

'No direct contact,' he lied. 'I'd say that we interpreted each other's smoke-signals correctly. If we hadn't, "Cliffhanger" could never have worked.'

' "Cliffhanger"?' Taylor asked, his eyebrows raised.

'Yeah. That was the name of the operation. Just my name for it, you understand. Nothing official. Appropriate wasn't it? The way things worked out.'

Falconer gave Taylor a sideways glance and saw that he seemed to be more puzzled than entranced by the deviousness of the operation. Yes, his suspicions seemed to be justified. Perhaps he was not the right man to succeed him. By nature he would be too inclined to play everything straight. Too hamstrung by what ordinary people, who didn't have to deal with the KGB, called 'decency'. He would need to check on him further.

'As you know, Ed, because you forwarded the information to us, we got wind of the split between the top Kremlin leadership and the Yakovlev–Dominowski faction through Quinn's source, "Uncle Vanya". So it suddenly happened that our interests and the KGB's were the same.'

'You mean to kill Borisenko?'

'Certainly not! To prevent the attack in Europe. I wasn't sure how Yakovlev would play it. I expected him to persuade Borisenko that the war should be delayed on the neutron bomb evidence. Dominowski would undoubtedly have insisted on that. But obviously it didn't work. I assure you Ed, that "Cliffhanger" didn't start as an assassination operation but, if our central strategic plan is to encourage the Soviet Union to destroy itself from within, a little outside help should never be denied.'

Taylor did not know whether to believe him or not. He sucked at the pipe which had gone out while he had been listening to Falconer with ever growing astonishment.

'You amaze me, John,' he said finally. 'And you dared to do all this behind the President's back!'

'There was no other way, Ed. "Cliffhanger" was obviously going to be a high-risk operation politically. I didn't even tell the Director. If I'd told anybody I would have been stopped in my tracks. It was crystal clear after that last National Security Council meeting that the hot-line between the White House and the Kremlin wasn't working. Either the President wasn't making the calls, or Borisenko had gone deaf. Their hot-line wasn't working. Mine was. So I used it.'

'So "Cliffhanger" was entirely your initiative?'

'I'd like to think so, Ed, but one can never be sure of anything in this game. I'm not sure the initiative wasn't Yakovlev's.'

'Yakovlev's! The KGB's?'

'Yeah. It all started with that defector, Kovalsky, who came over with the information that King-Lander was a spy.'

At the mention of King-Lander's name Taylor almost squirmed. He had been told about the surveillance operation against the Prime Minister's doctor only after it had been completed. While Falconer had explained that his intention was to avoid involving the resident CIA mission, in case the operation went wrong, Taylor knew that the real reason was security. Falconer had not trusted him.

'Kovalsky could have been a plant sent over deliberately to blab on King-Lander and set the ball rolling,' Falconer suggested. 'We'll never be sure now, but that would explain why the KGB wanted him silenced once he'd spilled the beans – in case he revealed that he was a double.'

Taylor looked more and more disturbed, his florid forehead furrowed with concern. He did not believe what Falconer was telling him. 'The reports about Kovalsky's assassination make it look as though not much effort was made to protect him,' he said. 'Any results from the "inquest" at Langley?'

Falconer shook his head in a way suggesting that he did not want to discuss it further, but Taylor felt that he must probe more deeply for his peace of mind.

'In view of what you called the smoke signals from Yakovlev, is there any possibility that the Agency went out of its way not to interfere with the KGB? I mean that maybe it was no coincidence that the case officer was missing when the hit-man called?'

Falconer pursed his lips at this further trespass on to dangerous ground. 'I really don't know, Ed. I was here in London, wasn't I?'

Wondering if even that were true, Taylor recalled a peculiar telephone call which his companion had taken, with evident relief, shortly before they had left his Washington home.

Falconer stared down at the water. The details of Kovalsky's death occasioned him no more concern than the erratic movements of the lump of driftwood swirling about in the eddies below, itself at the mercy of decisive forces. It was only with the satisfaction of an unfortunate complication well taken care of that his mind recalled the circumstances of the defector's demise.

It had been that last meeting with Kovalsky, coupled with his need to visit London, which had firmed up the decision. Falconer had dealt with many defectors but never one as restless.

'Take it easy Mr Kovalsky,' he had cautioned. 'You, of all people, must know that your interrogation can't be hurried ... '

'But, Mr Falconer, you know who I am, you know my rank, the value of my information. You are not doing enough for me. I'm getting very bored, very frustrated ... '

Falconer had left him with the case officer with a growing fear that, either in a bid to improve his standing with the CIA or even in the hope of being returned to Russia, Kovalsky could break down and admit that Yakovlev had sent him over as a 'mole'. And that could have meant disaster both for himself and for 'Cliffhanger'.

Suppose he does break down while I am in London, he had

asked himself as he was taking one of his solitary 'thinking walks' during a weekend break in Virginia. It will be immediately assumed by my enemies in both the Agency and in the FBI, especially the FBI, that not only have I been sold a double but that I have taken extreme action on what may be false information about the British Prime Minister. There will be an immediate investigation. I will be recalled. And some nice friend will undoubtedly leak the circumstances to the Press or to Congress.

I can't take Kovalsky with me to London, he reasoned. Apart from the problem of his security, I could only take him if I was going to hand him over to Quinn and that would be far too dangerous. Neither can I leave him here out of control.

Kovalsky's fate had been settled before Falconer had reached his elegant home, with its splendid views over the paddocks, grazed by his beloved horses. On his return to Washington he had taken 10,000 dollars in used notes from the safe concealed behind his grandfather's portrait, and then made a cryptic telephone call to a skilled, freelance assassin. A loner of German origins, he was thorough and could be trusted to obey instructions to the letter and, most important-ly, keep his mouth shut. He had been hired before on behalf of the Agency and would be allowed to assume that this would be a repeat performance with the guaranteed safe-guard of minimal investigation into the murder. In fact, Falconer would be paying for it privately out of his ample purse – an investment, as he had cared to consider it, in his own future freedom and that of the Western world.

Personal contact with the assassin had regrettably been essential, and they had talked in the hit-man's black limou-sine after he had picked up Falconer in a side street. The meeting had been brief and professional with the minimum of questions asked, no reasons given and the money handed over on the understanding that a similar sum would be paid when the mission had been accomplished.

Falconer had been disappointed with the assassin's failure to dispose of Kovalsky by a hit-and-run 'accident' but, with his customary prudence, he had a fall-back position and, for his peace of mind, this had to be accomplished before his departure for London, which had become imminent. Falconer's first move had been to use the failure as an excuse to replace

Kovalsky's case officer, deliberately choosing a quiet, middle-aged bachelor who lived alone in an apartment in Washington, and who was known to be working hard on a Russian language crash-course prior to taking up his first assignment in Moscow. That CIA colleague was the only cause of any minor qualms as Falconer retraced the Kovalsky episode in his mind.

'There is a complication this time,' Falconer had explained to the hit-man on their second meeting, at which he had handed over the Luger Parabellum pistol, taken from a selection in his safe and wrapped, after careful polishing, in tissue-paper. 'You will have to take steps to make sure that the case officer is not with Kovalsky when you call at the hotel. Up until midday he will be in his apartment working on his Russian course. Make a note of his address.'

He had dictated the address and revealed the coded CIA door-knock, which was changed each day.

'Knock that way and the case officer will come to the door believing it's a colleague.'

'And what then?' the hit-man had asked.

'Say nothing. Not a word. Communicate solely by waves of your gun. Take some cord and a gag, truss him up then pull out the telephone and leave him.'

'And if he fights or attempts to draw?'

'He won't have a gun. If he tries to fight – well, you'll have to defend yourself, won't you?'

Yes, Falconer admitted as he continued to stare at the surging Thames, the operation could have cost the case officer's life, but what was one life compared with the millions then at stake? However, the eventuality had been avoided. The hit-man had been brutally efficient and the officer had been sensible enough to avoid forcing his assailant to shoot him.

The case officer had also reacted as Falconer had forseen in other ways. He had reported that the killer seemed determined not to betray any accent by speaking, though he had tried to reason with him, even in Russian. That, along with the other sparse clues, including the bullets from Kovalsky's body fired from the type of pistol favoured by Soviet execution squads, had made it look like the work of the KGB.

In those circumstances, as Falconer had also anticipated,

the case officer had been instructed to say nothing to the police, or to anyone else outside the Agency. The Director, who had been furious at the ease with which Kovalsky had been liquidated, had not wanted the defector's name in the newspapers with all the consequent probing under the Freedom of Information Act, and the ridicule and ignominy for the Agency, it would engender.

As for Sergei Yakovlev, Falconer reckoned that he would understand what had happened without having to be told, and would appreciate why. He would certainly never generate any publicity about a KGB defector, dead or alive. They weren't supposed to exist.

Falconer would never have gone into action on Cliffhanger without a real, live defector in hand. A personal tip from Yakovlev about the King-Lander-Henderson connection, which could have been presented as coming from a defector still 'in place' in Russia, would not have been enough. With an involvement as sensitive as a British Prime Minister there had to be genuine collateral in case of political trouble if the operation went sour. Like reports of interrogations of the defector by case-officers in CIA files. And other evidence of his existence, like hotel bills and the reports relating to his murder.

He had briefly wondered why Yakovlev had chosen Kovalsky for the 'defection'. It had to be somebody very senior to know the information about King-Lander and Henderson, for that would be kept within extremly close confines at the Centre. It also had to be somebody senior for it to be believed in Washington. But why a man as senior as Kovalsky? Maybe Sergei had really been offloading dangerous competition. Apart from being an ambitious thruster, Kovalsky had also been something of a protégé of Premier Volkhov, so he might have caused trouble, especially in view of what had happened.

So far as Falconer was concerned, the defector had been such a dangerous enemy to Western freedom in the past that his death was thoroughly deserved. No, he had nothing to reproach himself with. In the best of worlds what he had done would be deemed reprehensible. But when the world's fate depended on the whims of a few old men sitting behind grim fortifications in Moscow it was far from being the best.

'As regards Kovalsky, we'll just have to see what the inquiry at Langley produces,' he remarked to Taylor, making it clear that there was nothing further he wished to say on the subject. Familiar with internal CIA inquiries Taylor felt sure that this one would produce nothing that his superiors wished to remain concealed. 'Cliffhanger' had clearly gone so well that, if anything implicating Falconer came to light, no VIP, either in the Government or the Agency, would be inclined to attack him – unless there was outside publicity when, of course, they would throw him to the Washington wolves.

'Just tell me one final thing, John,' Taylor essayed with some courage. 'Would I be right in assuming that you heard of Kovalsky's death with some relief?'

Falconer paused then watched his companion carefully as he answered, 'I'm prepared to admit that at that moment the KGB's interests and mine happened to coincide.'

Taylor was visibly sickened by what he rightly interpreted as something of a confession. At least Falconer must have known what was likely to happen to Kovalsky and could even have connived at it. Still, in the Intelligence game a successful end justified every terrible means. He had sensed that Falconer might have been sounding him out as a possible successor, but after what he had just heard he wanted no part of the job. The demands on his integrity would be too heavy. He was prepared for some degree of deception and general ruthlessness. Oherwise he would never have stayed in the CIA. But could he have conceived 'Cliffhanger' and carried it through? With the violence, the frame-ups, the lies? It was odd to be thinking of ethics against an opponent like the KGB. But for him there were limits.

And what would the job do to his character? There was also his wife and children to consider. What would it do to them? No. It was a post for a bachelor of a very peculiar kind. There must be something about the wiring in Falconer's cerebral computer that was utterly different from his own.

In Falconer's mind Taylor was also out on every count. Definitely too soft, mediocre at dissimulating, short on imagination and overly concerned about individuals. He was the sort of guy who could even get religion! And, leaning there with his elbows on the parapet, he somehow looked fatter than usual, another symptom of inadequate personal discipline.

No, Taylor wouldn't do for promotion of any kind. Mission chief was definitely his limit, and it would be his duty to make that known in the right quarter before he quit the Agency. And he wouldn't be telling anyone at Langley that Taylor had been responsible for discovering the identity of "Uncle Vanya".

He picked up the parcel from the parapet and tucked it under his arm, casting a glance at the Mother of Parliaments and the Whitehall complex that could so easily have become a mini-Kremlin. It still might one day, he thought. God knows what absolute power could do to Yakovlev.

'Come on, Ed, let's walk across to Century House and say my farewells to Quinn and his lady friend.'

Chapter Eighteen

'That bloody computer's playing us up again,' Quinn said angrily to Angela as he twiddled with the remote-control operating the display terminal by his desk. 'Is this the age of electronics? I say no! We were far better off with a card-index. It always worked and you couldn't bug it.'

Quinn was referring bitterly to the inroads he had been forced to make into his limited funds to enclose the whole computer room downstairs, complete with staff, in a huge copper cube. Intelligence had been secured showing that the Russians had devised a means of picking up the weak radiation emitted by a computer and so might be able to decipher its secret contents.

He had been busying himself with one of his Sequence of Events exercises on a foolscap sheet. As he burned it he remarked, 'You know, Angela, I'm as certain as I am ever likely to be that Henderson was framed by John Falconer.'

'Framed?' Angela asked incredulously. 'But I thought ... '

Quinn interrupted her. 'I think that all Falconer knew for

certain was that King-Lander was a spy. He got that from the defector Kovalsky, who is now conveniently dead. Then when the boys from the National Security Agency investigated King-Lander they discovered that Henderson confided in him as a sounding-board, like I suppose I use you. Someone to think aloud to. Someone independent of the bureaucratic channels. Someone outside the Whitehall machine. After all, political leaders have always done it. Roosevelt had Harry Hopkins ... '

'And if you can't confide in your doctor who can you trust? I mean would it be a breach of security to confide State secrets to a priest?'

'It certainly would in Northern Ireland,' Quinn said. 'But I agree that talking to your doctor if you are Prime Minister is safer than talking to most of the other members of the Cabinet. At least doctors are trained to keep their mouths shut and usually do.'

'But why should Falconer want to frame Henderson?' Angela asked. 'Why should he tell you categorically that he was a spy if he wasn't sure of it? Was it that Washington wanted rid of him because he was too friendly with Russia?'

'I am sure there was much more to it than that. Shopping Henderson was just a means to an end. And I strongly suspect that end was the assassination of Borisenko.'

'But surely we know now that Borisenko was killed by Yakovlev,' Angela pointed out.

'That's right,' Quinn replied, wondering whether she would draw the right deduction.

She immediately obliged by saying, 'Then that means that there must have been some sort of collusion between the CIA and the KGB.'

'Between Falconer and Yakovlev is how I'd put it. And I'd say conspiracy rather than collusion. It wouldn't be the first time that the CIA and the KGB have pooled their interests.'

'But that's fantastic. When did you first suspect it?'

'When Falconer gave me that dossier on Henderson. It was a concoction. I've faked too many myself not to recognize one when somebody else does it. Anyway Henderson didn't have the courage to be a spy. For my money he was just a sacrificial stooge in a CIA–KGB operation.'

Angela never ceased to be surprised by the machinations of her master's mind but this one had shaken her.

'If you knew it was a fake why did you go along with the move to get rid of the Prime Minister?' she asked.

'Because it suited me,' Quinn said. And before Angela could suggest that he had taken advantage of a sudden opportunity to capitalize on his animosity for Henderson he added, 'And it also suited the Service. On both counts Henderson was expendable.'

He picked up his pen which was a signal that he was not in the mood to offer any further explanation, but he had signed only a couple of documents before the arrival of Falconer and Taylor at the entrance to Century House was announced over the telephone.

There was a brief delay while the gift-wrapped parcel was scanned by an X-ray machine. Taylor was well enough known to the security guards, but no exceptions to the examination were permitted since a booby-trapped parcel, which fortunately failed to explode, had been delivered to a Middle East Intelligence officer in Century House some years previously.

'Just a farewell social call, Mark,' Falconer said jovially as he entered the Director's office. 'I'm back to Washington on the Concorde flight. For good this time.'

'You are determined to retire then?'

'Absolutely. I've had enough.'

'What will you do?' Angela asked. 'Daddy says that retirement is doing twice as much work with a quarter of the resources.'

'I'll grow tobacco and breed horses.'

'A pity you are forbidden to write your memoirs,' Quinn said. 'Especially as you are going out on the crest of a wave – the worst crisis since 1939 resolved. There shouldn't be any major trouble with our Russian friends for a year or two. So perhaps you can be spared.'

Falconer smiled. 'Yes our reports show that Yakovlev and Dominowski are firmly in the saddle. How do you feel about that, Mark? I know how much you despise Yakovlev.'

'Despise isn't the right word, John. I have to admire him as an operator. But if he follows his nature he'll be the most ruthless dictator since Stalin.'

Falconer raised his hands in mild protest. 'But I know the man, Mark. Compared with Borisenko he's a dove.'

'Some dove!' Quinn commented bitterly. 'I happen to know him, too, as you well know. In any case, power will corrupt his judgement. It will be the same general policy under new management. The Kremlin will never relax its Imperialistic aims.'

'You may be right,' Falconer conceded. 'But at least we'll have a breathing space. The West will have a couple of years or so to strengthen NATO – if the politicians have the guts to do it.'

He felt in his pocket and handed Quinn two tape cassettes. 'The record of your conversation with King-Lander. I think you handled him brilliantly – with one exception.'

'What was that, John?'

'Your mention of the possible CIA interest, and the possible intervention by the President.'

'Yes, a pity about that but I suddenly needed it. For a moment or two he seemed to be hardening.'

'I think he was,' Falconer agreed. 'But let's hope he hasn't spilled any beans to the "White Lady". What's the latest on the Prime Minister?'

'He's resigning all right. He's telling the Cabinet now, and it will be announced immediately afterwards. Otherwise the other ministers would leak it. They say his wife almost danced for joy when she heard the news from King-Lander.'

'Just like a woman,' Falconer commented. 'Or so they tell me,' he added hurriedly, seeing the disapproving frown on Angela's normally creaseless brow. 'As you know I have no practical experience.'

'I'm only sorry I can't reciprocate with a tape of my interview with the Prime Minister,' Quinn lied. 'The way things have gone I must have handled it quite well, although one says it who shouldn't.'

'You must have done but in a way I feel sorry for Henderson. I suppose that he was more of a fool than a villain. Still, the exercise deprived the KGB of a major source – and that's always great news.'

'Yes,' Quinn agreed, exchanging glances with Angela at Falconer's expression of regret. 'But, sadly, we lost "Uncle Vanya". Poor old Rakitin. He's been arrested and there's no doubt that he'll be shot. He'll protest his innocence but it won't do any good. Still, we'd have lost him anyway. He's about seventy and Yakovlev would never have kept him on for long.'

Falconer looked at Quinn with a mischievous expression. 'I'm afraid you've lost another major source, Mark. You won't be hearing again from "Diamond Jim".'

Quinn had trained himself never to blush but he was unable to keep his features entirely free from an expression of shock.

'You know that was very naughty of you, Mark,' Falconer continued, playfully wagging a finger.

'Ah, John, we live in a naughty world. But I can tell you, in all honesty, I didn't go behind your back and recruit him. He volunteered. Would you have rejected a gift like that?'

'No comment. But did you ever discover his identity?'

'I never tried, John. So long as information like that was flowing my way I had no intention of probing. But maybe you can tell me now who he was – if you've neutralized him.'

Falconer paused. 'I can't tell you now. But I promise I will later. I can also promise you that there will be no publicity. Like Henderson, he's much too important for that. He'll just be put quietly out to grass.'

'With honour?' Quinn asked.

'Certainly not!'

'Ah, we are more civilized here, John. You're a betting man. I'll lay you odds that both Henderson and King-Lander become Lords.'

'Good grief,' Taylor exclaimed.

'Yes, but there ought to be some reward for them,' Quinn said, half in jest. 'After all, John, you couldn't have stopped the war without them.'

It was Falconer's turn to be startled. From Quinn's expression he realized that he knew at least part of the truth about 'Cliffhanger'. He averted his eyes and commented gruffly, 'Thank God we don't have honours in the United States.'

'No, but they'd make fortunes out of their memoirs and television appearances,' Quinn said.

Falconer shrugged his acceptance of the gibe. With Watergate in mind it was legitimate enough.

194

'I suppose you'll be going back to a round of farewell parties, after all your years in the CIA,' Angela suggested.

'Not me,' Falconer replied vehemently. 'To me a cocktail party is a room full of smoke and boring people. Except when duty demanded I've stayed out of the diplomatic cocktail round. Anyway, I think that, like old soldiers, old Intelligence men should quietly fade away and that's what I intend to do. But if you are ever in Virginia come down and see me on my farm.'

'I'll do that,' Angela said, shaking his outstretched hand.

'Well, goodbye, Mark. It's been great working with you. I hope you establish the same relations with my successor.'

He was making for the door with Taylor when he turned round towards Angela and said, 'I almost forgot. Here's a personal present to you from me. Just a token for all your many kindnesses.'

He gave her the gift-wrapped parcel and departed with a final wave.

'That's a sad parting, Angela,' Quinn said, returning to his desk. 'A dog you know is always better than a dog you don't know.'

'I suppose he's one of the greatest Intelligence officers of his time,' Angela remarked as she unwrapped the parcel.

'Greatness is only other people's opinions of what you've done,' Quinn said. 'But I would have to agree, I suppose. What have you got?'

Angela opened a red box and produced a vintage bottle of Dom Perignon with a card tied to the neck with a red ribbon.

'It's a superb bottle of champagne. Let's see what the card says. "To Angela with love from 'Diamond Jim!' " '

' "Diamond Jim" '! Quinn exclaimed, as the full implication struck home. 'Falconer is "Diamond Jim"! The incorrigible bastard!'

Angela succeeded with difficulty in suppressing her laughter, for the one thing her master hated was being derided. In this instance, however, Quinn himself saw the funny side of the situation because he had secret reasons for satisfaction.

'He thinks he's taken my trousers down,' he said. 'Well let him, if it gives him pleasure. At least I had a fair idea of what he was trying to do. He hadn't the faintest idea of my

195

objective and he still hasn't. He thought I played ball with him just to get rid of the "Prince of Peace". I confess that gave me pleasure but it was ancillary to my main purpose.'

'What was that?' Angela asked, taking what she rightly thought to be a deliberate cue. There were occasions when Quinn's vanity overrode his discretion, and this looked like being one of them.

'I have to put you in the picture, Angela, because you'll be finding in the course of the next few days that we haven't lost "Uncle Vanya". He'll be reporting more usefully than ever.'

Angela did not reveal by look or word that the remark failed to surprise her. She had known for some days that Rakitin, an old man, could not possibly be 'Uncle Vanya'. The voice she had heard on the tape during her surreptitious moments of listening to it had not only been that of a younger person. It had been the voice of a woman.

'I thought you told Falconer that Rakitin was going to be shot,' she said.

'I did. But Rakitin isn't "Uncle Vanya" and never was.'

'Then why did you ask me to let Ed Taylor know that Rakitin was "Uncle Vanya"?'

'To cover the real one,' Quinn said. 'I suddenly needed some extra cover.'

'And now poor old Rakitin, who was no traitor at all, is going to be killed.'

'I'm afraid so,' Quinn replied without feeling. 'He was a good Communist and, so far as I am concerned, the best Communists are dead Communists.'

Angela was sickened by the thought that she might be an accessory to the execution of the old man, but consoled herself that this could hardly be.

'How on earth did telling the CIA give any cover to your real "Uncle Vanya". I don't see it.'

'Because I knew that Taylor would tell Falconer and that as sure as fate he would tell Yakovlev. And that's exactly what happened. I read Falconer's mind perfectly. In this game, Angela, reading your friends' minds is as important as reading your enemies'.'

The statement seemed incredible in view of the steady dependence of the CIA and, through it, the Washington machine, on the information supplied by "Uncle Vanya".

'Are you seriously suggesting that John Falconer, that friend of yours who's just left this room, would blow your best source to the KGB? It makes no sense.'

'It makes all the sense in the world, my dear girl. And I don't blame him for doing it. He was involved in a crucial operation to help Yakovlev assassinate Borisenko, and so stop or at least delay the war, which the West was likely to lose. When he found out that Rakitin, who was always in Borisenko's office, was an active British agent he was terrified that he might interfere with the operation and ruin it. So he warned Yakovlev of the danger. It was fair enough. John knew that once Borisenko was eliminated Rakitin would be finished as a source anyway. He was expendable. I even know how he did it. With a coded message sent as a racing tip through a KGB agent he met by appointment on the racecourse at Epsom.'

'Which was why he was so keen to go to the Derby! But I don't understand how you know these details.'

'Because the real "Uncle Vanya" told me. I knew that Yakovlev and Marshal Dominowski were likely to try to assassinate Borisenko before they'd finally made up their minds to do it. And I knew that Falconer had been part of the conspiracy from the start.'

'Why didn't he ask you to join it?' Angela asked.

'Because he knows I could never co-operate with Yakovlev in any situation. Dialogue with the KGB is one thing. Tête-à-tête is another. In any case he knows I don't like conspiracies. I'm a cat that walks alone. History is littered with conspiracies that failed because, once several people are involved, secrecy flies out of the window.'

'Well you know best but I must tell you that I don't relish being used to help to kill someone I don't even know,' Angela complained.

'Too bad,' Quinn commented curtly. 'You knew what this business was about when you came into it and I needed your help. We're not bloody social workers, you know. Now be a good girl and bring me some coffee. Don't lose any sleep over Rakitin. He was an enemy. Every bit as bad as any of the rest of them in the Kremlin.'

'Including "Uncle Vanya"?' Angela asked archly, as she filled Quinn's coffee mug.

'I didn't say that "Uncle Vanya" was in the Kremlin. Type out this report for me, will you?' he asked, giving her a short, routine document for the Foreign Secretary written in his own hand.

Angela could always tell when Quinn was about to wrap himself in the cloak of preoccupation. As she disappeared into the ante-room he stretched out his legs, put the mug to his lips and felt the warm glow of satisfaction, letting his mind range over the long succession of events, which had produced such splendid results.

It had been many years since the 'Uncle Vanya' coup had first germinated, but he could recall the circumstances vividly. Like so many of the events which had dominated his life, it had arisen unexpectedly, almost accidentally, and there had been a strong sexual component.

Ever since the phenomenal success of a spy, code-named Cicero, who had served as a valet to the British Ambassador in Ankara, it had been standard practice for the MI6 men on the spot to keep close check on the activities of all foreign servants employed in the ambassadorial residences. It had fallen to Quinn to be responsible for that task in the residence of the British Ambassador in Moscow during his two years of service there. Because of some diplomatic agreement, which he could never understand, the Kremlin insisted that most of the domestic staff of the Residence should be Russians, a situation which was not reversed in the Soviet Embassy in London. Inevitably some of those Russians were selected and planted by the KGB, and tended to be far more astute and better educated than they seemed.

Quinn's interest had been immediately aroused, in more ways than one, by the appearance of a replacement in the form of a tall and most attractive servant called Nadia, who could speak a little English and understand even more. Like the rest of the Russian domestics she affected an almost peasant style of dress, but wore it with such grace that it stimulated Quinn. He was greatly entranced by those long legs in their black woollen stockings which, he guessed, would be brief enough to produce a glimpse of alabaster thigh as she stretched across the bed to straighten the sheets.

During his visits to the Residence, which was conveniently located along with the Embassy and his own small office inside the British compound at Number Fourteen, Naberez-hanaya Morise Tereza, he made efforts to speak to Nadia, but she showed no interest. He guessed that her quarry was rather more important – the Ambassador himself.

Fortunately Quinn had managed to make friends with another chambermaid, sadly a much plainer and dumpier girl called Zina, who, he guessed, had taken something of a fancy to him. When skilfully questioned she had admitted that she was with the KGB, although insisted that she had joined as a shorthand-typist and resented her current assignment. This had been organized by her previous boss, who wanted to install his girl-friend in her place. Quinn noted this admission with considerable reserve, realizing that Zina was much brighter than she looked. On one of his routine afternoon visits to the Residence, which he usually made during the Ambassador's absence because the presence of MI6 there was never relished by the diplomats, she had startling news for him.

A few hours previously, quietly entering the Ambassador's bedroom, believing him to be out, she had seen him 'up to the hilt in Nadia', as Quinn later described it to his chief. A believer in securing the maximum detail, and in this instance finding it highly stimulating, he had induced Zina to give a graphic description of all she had seen as they sat on the bed in one of the rooms reserved for visiting VIPs.

Quinn had always admitted to himself that on a hot afternoon, after a good lunch, in the right conditions, any woman would do and as Zina, haltingly and with much prompting, described the literally moving scene with the Ambassador's trousers half down and Nadia's skirt up to her neck with her legs wrapped round him, he had made his pass. To his surprise Zina, though shyly passive, had offered no resistance and he had been disturbed, then rather gratified, to discover that she was a virgin.

Quinn had felt sorry in a way for the Ambassador who was near the end of his career and had a dreary wife who hated Moscow and spent most of her time in London. He was only too aware how the sheer dullness of living in Moscow could blunt all caution and exacerbate the 'It couldn't happen to me' syndrome. If chance excitement offered it was difficult to resist. Still, Quinn had been in no doubt what he had to do and what the consequences would be.

The Ambassador had first to be informed before his lust could be tempted outside the Residence, at Nadia's flat or some such place, where the KGB would have their photographers installed. There had been a few weeks of high-level shock in the Foreign Office before His Excellency's inevitable summons to London, and the eventual quiet announcement of his routine replacement.

In that time Quinn had done all he could to consolidate his relationship with Zina. 'I screwed for England!' he told his colleagues, who had ribbed him about her plainness. The love-making during their discreet meetings had quickly become such a chore that, while with her, he had been driven to concentrate his thoughts on Nadia, who had turned out to be a prostitute specially trained at the Lenin School of Subversion. As events developed, his boast had been well justified, paying far richer dividends for England than the Residence gossip and the KGB titbits he had expected. However, his intimate relationship with Zina was brought to a close by Sergei Yakovlev, then a middle-rank operator who had been responsible for fixing the Ambassador. Yakovlev knew nothing of their affair but saddled with a failure, which the Soviet Foreign Secretary had to know about following the Ambassador's recall, he had taken vengeance on Quinn whom he knew must have been responsible.

As Quinn sipped his coffee he shuddered as he recalled those dreadful hours in that claustrophobic cubicle, unworthy of the name of cell, into which Yakovlev had plunged him. Reaching out more than six inches anywhere in the darkness he had touched rough, damp concrete and the slow incessant drip was of water deliberately introduced through a bore-hole.

He had been interrogated to exhaustion in Yakovlev's efforts to identify his contact in the Residence, but he had stuck to his story that the Ambassador had voluntarily confessed. Zina, too, had been questioned brutally along with others but had held her ground so well that Yakovlev had been impressed with her composure and sincerity.

After her lover had been hounded out of the Soviet Union, Zina had been assigned as an assistant secretary to Yakovlev.

She detested him, not only for what he had done to the only man she had ever loved and who, she was convinced, loved her, but for what he was. Thus, throughout her career in the KGB, she had taken her revenge and demonstrated her continuing love by feeding Quinn a stream of information which steadily increased in importance as Yakovlev rose in the Service, taking her with him.

The dowdy girl, whom Quinn had secretly derided, had turned out to be not only limitlessly dedicated, but brave beyond belief. From the start, when she had continued to send information to Quinn in London, hoping that one day he would find some way of getting her there, he had insisted on handling her case. It was this which had kept him so many years at Century House, and eventually led to his appointment as Director, for he argued that Zina would work with nobody else as she took the risks not for Britain but for him.

Zina was also his secret reason for remaining unmarried. News of his marriage could not have been kept from her because she had access to his KGB dossier which was regularly updated by reports from London. He had never seriously contemplated matrimony but he had convinced himself that he would have sacrificed that prospect, however attractive, to avoid alienating Zina. She still expressed hopes, however forlornly, and he did his best to keep them buoyant.

Their communication was intimate and regular, his brief messages being so redolent of continuing love, that he had urged her to resist, for both their sakes, if Yakovlev, in his secure position, should try to take her to his bed. While believing that she would hate every minute in her boss's arms, she had offered to submit rather than risk losing her position. With studied reluctance Quinn had agreed, for he felt that a relationship free from emotional complications could be more lasting.

For her part she readily forgave him his relationships with Angela and her predecessors, which all appeared in his dossier, for having experienced his aggressively passionate embrace, she appreciated his compelling need for physical intimacy. In his unremitting effort to defend his star source Quinn overrode established practice by reserving the latest and most ingenious ideas and devices exclusively for Zina, their use in any other theatre being forbidden in case their discovery there might lead to checks in Moscow.

As many of her messages as possible came through in codes based on one-time pads. Normally in that system the person sending the message and the one receiving it each had indentical pads composed of small pages covered by lines of letters chosen at random. The encoder used letters from the top page to encypher a message, and the decoder used his to decipher. Provided each page was used only once, and then burned, the code was virtually unbreakable, but the discovery of one-time pads in a person's possession was damning evidence of involvement in espionage. To this end Quinn's technical department had come up with the idea of disguising the one-time pads supplied to Zina as wads of tea-bags. The lines of letters were pricked out into the paper of the bags, which were made to the Russian style, and the perforations were then filled with a white substance that dissolved in the tannin of the tea when the bag was placed in hot water. The numbers then became apparent, but only to the practised eye.

In a recent report to Century House, Zina's accompanying Moscow joke, which had tickled Quinn more than any other, had been a very private one – Yakovlev's remark about her ability to make tea so well!

Quinn saw to it that the best available field officer was in post in the Moscow Embassy to organize the safest possible protection for Zina. The location of dead letter-boxes – hiding places for her photostats and tapes – was contrived with particular cunning on the Metro system, which she regularly used, in the GUM store where she shopped, the parks where she fed the birds and other public places. The commonest was in a tiled cubicle which she, and the several women from the British Embassy detailed in turn to pick up her material, could visit without suspicion and in privacy. The clean, soft, white container in which Zina had been advised to conceal her tapes – unwound from their cassettes and tightly wrapped round a flexible plastic rod – the method by which she and her couriers carried it, and the bin in which she deposited it and from which it was retrieved, were repugnant. But the system worked so well that Quinn had a very private joke-name for it – the 'two-time pad'.

Her 'drops' included copies of KGB tapes so secret that they were kept in the combination safe in Yakovlev's office, a safe to which nobody but the Chief himself and his personal assistant had access, and which was not only locked with a different combination each night but sealed with wax so that any attempt at breakage would be visible. In addition she sent much of her remembered information on tapes which she recorded in her flat at night. These afforded Quinn particular, almost childish, pleasure with his knowledge that the machine on which she had made them had been a gift from Yakovlev for 'faithful service'.

As evidence of authenticity each drop she made was accompanied by the latest anti-Communist joke and by one tiny piece of a jigsaw puzzle showing Red Square on May Day.

The danger that Zina might be detected and arrested had been ever present, and in that sad eventuality Yakovlev would undoubtedly try to reverse some of his losses by using the contact to feed misleading information to Quinn for as long as he could. So Zina had promised that she would never reveal their jigsaw arrangement, even under torture. If a 'drop' arrived on his desk with no piece of the jigsaw he would know that Zina was finished.

The size of the half-completed puzzle in the far corner of the room was evidence of her tremendous contribution and of her courage. Her close relationship with Yakovlev had continued to keep her above suspicion, particularly when he had become chief of the KGB and, while efforts to account for odd leakages had been made, nothing had ever been traced to her.

Her immunity to date owed much to her long-established position of trust, as it had with Philby, but it was also a tribute to her astuteness and iron discipline in never taking chances. Like *always* using the voice-disguise attachment which Quinn had given her when recording her tapes; like *never* handling the tapes, or the packages containing them, without rubber gloves because of her inside knowledge about the invisible powder dusted into the pockets and handbags of KGB suspects, each with its identifying character when examined under fluorescent light; like leading a lonely and a temperate life because she knew, from observing so many others, that the most dangerous hazard in the most hazardous of all professions was the spy's own unguarded tongue.

Yes, as Quinn was fond of putting it, ' "Uncle Vanya" made Kim Philby look like a village sneak – and a drunken one at that.'

There was a further comparison. Like Philby, Zina had come to enjoy the excitement of living 'under the gun' but her position was far more dangerous, the death penalty being exacted for serious espionage in the Soviet Union. After the occasional near-disasters which, over so many years, had been inevitable, she had made up her mind to finish with clandestine work. Enough is enough, she had convinced herself after contemplating, in all its hideous detail, what would be her lot if she was caught. But the euphoria of escape had soon stifled fear and, to date, she had always decided to continue for a little while longer – to complete the immediate task which Quinn had set her. She knew there would always be another task and then another, but she had come to welcome them. They gave each day much more than routine purpose. To lose them would be like being deprived of some drug which heightened experience. It was easier to go on than to give up.

Lying in bed alone after a safe and successful drop, Zina had wondered how Quinn would behave if she suddenly appeared in London. It had been so long and they had both changed so much. Best, perhaps, not to risk finding out, she told herself. Anyway the question was academic. There was no way she could leave Moscow without raising suspicions, and that was the last thing she dared to do.

At his end of their secret line Quinn had often wondered how he would behave if Zina decided that she had done enough. He knew what the KGB would do in comparable circumstances – blackmail her into continuing or face exposure. Not a rouble had been paid to her in Russia, to eliminate the risk that she might be tempted to live beyond her means and so arouse suspicion, but money had been accumulating for her in a British bank and the details could be used as evidence of her treachery, but he couldn't behave like Yakovlev. Or could he? When he gave himself an honest answer he admitted that he didn't really know. At least he could not be sure. He would face the problem and deal with it depending on the prevailing circumstances on the day if it ever dawned. Hopefully, it never would.

The realization that, if Falconer's conspiracy succeeded, the hated Yakovlev could become virtual dictator of the Soviet Union had irked Quinn, and there had been a few hours in which he could have prevented it by arranging an anonymous tip-off to the Russian Ambassador in London. But his personal animosity had been quickly overridden by the glittering prospect of having a prime source of top-level intentions and planning right inside the highest office of the Kremlin.

Zina had sought his advice and he reckoned that his response had been brilliant. There had been no chance that Yakovlev might take on Rakitin as his personal assistant once his loyalty had been so heavily impugned, in spite of his unparalleled experience of Kremlin routine. With Rakitin eliminated, the odds were high that Yakovlev would choose a personal assistant whom he knew and trusted. Who better than Zina, who improved her chances by taking Quinn's advice – 'There's nothing like a bit of collateral' – and infiltrating some fake evidence against Rakitin into the KGB machine to reinforce the tip Yakovlev had already received from Falconer.

She had been rather proud of the 'dirty trick' which she had devised for the purpose. The KGB's Technical Directorate had produced a complex electronic wiring diagram to improve the security of the Secretary-General's office, among others, and Yakovlev had forwarded it to Rakitin for Borisenko's formal approval. Borisenko had initialled the diagram, with no more than a grunt, and Rakitin had promptly returned it to Yakovlev's office. All Zina had done was to make a carbon copy, pressing rather heavily on the stylus she used to do the tracing and making sure that the line wavered slightly.

Then, after burning the carbon paper and the copy, she had drawn Yakovlev's attention to the fact that when the diagram was viewed in an oblique light it seemed as though someone had made a tracing of it. Further it looked as though it had been done by someone with a shaky hand. Yakovlev's suspicion had immediately flown to Rakitin, particularly when forensic examination showed traces of carbon paper.

While Rakitin had been as good as condemned for his treachery, Zina had been complimented on her vigilance.

'That's my girl!' Quinn had murmured when he heard what had happened. She had also acted on his further advice. 'If he offers you the job, Zina, play hard to get. It will help your cover to be seen to be a little reluctant.' And that touch of his about being torn between loyalty to her leader and to her boss! Yakovlev had bought that beautifully.

It was indeed the sweetest revenge on Yakovlev that he could have conceived. Far more satisfying than having him subjected to indignities more savage than incarceration in a narrow cell before being shot, which he could so easily have arranged before the coup by a note through the door of the Russian Embassy in Kensington Palace Gardens.

He had been tempted. By God he had been tempted – enough to draft the note in his mind. Instead of quick vengeance he had brought off a Willi Brandt situation in reverse – a Western spy as confidant to the political chief of the Soviet Union. His frequent boast that the Lord would one day deliver Yakovlev into his hands had not been idle. He walked over to the jigsaw puzzle which now contained both the gigantic red star glaring from the pinnacle of the Kremlin Tower and one of the decorated onion domes of St Basil's Church. Would 'Uncle Vanya' be able to complete it?

He made a mental note to devise a new code-name for what the CIA would be told was an entirely new 'source with excellent access' brilliantly intruded by the British Secret Intelligence Service, another source so precious that the Director-General himself would be dealing with it, personally. To support the illusion that 'Uncle Vanya' had dried up with the demise of Rakitin there would have to be a decent interval of a few weeks before he could pass any information to Washington. Well, there was no harm in that.

Zina would slip up one day, or her case officer would. That, surely, was inevitable but, with care and luck, it could be many months, perhaps years, away. And during that time he would have regular access to that most valuable of all Intelligence commodities – Soviet intentions.

'Almost day by day I shall know what's going on in Yakovlev's mind,' he assured himself.

There would be little hope of getting Zina out if she was

detected, but she herself no longer entertained illusions about that eventuality. She was professional enough to understand that whatever Quinn's personal feelings about her might be – and she remained deluded on that score – he could not possibly put them before the needs of his Service, which she was fulfilling so uniquely. It was his duty to encourage her to remain 'in place', indeed to make it impossible for her to do anything else.

She had come to terms with the stark fact that she was expendable. She had accepted that her best course then would be to take the poison pills which he had provided because both knew that, if and when the awful moment arrived, Yakovlev's revenge would be terrible. It would also be quick and very private. He would never admit the treachery of his personal assistant to anyone outside the organization, or inside, if he could avoid it, because it would redound so harshly to his discredit. So immediate demise after ruthless interrogation, through some 'accident' or other, would be inevitable.

As for John Falconer, well he was finished anyway. Worn out. As good as gone. Had he been staying on, Yakovlev would have cut off all contact with him now that he had achieved the prime position in the State. Yet his own situation could hardly be more promising.

'Poor old John,' Quinn said aloud, as Angela brought the typed report for his signature and he returned to his desk. 'He thought he'd sold me a gold brick and it's turned out to be twenty-four carat. The CIA has a worldwide reputation for "dirty tricks" but we are far better at them you know. And we ought to be. We've been at it for centuries.'

'So how would you rate the final score – between yourself and Falconer, I mean,' Angela asked.

Quinn pondered for an appropriate answer. 'Let's give the old boy some credit. Let's call it "Dishonours even"! Now how about opening that champagne. We've a lot to celebrate.'